JUSTINE KILKERR

Advice for Strays

VINTAGE BOOKS
London

Published by Vintage 2011

2 4 6 8 10 9 7 5 3 1

First published in Great Britain in 2010 by Jonathan Cape

Vintage
Random House, 20 Vauxhall Bridge Road,
London SW1V 2SA

www.vintage-books.co.uk

Addresses for companies within The Random House Group Limited
can be found at: www.randomhouse.co.uk/offices.htm

The Random House Group Limited Reg. No. 954009

A CIP catalogue record for this book
is available from the British Library

ISBN 9780099535263

The Random House Group Limited supports The Forest Stewardship
Council (FSC), the leading international forest certification
organisation. All our titles that are printed on Greenpeace approved
FSC certified paper carry the FSC logo. Our paper procurement
policy can be found at www.rbooks.co.uk/environment

Mixed Sources

Product group from well-managed
forests and other controlled sources
www.fsc.org   Cert no. TT-COC-2139
© 1996 Forest Stewardship Council

Printed and bound in Great Britain by
CPI Cox & Wyman, Reading, RG1 8EX

ADVICE FOR STRAYS

Justine Kilkerr was brought up in South London, lives in Brighton and is currently working on her second novel.

For BCG. Be at peace.

Wake, butterfly –
it's late, we've miles
to go together.

Matsuo Bashō, 17th century

If a lion could talk, we could not understand him.

Ludwig Wittgenstein, *Philosophical Investigations*, 1953

Lost cat: SANDMAN (SANDY for
short) – missing from Lloyd Park
area since early September but still
holding out loads of hope.
Ginger seven-year-old tom, long-
haired, white back socks, yellow
eyes. Very vocal. REWARD.
Call me on . . .

My father named me after a kleptomaniac man-hating liar. Marnie. Not the best start in life, you might think. Though I could have had as a namesake one of de Sade's famously degraded leading ladies. I am thankful for small mercies. I've always thought it would have made more sense for a writer to name his daughters after literary heroines. Rebecca or Clarissa or Tess. I like Tess, it has a romantic, highbrow feel. Having said that, you could hardly confuse my father's writing with highbrow literature. In much the same way that you could hardly confuse me with a legendary literary heroine.

From my bedroom window three-stories up I can see a tiny pink tutu hanging in the top window of the house which backs onto mine. It's delicate, insubstantial; the kind of thing little girls dream of. I see its owner most days, running in circles around her living room or bouncing up and down on her bed, hair flying. There she is now, forehead pressed to the glass, watching her mother, who sits perched on the edge of a wooden bench in the tiny garden below, nut brown and crop-haired like a squirrel in a bathing cap. Her garden glows golden in the autumn sunshine. The few plants on my side of the low wall look weary, though it is October. Still, they should be revelling in the late surge of heat. I mention this to them often, as I've heard that talking to plants encourages them to flourish.

Do you think swearing at them would have the same effect? I try a different expletive every day to find out.

He's gone. It's only been five days since I found his house empty, but he's definitely gone. Disappeared. Everyone tells me not to worry, look at what he got up to in the past, he's always turned up in the end, and anyway, he's so much better now and it's really not been that long. Trust him, don't worry. Trust him.

When was I ever able to trust him?

I lean back from the window and push my knuckles into my eye sockets, rubbing until my eyeballs ache and colours shimmer on the inside of my lids. The sheets have wound themselves around my feet and I have to struggle and kick to get out of bed, almost tripping when a crafty loop in the blanket snags my toes. My hair snakes into knots around my fingers as I try to untangle it. A breath of lavender follows me around the room, souvenir of Shiulie's prescription for a peaceful night. It doesn't work.

I'm already finding it hard to keep my eyes open. Let me sleep tonight.

I knew all along this was going to happen. What went before was only a rehearsal. Where are you, Father? Father. The word looks odd, unreal. I've looked at it written down so often in letters I will never send, whispered it aloud to myself in the night. It loses all meaning when you repeat it too many times, gets caught in the throat and stuck on its way to the brain. Father. Father.

Yawning, I drag a wedge of air into my lungs, air that is thick with uneasy dreams, uneasier memories.

Please let me sleep tonight.

When I see her this evening my sister will ask again, as she chews at her fingers, why I've always been so hard on him. Her pale eyes will blame me for his vanishing. Yes, he is ill. Yes, he's been locked away, more times than I can remember. Yes, they've tried everything, first talking, then drugs, then electricity. I see him gesticulating furiously at the therapists, doctors, laughing at them. I see him, eyes and belly swollen, hands limp like squashed-open fruit, brown-backed and pink-palmed on his lap. I see blue and white threads of light coursing through the soft tissue of his brain, burning, cauterising, erasing the memory of the pain that keeps him locked in his dark cocoon. And then him, my father, fighting his way through a fog of anaesthetic to surface finally, a benign look, a sweet, quiet word on his lips. All forgotten, all gone. All gone.

My father would take me and my friend Shiulie to the circus whenever it came to town, which seemed to be every month or so. Although it couldn't have been. I've no idea why we went, why he'd take me but not my little sister. A special treat for the first born, even if that particular first born cried and screamed and hid her face. He hated it too, but seemed to take some kind of strange pleasure in torturing both himself and me.

The crowds heaved – children squealing, parents complaining – and I'd always get knocked about, by umbrellas and heavy coats in the winter, picnic baskets in the summer. The air was always close, the wide-eyed ringmaster's gaze manic and his voice permanently on the verge of hysteria.

'Laydeez and Gennelmen! Boyzz and Girlzz!'

I would look up at the canvas far above us, concentrate on the blue and red stripes, the ropes, imagining myself floating up and away. Leering clowns tumbled into the pools of light. Was I the only child ever to find them terrifying? Shiulie adored them. She would shriek with fright when they scoured the audience for volunteers, digging sharp elbows into my ribs to encourage me to share her delight at hats being set alight, buckets of water being emptied over yellow-wigged heads.

The clowns gave me nightmares, but the animals made me cry. When a horse with a side like a wash board, or a moth-eaten lion came into the ring my eyes would sting. I'd cover my face with my hands. But once, when it was all over, a lion cub was brought out and paraded by its young handler. I had no idea how old it was. The boy was shouting as he struggled out of the circus wings with his warm sleepy load, his flimsy voice rising to the top of the tent and becoming entangled among the coloured stripes and ropes of the huge canvas.

'Anyone wanna hold a lion cub? Have your photo with him before he gets big enough to fit your head in 'is mouth! C'mon, give Jericho a cuddle!' he shouted, trying to fan the dying embers of the audience's attention before they emptied out into the cold night. My father waved to catch his attention and the boy made his way towards the flapping hand, as if the cub were a life jacket to be thrown in to save a drowning man. The animal was huge to me, lying like a folded rug over the man's shoulder. He manoeuvred the cub with some difficulty up the row of benches towards us, then bundled it on to my lap. I hesitated to touch it at first, but then slowly wrapped my arms around the warm body which fidgeted for a few moments, and then, with a frame-juddering sigh, was still. And so was I.

A hand on my shoulder squeezes, and Leo, my boss, is calling me away from the circus ring to the office at the end of the day. I raise my face to his and blink the sawdust and greasepaint out of my eyes. He asks if I am all right, lines deepening on his forehead. I must have been staring at that stapler for ages.

Please let me sleep tonight.

Try not to make too much noise, breathe normally. Can't let her see me. Not yet. Look at her. After all this time she's not changed. She's older, obviously. Grown up. Prime of her life. Like I once was. But she's tired. Her eyes were green, but they've dimmed to grey-brown. Her cheeks are hollow. A crease between her eyebrows. Hair seems leached to dusty mouse. The hunted look she had when I first met her still lingers in her eyes. That smile she puts on could have been borrowed from a friend; it's too large for her small face. Unconvincing. She's walking home in the afternoon sunshine, shoulders hunched up under her ears. Smell of sleep trailing behind her. I can taste it behind my teeth.

Remember the time I first saw her. She was only four or five. A small thing, such a little scrap of life, with her tiny heart like a bird's, hammering against my side. Not sure she really wanted her photograph taken with me. Could smell the fear, the hesitation in her breath. Still, she clutched me as the man ordered her to smile. The photograph was taken. The sudden bright light hurt my eyes, red blooms opening against my eyelids.

What does she want me here for? What use can I be to her? My teeth rattle in my head; my eyes are cloudy and vague.

No bark, no bite. My knuckles hurt where they took my claws. Some injuries never fully heal. I'm getting old.

How can this be, you ask? How can it? How are you here suddenly, from nowhere? Things happen, I suppose. Things just happen. Who knows?

Concrete rough on my feet, I have to follow carefully. Scents of a thousand creatures rise to my nose: reek of stale meat, rubber, oil, burning tang of piss. Don't remember it stinking so bad. The speeding engines deafen me and I try to concentrate on the stench coming from the damp pavement. There are rats around here. I feel them watching.

A dog – small, white, mean-looking – stops as I approach, hackles raised. It begins a low whine, which gets stuck in its throat as I swing round to look into its eyes. It wouldn't dare. A man bends to stroke its back, mutters to it. I swallow my anger, push it deep under my ribcage, but the taste still lingers. Keep going, keep up, don't get distracted by sounds that clang in my head, yellow, blue. Mustn't let her out of my sight; I might never get out of here.

Reached her front door now. There's that cat. Hate that bloody cat. Orange eyes, orange fur. It's gone to skulk in the shadow of the rosemary bush, like I don't know it's there. My eyes aren't that knackered, idiot. Could smell you a mile off, even over the scent of herbs. And she loves the animal, like it's one of her own kind. Even though she doesn't know it. Even though it's just using her, soft opportunistic bastard. Yeah, you heard me. Right, and those are really impressive teeth. Scowl as much as you like. Do I look scared?

She picks it up, buries her face in its fur for a moment. Then drops it, goes inside. The little bastard scrambles past her legs, through the door, straight towards the warmth. The food. I'll wait outside the house tonight. The thought of going into that cramped space makes my skin shiver. Hate these bloody house cats. Second-rate runts and liars, all of them. I hate cats more than I hate dogs. In fact, I hate cats more than I hate bloody humans.

LOST CAT
NAME BOB
BLACK AND
WHITE FRONT,
POORS AND
CHEEKS IF SEEN
PLEASE RING
THANKYOU

Despite the lack of sleep, I know this piece of copy is some of my best work. I also know that I've spent far too much time on it. Five days was what I was given, and that was more than enough time for a good job. But I've been taking it home. Working until three, four in the morning, my hands shaking from too little sleep and too much coffee. Falling asleep on the bus in to work, head rolling on to strangers' shoulders as if for comfort. Is an instruction manual for a 'Revolutionary New Upholstery Cleaning System' really worth this? I doubt it. But I have to try and still the voices somehow. I have to stop thinking about my father. And it sounds ridiculous, but sometimes in the night I feel I am being watched.

Once Leo's talked the copy over with me he'll probably give me the rest of the day off, even though it's only mid-morning. He's already remarked on the dark smudges circling my eyes. I must try and get some sleep tonight.

Here he comes. Look, you see; there are my words, held against his pin-striped side by one elbow, the paper clutched to him as if it were a wild thing which might escape. He smiles at me as he sits down.

'Here we are then. You OK?'

'Yes thanks. How you doing, Leo? How's Julia?'

'Yeah, fine thanks. Both fine. Good. Marnie, this is great stuff.'

He flips the first page over, then a couple more.

'The introduction really sums up the product well, it's pitched just right, really well done.'

He glances at me. He turns another page. Halfway down the typewritten sheet there is a thick red line through a short phrase. A barely legible substitute hovering just above it.

'Here, we've got to work on this more. Yes? Let's try . . .'

He makes another mark.

'I think that probably makes more sense. Do you see?'

He doesn't wait for a response, flips over the page. More red marks spike my words. More red curlicues in the margins, wedged between my ordered lines.

'You see, if I'd been asked to write this section I'd have started with this . . . That's better. And now that should go there. And look, you've used totally the wrong word, I'd have this . . .'

A sentence is added. Red scribbles appear on one side, on both sides, but I can't read them. My words are disappearing under his. My fingernails are digging into my palms; if I don't breathe this won't really be happening. And all the while my dad is lost in my words, muttering under his breath, talking to himself, not me.

'No, that part won't do, this'll be much better . . .'

My chair is suddenly rigid, uncomfortable. I shift and cross my legs but the desk is too low and I bang my knee, hard, against the desk top.

'You all right? That was quite a knock.'

'I'm fine. Sorry, what was that?'

'The conclusion needs a little more work, but once you've re-iterated the main features . . .'

And me silent. I'm not sure my heart is beating any more, but my face is still smiling. I can feel my mum behind me, holding her breath. Her hand hasn't moved. I don't think she's smiling.

My poem, the first I've got into the school magazine, the one my teacher loves, the one my mum kissed me and called me her little Emily Dickinson for. This is the first one I've ever shown to my father. He's come to visit, the first time for three weeks. My dad. I'd sat drumming my socked feet against the table leg waiting for him. His knock at the door shocked me from my chair. He stood over me so the light from the dining room lamp couldn't get to me and bent down and kissed the top of my head. His breath was warm on my scalp. He smelled of aftershave and his damp wool jacket.

'I've written a poem. Do you want to see it?'

And my hands were shaking as I laid the paper out on the table, trying to smooth out the creases they've made. They hadn't meant to. They were as nervous as I was.

And now. I'm sorry, I didn't know it was so bad, I didn't know those words were wrong that I should never have written them that I shouldn't I shouldn't.

'Marn, are you sure you're OK? You're looking a bit pale.'

'My poem . . .'

'You've written a poem as well? Great. Let's stick to this for now though, eh? Marnie?'

The light from the long office window seems too harsh and flat suddenly. I look at him silhouetted against the slatted brightness pouring in from behind the Venetian blinds and have to blink hard to focus.

'Yes, sorry. I'm just a bit, just a bit tired.'

'Mm, I can see that. You're off home, I think, after we've done with this.'

His look lingers on my face, searching. I pull my mouth into a smile and contain the sigh that threatens to blow the pages from his grasp. My hands are squeezing themselves together in my lap like small animals trying to hide under each other. He lowers his gaze to the paper and continues to read down the page, explaining his changes.

'Yes, yes, and this phrase here . . .'

At last he's finished. He turns to me. He looks pleased with himself and shows me his white, white teeth. He has brown eyes that turn down at the corners so he often looks a little sad, but now he's looking excited and wants to show me what he's done. He reads out his words, carefully, slowly, making sure not to mess them up.

'Dad?'

He asks me not to interrupt. I listen to his words.

'Um, look, maybe you should go home, get some rest. Let's leave this 'til tomorrow. Marn?'

I'm looking at the single sheet it took the whole day for me to type, one-fingered, on my mum's old Brother typewriter. My poem has sunk under the weight of his pen marks and his words have become hard and solid in the room as he reads them. I can't see past them. I can't remember my own words either. They slipped out of the open window into the rain. They've gone.

'There. That's a much better poem, don't you think? Do you like it? You do, don't you? I wrote it for you, Marnie.'

I'm good at pretending so I lean over the paper and nod, and smile.

'I'll call you a taxi. Where's your jacket? Marnie?'

'Yes,' I say, 'You're right. It's a lot better.'

I smile and smile. Something inside me has curled up and stopped. And my nails have left perfect red crescents in the palms of my hands.

Missing: ELLIOT two years old,
Tonkinese male cat, very sweet &
shy. Please ring . . .

I won't think about him any more today. I can't. Leo was trying to smile as my taxi pulled away from the kerb yesterday, but he's not an idiot. He can see something's up and has given me a few days off work. The rest of the week is mine. I was planning to go home and crawl under the covers, but called Shiulie instead. She has taken me for an 'emergency day out in the country', cycling. To distract me, cheer me up. I didn't even know she could ride a bike. She jokes that the countryside is filthy, packs of feral dogs lurking in every thicket, semi-literate ruffians lying in wait for lone women. She can still surprise me.

And now we're here standing on a low hill, the damp grass leaving the hems of my jeans heavy with wetness.

'It'll take your mind off your dad, for a while. Bit of country air, bit of exercise, surrounded by country-type things, you know. Healthy stuff. You'll love it, you'll feel so much better soon. Promise.'

This said with such finality, such authority. I wish I could believe her. She flashes me a gleaming smile and secures her loosely-woven, scarlet shawl around her shoulders. I think she has one in every colour. Not the best clothing for cycling in the country, but there's no telling her. She could at least have put some flat shoes on. Her helmet has been dumped on the ground by the car and she's off down the grassy slope on a barely visible track. I'll wait a while at the top of the rise and think about the wind in my hair for a moment. Nothing more. I'll breathe in the clean air, breathe in deep, let it scour my brain of wintry thoughts. A bird is singing somewhere, high and sharp.

Shiulie's heading straight for a tightly knit group of sheep in the valley below. One hand steering, the other waving at the flock. They've raised their heads to look at her now, white faces bobbing up together as if joined by an invisible thread. She stops, expertly, and sits with one foot on a pedal, shawl draped across her back and one hand raised as if in salute to the flock. A human ambassador to the ovine race. The sheep stare as one for a moment, grass-stained muzzles sawing sideways, then they jog away like clouds scudding across the heavens.

My friend's voice forks like lightning suddenly from below me in the valley. I tighten my ponytail and zigzag down to meet her, almost hurling myself over the handlebars as I stop. She's standing astride her bike, chewing her lower lip furiously.

'Try and use both sets of brakes when you stop quickly, you'll end up needing reconstructive surgery using only the front ones like that. And then you'll come to me for counselling for Posttraumatic stress disorder. And then it'll just get ugly.'

'OK, I'll try.'

She frowns.

'You'd think they'd be OK with me, no?' she hisses.

I look around.

'Who?'

'Them. The sheep.'

'What are you talking about? They're sheep, Shiulie. They're *meant* to be scared of you.'

'No they're not. Not of me. They're meant to have a sixth sense type thing. You'd think they'd know.'

'Know what?'

She turns to glare at me as if it were my fault the sheep are keeping their distance. Then turns to the swaying woolly rumps and yells against the wind.

'I'm a vegetarian, you lot. Vegetarian! I. Don't. Want. To. Eat. You. You could at least have the decency to come and say hello. Idiots.'

She sighs heavily.

'I mean, I can understand why they wouldn't want to get near you. You probably smell of dead animal to their keen little noses. Of all the dead animals you've ever eaten.'

'Right. So you don't think their farmer eats meat then? He'll be a vegan then, will he? A soya-milk-on-the-organic-cornflakes type of bloke.'

I stop.

'And since when have you been a vegetarian, anyway?'

'Since . . .'

She snorts laughter into the corner of her shawl.

'You're taking the piss, aren't you?'

"Course not. I'm absolutely positive that – *were* I a hippy – I'd believe that animals would be able to pick up on my soft and fluffy non-meat-eating vibes. That they would be able to sniff out the fact I was wearing "vegetarian" shoes, that nothing in my life was connected with the exploitation of animals in any way. That they would instinctively know I did not cover myself in lard every morning before I went to work. Not only would they know all this, but they would actively seek me out to thank me for not being a carnivore, fur-wearer, user or abuser of animals. *Were* I a non-meat eater. I am, however, a head-shrinker, so none of the above applies.'

Another blinding smile is flung my way. My Shiulie. She is like an exciting new toy, lots of electrical moving parts and accessories, the latest features, the brightest colours. Everyone wants to play with her. I'm more your wooden train set. I don't mind that she gets the attention, turns the heads, grabs at life while I watch. I don't mind.

'Just trying to take your mind off things, Marn. Thought you could have a few moments off and think *I* was bonkers rather than . . .'

Shiulie's voice trails off. She turns and looks towards the horizon. As I follow her gaze I notice that the sheep are again alert, ears twitching. But they are no longer chewing their grass. They are expectant, quivering.

'Look, maybe this was a stupid idea. It's getting cold. You cold? Come on, I'll take you home. Head massage? Rub all those bad thoughts away. What do you say? Or just good old-fashioned alcohol? Ask. It shall be yours.'

And suddenly the flock scatters, white bodies leaping, trying to fly over each other, scrambling madly for escape. Two bolt away from the rest, then swivel on their hind legs like ballerinas and gallop back to join the herd, barging head first into a moving wall of woolly backsides.

'Christ.'

The sheep are hurtling around the field, ears flat against their heads, eyes rolling.

'God, look at them go. Burning off those calories.'

'Give it a rest Shiu. They're scared of something.'

She squints at the fleeing knot of sheep.

'My professional opinion would be that they're actually bloody terrified.'

Shiulie turns and looks at the sky. Clouds are gathering low on the horizon.

'Maybe we should get back to the car. We've had enough fresh air for one day, and you're looking better, you really are. Told you it would work. Home, drink, food. Shall we?'

The sheep wheel round at the end of the field, rush headlong along the stone wall, a tightly-packed ball of fish swerving to avoid hungry dolphins. I feel the drumming of their hooves through the soles of my shoes. Shiulie turns to look at the galloping flock one last time and hurls some final words their way.

'You're all just a bunch of *sheep*!'

She shoves off on her bike, a small brightly-coloured skiff launching itself against the wind. She stands on her pedals and pushes powerfully uphill, her hair streaming, raven-blue in the sunlight.

Shiulie has dragged me out of myself again. She has always coaxed and wheedled me out, has perched me atop a hill with a huge box of white chocolate truffles and a flask of hot whisky; has sat me in an empty art house cinema to watch a French film set in the Middle Ages with a soundtrack played entirely using the instruments of the time while feeding me toffee popcorn; has taken me to the beach to picnic in howling autumn winds with Dylan and Ruth.

I have vivid memories of that day. Of the feeling of wrongness and then the feeling of rightness. Of the way the sun was swallowed whole in the throat of a sea mist which reared up suddenly and without warning. Of a cricket bat made from driftwood. A trail of empty clothes leading to the water's edge, gooseflesh meeting the stinging sea, shrieks and squeals and peals of laughter wrung from cold-shocked lungs. But most of all

I remember the clinging insistence of the sand, and the last tuna sandwich left untouched.

That Sunday morning saw me drag myself from the fug of my bed with streaming nose, sore eyes and a bouquet of barbed wire lodged in my throat. The thought of sitting on a windswept beach sent me scurrying back to the safety of my duvet with a hot honeyed drink, but the telephone wouldn't stop ringing. After half an hour I relented. Shiulie's voice pleaded, cajoled. I was promised the most beautiful stretch of sand in the northern hemisphere, studded with the rarest of shells, fossils and stones. I was guaranteed the most sublime of sunsets, over the most impressive of oceans. We would see the brightest of starry starry nights, the Milky Way and a meteor shower. I would be granted whatever wish I wished on my lucky star. I would be the sorriest of sorry fools to miss it.

I peered through the curtains at the low, dull day and its blanket of grey which seemed to hover below the sky at the level of my bedroom window. I'd give it a miss this time, I was sure they'd have a lovely swim and that they would bring me some pretty shells back from the trip. This did not deter Shiulie and after a few minutes of her haranguing I was unable to fight any longer. She was, after all, the doctor. I was to get up and get dressed. I would be picked up in ten minutes. I would not regret it.

I began to regret it as soon as I stepped out of the building. My cheeks were immediately chill and damp and my hair began to frizz. I folded myself next to Shiulie on the cold vinyl-covered back seat. Dylan twisted round, his shock of white-blond hair grazing the headlining of the car, and threw me a wide grin from the driver's seat.

'Ready to battle the wind and the waves Marn?'

I gave him what I hoped was a truly piteous look and coughed into my balled fist. What on earth was I doing?

'Going to have fun at the beach,' came the reply from Ruth, who sat in the front on the passenger's side. She reached around her seat, squeezed my knee and winked. I hadn't realised I'd actually voiced my misery. I sighed and sank further into my heavy jacket. Shiulie hummed to herself and tapped her long fingers on her knee, keeping time to some internal rhythm.

After a long grumbling car journey we rounded the final bend of a single track lane which led to the beach. The sky had not lifted and the wind had picked up, was whipping the coarse grass about our legs as we unfurled ourselves from the car. Sand scoured the wide expanse of beach, hurried along by the wind as if trying to discourage trespassers. One lone surfer rolled in on the breakers and disappeared into the froth of waves.

'Jesus. You sure about this?'

No one answered. Dylan was already semi-naked and bounding towards the water. Shiulie and Ruth unrolled blankets and pinned them to the shifting sands with the food basket and Dylan's enormous boots. I retreated to the safety of the back seat of the car and held the door open with my foot, battling against the wind and watching the others' meticulous preparations. Once they'd satisfied themselves that our little patch of beach was properly habitable they stripped off to reveal one plain black swimming costume against dark skin (Shiulie) and one orange crocheted bikini against pale, freckled skin (Ruth).

'Not coming in?'

I looked at Shiulie. I looked past her at the sea, where Ruth had just dived into a wave. I looked back at Shiulie.

'I guess I didn't really need to ask.'

She turned and walked determinedly to the water's edge, with a final 'Keep warm!' flung over her shoulder towards me before wading in to waist height and ducking her head under.

'Jesus.'

I clambered out of the car and dropped onto the blanket, leaning back against the old car and trying to make myself as small a target for the wind as possible. Watched the swimmers shriek at each other and splash about for a few moments and wondered how much of my clothing I could bear to remove. I began to shiver.

After ten minutes of splashing about in the churning waters of the Channel, Shiulie, Dylan and Ruth returned briefly to refuel with warm soup and sandwiches, trying to eat as they hopped around me slapping their arms and showering droplets of seawater on my head.

'Can't you sit down for a moment, you lot? You're going to make me have a seizure.'

Dylan rubbed his arms and lunged for the soup Thermos.

'Nope. We'll freeze. Hypothermia doesn't suit me, I go blue and that's Ruth's least favourite colour, isn't it? Bit of soup, all will be well.'

He unscrewed the lid while skipping around the blanket, stopped briefly to gulp at the steaming liquid. Then a loud belch and a satisfied sigh.

'There. All that's needed.'

I wiped my nose on my sleeve. I was feeling uncouth, and didn't much care who saw.

Dylan threw the crusts of a sandwich into his mouth.

'I'm going to go coax some pearls from oysters for my woman. Would you like that, Ruthie?'

Ruth reached out and put her hand against his cheek.

'Yes, sweetie. I'd love that.'

They stood that way for a few moments, eyes locked. Then Dylan turned his head, kissed the open palm of his young wife. Grinning, he slapped his flat white belly.

'And we're off!'

He strode towards the water again stooping once to pick up something from the sand. A dark young man, skinny to the point of emaciation and whooping wildly, was running in circles on the shoreline, a large shell clasped in his raised hand. Dylan hefted the piece of wood in his hands. A shout from the water's edge and an object came flying towards him. He steadied himself, swung the wood and hit the airborne shell back out across the sand.

'Howzat!'

The man lined himself up again and, with a hop and a jump, launched the shell back at Dylan. Who missed it with his makeshift cricket bat and dropped to his knees in mock anguish.

'Anyone for cricket?'

Shiulie wiped her mouth, grinned at me and trotted with Ruth down to where Dylan and his new friend were examining the driftwood bat, discussing the pros and cons of using seashells as balls.

In the spirit of joining in with the day's fun and games I had got as far as taking my shoes and socks off and burying my toes in the damp sand. It sucked at my feet. I imagined them sinking deeper, my ankles, my calves disappearing into the cold wet, my thighs, my waist, my chest surrounded by the sucking coolness. It would pass my shoulders, grasp my neck and creep towards my jaw, taking in my earlobes, finding its way into my ears, into my head and finally my nose would be under and my eyes would be closed and I wouldn't breathe but that would be OK and I would be in the cool darkness and it would be so quiet and so calm.

But the sand would not take any more of me than my toes, which were now a greyish shade of purple. I sneezed, wiped my nose on my sleeve again and was suddenly thrown into shadow. Cold droplets of seawater landed on my cheek as Shiulie flung herself down on the rug, towel-swaddled and rosy-cheeked. I half expected her to shake herself like a wet dog, but instead she hugged her long limbs to her chest, planted her chin on her knees and burst into tears. I watched her for a moment, then put a hand on her shoulder. I looked back out to sea. Dylan's pale form was pulling further away from us with each of his strong strokes, and could only be seen as he rose over each wave. Ruth paddled at the water's edge, her thin arms wrapped around herself. Shiulie sobbed silently, eyes closed. I shuffled closer on my bottom, wrapped an arm around her shoulders and held her. I drew sweeping lines in the sand with the fingers of my free hand, catching mounds of it under my fingernails. The tiny scraped ditches filled slowly with seawater and my body shook with her sobs.

I watched the heaving ocean and we sat sharing our warmth as Dylan disappeared further out and the cold damp seeped through the blanket and the seat of my jeans. I said nothing and neither did she.

After a while Shiulie's body stilled. She rubbed her eyes and nose viciously with the ball of a hand, let go a shuddering sigh. Leant her head against my collar bone. I breathed in the smell of salt and coconut hair oil.

'Last time I was here, at this beach.'

The sentence was not completed, but I knew what she was thinking. I nodded my understanding, but a deep cold that was nothing to do with the weather, began a slow spread upwards from the pit of my stomach.

'Will.'

The name I wished she hadn't mentioned was whispered against my skin.

'The bloody fucker.'

I nodded again, harder, agreeing. The low clouds began to

empty themselves on us, gently at first, then with more vigour. The iciness was rising, had gripped my chest.

'Shit sucker.'

Nod. I thought I should probably try and get Shiulie into the car but was afraid to remove my arm from her shoulders.

'Adulterous fucking wank stain.'

Nod. Nod. I concentrated on my breaths, slow, steady. Nothing to panic about.

'Sorry . . . you know.'

She pulled away and sniffed into her knees, crushing the tip of her nose against her kneecap.

'Bastard.'

I knew this. Shiulie didn't know how well I knew this. He had got away with too much. I blinked my eyes, hard, to rid my eyelashes of raindrops and coughed loudly to rid my mind of him.

'He was Shiu. He was.'

She sighed, bit her lip.

'He'll get it though, won't he? One day. He'll get what's coming to him.'

She turned to me, took in my soaked hair, my sodden clothes. I must have had the air of an old but faithful and long-suffering dog who has been left out in the rain: slightly reproachful but ultimately willing to put up with most things thrown my way.

Shiulie smiled with just one corner of her mouth.

'You not too cold sitting here?'

She lowered her nose to her knees again, but kept her eyes on me. I gazed at her through darkly-dripping hair.

'Nah. I live for this sort of thing. After all it's the most perfect beach, the most beautiful of oceans, the most delicious of picnics, everything you promised and more. I'm bloody loving every moment of it.'

My fingers scratched at the sand.

'Still waiting for my meteor shower, though.'

She snorted into her knees. Her eyes were red-veined and glistening, her nose was dripping, and suddenly she was trying not to giggle.

And then there we were. Laughing as the rain fell fat and hard against our upturned faces and the sand around us darkened. We clutched at each other, toppled sideways onto the wet blanket and guffawed at the racing clouds. Dylan had risen like a sea monster from the waves, found us sodden and sand-peppered and hiccoughing hysterically and, with many an eye-roll and much muttering, he and Ruth herded us towards the waiting car. Once we had settled Dylan threw the remains of our picnic in after us. Shiulie lay her head on my lap and fell asleep. I stroked her damp black hair and watched as the raindrops zigged and zagged across the windows.

From behind glass you can pretend you're not part of the world. The windscreen of Shiulie's Mini is my barricade as she weaves us home through green-fringed country lanes after our abortive cycle ride. She is quiet, for now, singing softly to the music

> And that smell of sweet perfume
> comes drifting through
> The cool night air like Shalimar

I am cocooned, apart. Safe. I watch these scenes slip by our small circle of warmth and music and gentle movement: sleeping swans in the corner of a field; a tunnel of trees, arching over us, pitching us into underwater gloom; a hillside of shaggy ponies, steaming in the weak low afternoon sunshine.

And all the little boys come around,
walking away from it all
So cold
And as you're about to leave
She jumps up and says hey love,
you forgot your gloves

A row of tiny, box-like back gardens, in one a tarpaulin-shrouded boat hull, its naked mast pointing forlornly at the sky; a dead fox at the kerb, shatter-backed and twisted like a discarded fur stole.

'Listen, Mum's cooking Methi mutton tonight, I said I'd go over. You want to join us? She'd love to see you. She's been asking after you. She's worried.'

A cat's cradle of electricity cables snaking over the fields; a hook-beaked bird hovering over a hedgerow; muddy water pooled in a tractor tyre track.

'Marn.'

A lifeless tree, bare shoulders drooping towards the freshly-ploughed soil in which its roots rot.

'Marnie?'

It takes me a moment to focus on my friend's voice.

'Sorry. She's worried, your mum. Why's she worried?'

'Marnie, I know you're not sleeping, what with everything . . .'

'Look, Shiu, she shouldn't be worried. There's nothing to be worried about. I keep telling you. I just need a night, a couple of nights' sleep. That's all. Why's she worried about me?'

A stupid, stupid question, but you have to put off the inevitable, don't you? You have to pretend everything is fine, that there's no reason for people to be concerned, move along please, nothing to see here. You have to stall the moment when you are forced to look the situation in the face, get to grips with it. I am dishonest with my concerned friend. I play daft.

'You've hardly been yourself recently, have you? Understandably, of course.'

I rub the knuckles of my right hand, which started aching a few days ago and seem to be getting gradually worse. I wonder vaguely whether I'm too young, at twenty-nine, to be getting arthritis.

'God, I forgot, Ravi's having some of his friends staying over tonight, I think. Can't remember. Anyway, we can banish them to his room. Please come. If only to save me from my little brother.'

'It's sweet of you Shiu, but I'm exhausted. I just need to get some rest. Please don't worry. That goes for your mum too. Say "Hi" from me, yeah?'

Her glance has lingered on my face for a fraction of a second too long. A car horn blares. Too near.

'Shit! Where did that come from?'

'The road in front of you.'

'Funny. Alright. I'll drop you home and you get an early night.'

'Thanks Shiu.'

She glares through the windscreen at the red lights snaking up the road in front of us.

'Oh, and if you tell me you're OK once more I'll scream.'

She returns to her music.

> Say goodbye in the wind and the rain
> on the back street
> In the backstreet, in the back street
> Say goodbye to Madame George

I smile at her profile as she mouths the words. I know I'm smiling because I feel my cheeks rise. I just don't know why.

And now I'm here. Here. Out in the light that hurts my old eyes. I'll just have to wait. Bide my time. Behind bars you learn to be patient. Watch. Listen. Pore over the smells that rope you, pick through them, one at a time. Turn them over and over: a rat on a rubbish tip examining old boots, old bones.

Did I say it was easy? The waiting? It is. Once you've worn the youth from your hide, like you rub the hairs away from your flank by constant licking, hour after hour. Once you've swallowed and digested your pride, even though you know it'll threaten to burst from your guts. Did I say it was quick? Because it is. One day you wake and the pads of your feet, once tender, soft, have hardened from pacing, pacing along draughty concrete floors. One day you wake and the flame behind your eyes has dimmed so much that a casual observer – there are many – might think it gone. On this day, this calloused, dimmed day, you wake and, instead of jumping up to snarl at the bars and start your endless back and forth march, you stretch your legs, yawn. You watch the clouds come from your mouth in the cold air. You lay your head back down. You close your eyes and wait for breakfast.

Did I say how easy the waiting gets? After months, years. After lifetimes. So when you find yourself free what do you do? Creep back to the bars of your cage, beg to be let back in? Because sudden freedom is blinding, deafening. Terrifying. Do you decide to become your own jailer, accept the lock and swallow the key, keeping it safe within your bowels? Or crouch low, crawl out, eyes wide, nostrils scanning the wind for signs of trouble or betrayal?

I was freed. Not that my liberator knew what she was doing. Not that I asked for it. Too many years inside. Makes you scared of sunlight. Of new foods. Of yourself. Old beast like me wants a bit of comfort, bit of rest and relaxation after a lifetime of service.

Still, managed to get a bit of exercise today. Brushing up on my hunting skills. Sharpening up this old nose.

Might try that cat tomorrow.

Leo my yellow cat is gone
MISSING
LOST CAT PLEASE HELP
Yellow-sand colour
Blue eyes
Male cat MISSING
Call me please if you see him.

My day of being cheered up has exhausted me. Back at my flat
I find my sister, Jess, watching TV. She's let herself in with my
spare key, the one she keeps for emergencies, such as escaping
our mother's relentless optimism. Mum seems to be able to draw
a blanket over anything she doesn't understand, anything which
frightens her. Jess needs to take that blanket between her teeth
and worry it like a dog. It doesn't make for a happy home life.
She should leave mum's place, I've told her, find a room of her
own, but she just shrugs and rolls her grey eyes.

From behind she seems to be on fire, the sofa back obscuring
all but the very top of her head and the rings of smoke blanketing her. A wildlife documentary. She loves them. This one is

about the sea. Blind fish, mouths bristling with needle-like teeth. Tiny underwater volcanoes belching blue-black smoke.

'Hi Jess. You OK?'

'Mhmm.'

To the casual observer this could mean anything, but I know she's not OK. I know this because she has been turning up at my flat at all hours of the day and night, saucer-eyed and monosyllabic, since Dad disappeared. Burying herself in TV and chain-smoking. When she runs out of cigarettes – which is not often, she seems to carry countless packs on her – she gnaws on her fingertips until they swell and redden.

The picture changes. Now we have the wide open plains of the Serengeti. More teeth, this time in the mouths of graceful sandy cats. Ears flickering delicately at clouds of fat black flies. And wildebeest. The cannon fodder of African wildlife documentaries. As if on cue two lions stand to watch the dust rise on the horizon, yellow clouds thrown up by thousands of dry hooves.

There is another feline presence here, but this one is noticeable by its absence.

'Seen the cat? Thought he'd be waiting for his dinner. Scowling for his dinner.'

'Nope. Not seen him.'

He'll turn up when he wants something. He's probably out with the ladies. I pluck at one of my guitar's strings and a tiny plume of dust rises from the vibrating steel. The instrument, a sixteenth birthday present from Dad, has been propped against the arm of my sofa for the three years I've lived here. It is only occasionally moved for hoovering. I have long since forgotten the five simple chords I once learned to please him. One day soon I'll pick it up and play again.

'You been back to his house today?'

The question is so casual, thrown over her shoulder towards

me. I've not checked his place for two days now and the guilt is beginning to nag. A wildebeest calf staggers to its feet on the screen behind her, balancing uncertainly like a novice acrobat on stilts.

'No. Shiulie wanted to cheer me up, she said, so she took me cycling. I'm not sure why she thought bikes would do it, we didn't end up doing much. We did watch some sheep go berserk though.'

Jess turns her head slowly to look at me. Raises an eyebrow. Behind her four hundred pounds of feline power crouches, muscles and tendons quivering beneath the tawny hide, readying itself for the chase.

'You're joking. Shiulie? On a bike?'

The thought of my friend engaging in any kind of physical activity other than shopping is, I agree, odd.

'I know. She just thought it would . . .'

'Cheer you up. Yeah. And I'm sure it did.'

The small grey beast disappears screaming under a mound of lion fur. My sister is six years younger than me, yet so much more cynical. How did that happen? The ashtray is, as usual, overflowing. I drop my jacket over the back of a chair and sit down next to her on the hard sofa. A strangled yelp and hiss alerts me to the fact that the cat has been sitting directly beneath the seat I've just dropped my backside on. Knuckles darts over to the window and jumps up onto the sill. He scans the street below and finally settles down to wash his paws. A simple life. He stops scrubbing his marmalade ear, forefoot hovering millimetres above the window sill; ears swivelling, pink nostrils flexing. Then turns to glare at me and gives a yowl of pure despair. The shock of the sound splinters the low mumblings of the TV. Jess's cigarette stub dangles from her lower lip as she finds her voice again.

'What's up with him?'

He carries on meowing, quieter now, pathetic.

'You'd think the bugger was caged and starving. Tell you what Knuckles, we'll sell you to a lab, yeah, so they can do experiments on you? How'd you like that?'

The cat looks away through the window briefly, then hops off the sill and flashes into my bedroom to disappear under the bed. Always under things, always slinking and sliding, never up front, on top, in your face. Below and behind. You've got to watch your ankles.

Jess's eyes are red. She's been crying again. I wish I could. The most I can manage is a tightening of the throat, a sudden prickling rush of heat behind my eyelids. And when that happens I beat it back, push my fingers into my mouth and bite, hard, until the pain makes me forget.

'So what are you watching?'

'Animals.'

She rolls her eyes towards the ceiling and sniffs. Rubs roughly at her nose with the back of a hand. I have a sudden urge to lean over and tuck a stray strand of hair behind her ear, but don't, and follow her gaze to the TV screen. The lions rip through their meal, snarling at each other and licking bloody noses with tongues the size of dishcloths.

> My name is Red – I'm LOST –
> Ginger tabby with orange eyes is
> missing from the Park Crescent area.
> He is only eleven months so he is not
> fully grown. Please look in your
> sheds and garages, we really miss
> him and want him home.

I'd tried to relax my grip on the phone receiver as the throbbing in my knuckles was getting worse.

'Ben Irving. I-R-V-I-'

'Yes, I know how to spell Irving, thank you. His age?'

'Sixty. No, sixty-one. I think.'

Silence.

'Hello?'

'I'm still here. Right. And when did you last see your father?'

A small boy in sky blue satin standing on a cushioned stool springs to mind. A large table. A kindly, questioning face. Royalists. Roundheads. A sobbing girl.

'Ms Irving, did you hear the question? You last had contact with your father when exactly?'

'Sorry. I was just thinking about a painting, do you know the one which . . . ?'

It's probably not the time to be talking art.

'Never mind. About a week? Well, I spoke to him. On the phone. I went to visit him on Thursday, and he wasn't there. So, maybe, I don't know, four or five days?'

I have no idea why this comes out as a question, as if I'm awaiting confirmation from the policewoman that I did actually see Mr Ben Irving a week ago. One point for a correct answer, well done, and your prize today is . . .

'How did he seem to you when you two last spoke? Did he seem in any way different?'

Different to what exactly? How much different could he squeeze into one day? The different when he told me about discovering his ability to walk through walls when I was eight years old? The different when on my eleventh birthday he called me a whore? The different when he described to me the mysteries of astrophysics driving me to my first sports day at school? Or maybe the different when he told me I was the most beautiful girl in the world. Maybe it was the different which made him believe the dead were trying to communicate with him from the depths of the sink plughole, when he held me over it so I could hear the voices coming from the depths until I cried to be let down. Or the next day's different, when he took Jess and I for a walk in the woods and showed us how the shy woodlice hid in rotting logs and the ferns gathered in the shady places under the trees to whisper their secrets to each other.

'Well, he seemed . . . he seemed like he usually is. No real difference, I don't think. I mean, he had his mood swings, like I said, and he's had his . . . problems, you know about those. But there wasn't anything particularly out of the ordinary, you know, *really* different, that day.'

I see now how pointless this is. He is a grown man. There is really not much that the police will be able to do. But I know I must try. Jess will never give me a moment's peace if I don't. She says she can't deal with the police herself, that she would get too upset, make a scene, turn things over, smash glass, howl. That sort of thing. The sort of thing I don't do. The sort of thing I can only imagine doing when I'm alone in my bed, the patient dark pressing against my swollen eyelids.

I'm the big sister. I know how to communicate.

'Well thank you for your call, Ms Irving. I'm sure you are aware that in the absence of any evidence to suggest foul play there's a real limit to what we can do. But we'll try our best. I'll let you know . . .'

The phrase 'foul play' gets lodged in my mind, and I wonder whether I have somehow slipped into an alternate reality, an earlier era, where policemen wear handlebar moustaches and ride sit-up-and-beg bicycles and no one has heard of riot gear and nylon stockings have only just been invented. The rest of her words slide and jumble, dancing away with their meanings tucked under their arms, not sharing. I hear myself say 'Thank you'. I think I repeat it, maybe twice. The phone goes dead, a click, a silence, the rasping burr of dial tone. The receiver remains at my ear. Thank you, I whisper. Thank you.

JULES

Short-haired tortoiseshell
Neutered female
Distinctive markings
Dearly loved and missed
Please phone

The light is cool, scraped thin over the early morning. I have not been able to sleep, have woken in the indigo hours of the day and waited, wrapped in my duvet, for the first birdsong to reach me. Eventually I dress in the two-day worn clothes which I've retrieved from the bedroom floor and leave the flat, intent on walking until my feet bleed. But I'm only just round the corner and a few hundred yards down the high street when my enthusiasm for exercise dissipates and I decide that what I really need is a strong milky coffee and something meaty for breakfast at Woodie's. Which is, happily enough, only a couple of blocks away.

The café is next door to an 'ethnic produce' shop called In'pirations – no one has bothered to replace the missing 's'. I position myself in the window of Woodie's on a high revolving stool

37

and order a full English with extra black pudding. No tomatoes. Or beans. I imagine my sister rebuking me for being a slavering carnivorous beast. I imagine myself teasing her. *Fruit and vegetables? What's them then? Never heard of 'em, sound like weirdy lefty rubbish to me.* I smile at the greasy laminated menu.

The place is full of people: cab drivers, labourers, aged couples and a droop-eyed group of students, still awake from the night before, all here for the cheap, plentiful food. The smell of frying bacon is making me ravenous. I blow on my coffee and try to distract myself by watching the morning rush hour cars crawl past.

Lessons in the junior school opposite have not yet started, and the playground reverberates with the shrieks of small, safely-delivered children with a day's worth of energy to burn. The school is encircled by a high wrought-iron fence, from which a number of young mothers hang, watching their little ones in the yard below as if they are animals in a zoo. One woman has both arms wrapped around one of the great iron posts, leaning her forehead against it. The slope of her shoulders, the crooked angle of her neck, the flow of her hair down one side of her thin back all speak of bereavement, as if her child has been stolen away from her and imprisoned.

A hot plate piled with food is placed carefully in front of me, red and brown plastic bottles and paper napkin-swaddled cutlery arranged at my elbow. I forget the children, the mothers, the jail.

I eat.

CASPAR THE CAT IS GONE
Please let us know if you see
A blue-grey cat who is
Very gentle and sweet
And loves people.

The spectacled man behind the desk is sallow. His perfect finger-nails tap, tap on the desk top, fly to the back of his neck to scratch, scratch, then return to their tarantella on the Formica surface. His eyes scuttle from my chest to my face and back again. The tip of a pink tongue flicks out to moisten each corner of his thin lips – one, two – and disappears again. I expect him to ask me what he can do for me. He doesn't. I smile at him.

'I'd like to speak to PC Boyce, please. If she's around?'

He addresses my breasts.

'I'm afraid she's not in. What's it about?'

His voice is surprisingly low, gentle. But those eyes are not.

'I was just checking about my dad, Ben Irving. Whether anything's been heard. Any . . . progress.'

Progress. This is the word they use. I know this because I watch

TV cop shows sometimes with Jess. *I'm contacting you to get the latest progress update.* That's what they'd say.

'Haven't heard anything, Miss . . .'

'*Irving.* Marnie.'

'Haven't heard anything Miss Irving-Marnie.'

'No, just Irving. Marnie's my first name.'

'If you say so.'

His mouth remains open, as if he was about to carry on talking but has suddenly forgotten what he was about to say. He's looking at the doorway just over my shoulder. I look behind me. Two policemen with dogs walk past. They stop. The dogs are long-haired German Shepherds, silky, iron-jawed and tooth-studded. They sit and grin and pant, their tongues curling at the tips, thin ropes of spittle dripping from the black hanging corners of their mouths. I turn back to the desk but he seems transfixed. His hand creeps up to his throat, circles it protectively. He has started making a soft, high-pitched whining noise.

'Are you alright?'

His ears flush red but otherwise he acts as if he's not heard my question. I have the sudden feeling that he's about to have a heart attack.

'Excuse me, are you feeling OK?'

I did a first aid course once, years ago, how to do heart massage, mouth-to-mouth, that sort of thing. What can I remember of it? Nothing. It's seven compressions and then three breaths. No, three compressions, no five, yes. No. I'm in a police station, I'll just call for help. Someone is bound to come.

'Hello . . . ?'

I don't know his name, he's not introduced himself. I squint at a note lying on the desk. It's marked for 'PC Earle'.

'Um, PC Earle, are you feeling alright?'

His eyes dart to my face, tiny black fish behind thick glass.

The rest of his body remains perfectly still. One of the dogs looks over at us. The man tries to fold himself smaller, whimpers again. The other dog's ears swivel in our direction.

'm fine.'

His whisper barely reaches me. He still hasn't moved. I'm not even sure if he's breathing. Maybe his heart really has stopped, and he's being kept alive by the sheer force of his fear. The same way the crumbling plaster on my living room wall is kept together by the strength of the paint which coats it.

'It's not right. The dog's looking at me.'

I'm not sure I've heard his strained mumble properly. I look back at the dog, who is alert, watching. PC Earle may indeed be right.

'Well, it might be something to do with that noise you're making. Dogs respond to high-pitched . . .'

A loud bark echoes through the foyer of the station. PC Earle flinches as if he's been shot. Surely he can't be frightened of a police dog?

'Is it the dogs? Are you afraid of them?'

It's as if a spell has been broken. He relaxes his shoulders, pulls himself taller. I've offended him, and he's going to order me away, politely but firmly, and tell me to come back later to speak with PC Boyce. *In fact, don't bother. We're not going to take your case any further, so don't call back. Ever.*

'Afraid?'

He is shrill. I imagine him having me escorted from the premises by two burly, sensibly-shod WPCs. Man-handled off the premises. Woman-handled.

'Afraid?'

He seems to be tasting the word, as though it were an exotic yet potentially poisonous fruit, then spits its pips out at me, one by one.

'Of course I'm bloody afraid! It's a police dog. I know what they're trained for. I've seen it. Seen it first hand.'

He slumps down behind the desk again, as if to hide from the prowling beasts.

'They're not trained for *protection*, you know.'

It is obvious that I will get nothing from this man today, but I do find myself wondering what it is these dogs *are* trained for? His eyes skitter from dog to handler. The dog sits, watching us for a moment, tongue bouncing, then turns away. A small cough from behind the desk.

'OK, can you just let her know I've been in, that I've been asking about Ben Irving, please?'

A nod.

'Right. Thanks.'

I pause a moment longer.

'Are you sure you're OK? You don't want me to call anyone?'

The tiniest tightening of his features. Nothing else.

'OK. Well, 'bye then.'

I leave the PC trembling at his desk, pausing only briefly to stoop and pat the dog's warm bobbing head as I pass.

Scaramouche
Where have you gone?
Please call with any info on my big
white tomcat
It's been a week
And he's only young.

The morning is full of cold shadows. I tuck my hands into the arms of my dressing gown and look at the phone. The phone looks back at me.

Knuckles, on the other hand, is making strange sounds. He is usually quiet, even when asking for his dinner. A strong, silent type my sister calls him. But curled up underneath the radiator he is wheezing, and his back legs twitch.

I bend and reach out my hand to touch his shoulder. This is not something I do often, as stroking cats usually means spending the next couple of hours sneezing and wiping my puffy, streaming eyes. Knuckles is also not the friendliest of cats. He will turn up at my kitchen window, scratching the glass for food, then wolf it down and disappear until the next time his belly needs filling. He does not like to be touched.

He appeared from nowhere about a year ago. A nowhere cat. Orange and white stripes, a nick out of one ear, tail bent at a jaunty angle. Orange eyes. I found him on the doorstep one day after work. Just sitting, as if he was expecting me, with a look on his striped face: *Where the hell have you been? Can't you see I've been waiting?*

'Hello puss.'

I had the feeling he was assessing whether or not I was going to be a soft touch.

He made no other movement so I returned his gaze for a few moments and opened the front door. Went inside and turned as I closed it to check on the newcomer. He'd gone. Up at my flat I opened the door and when I reached the kitchen found the orange cat sitting on the table. *What took you so long? Where's my tea?*

On that first day I approached him, making soft kissing noises, wondering at the same time why we make kissing noises at cats. He showed me with one long incisor that air kissing at cats is not a sure way to their hearts. Then he growled. I stopped, feeling vaguely insulted. I rummaged in my cupboards and presented him with most of the sardines from a tin. He ate them from a cracked yellow saucer on the floor by the fridge. I ate the last one sitting on the floor with my back propped against a cupboard door, oil dripping down my bare arm to my elbow. Once he'd finished the fish, he carefully cleaned his plate, then his paws, then his marmalade face. And then he sat and stared at me. I poured him some milk, though I wasn't sure if he would turn up his nose at semi-skimmed. But he drank it with tiny flicks of his pink tongue, washed his face and paws once more, vaulted onto the windowsill and was gone through the open window. I thought I'd never see him again. But he was at the window the next evening.

And the next. Each time I fed him scraps and milk, each time he ate, washed and left.

I tried to touch him only once. That attempt left the back of my hand in ribbons. I assumed that he must have been mistreated in some way, so would take it slowly, build up trust. But every subsequent approach has been met with that stare, that bared tooth, that low-pitched growl.

The sixth day of his visits found me standing in the pet food aisle of my local shop. How could there be so many different makes of cat food? I chose a tin – 'salmon and tuna in a tasty and nutritious jelly' – and took it home. I waited in the darkening evening at the kitchen table with a cooling mug of hot chocolate and the pink tin of jellied fish. He arrived at the appointed hour and I poured him half of the thick stinky goo. He sniffed at it delicately, ate it and disappeared again.

He's been with me ever since.

Now, as he lies in my kitchen he lets outs a piercing shriek and then carries on wheezing like an old man. Has he swallowed something? Is he choking? I drop to all fours and crawl over to him. I put out my hand to touch him. As my fingertips meet his fur it's as if they send an electric shock through his body. He yelps, jumps into the air and turns towards me in the same instant, lashing out with a fistful of needle-sharp claws which catch the back of my hand and drag down. He scrambles onto the windowsill and is gone.

Four shallow scratches run down the top of my wrist and hand, itching and throbbing. Tiny red beads dot the gashes. He must have been dreaming. Dreaming of soft rodents, his tail bottle-brushed in alleyway battles, or of canine teeth inches from his striped haunches. I lift my hand to my mouth, put out the tip of my tongue and taste the metal of my blood.

He must have been dreaming.

S he didn't want her photograph taken with me the first time we met. It wasn't her hand which shot up to answer the call. It was the tall man next to her. Her father. Could taste dampness in the air as I was heaved forward. The man waved at Jay, who carried me through the gaping people. How he heard the boy's cry among the din and clatter of people leaving is a mystery. Booming shoes, grunts of humans struggling with steaming coats, shouts of laughter splintering the air, elbowing the boy's calls aside. Smell of dead leaves blew in from outside the tent. Hot stink of human bodies and cigarette smoke. It clung to the back of my throat.

I was only a cub back then, but I was heavy. Could feel the boy's muscles tremble against mine with the effort of carrying me. I tried to stay still, though his sharp shoulder bruised my ribs and I found it hard to breathe. My knuckles throbbed where the claws had been cut out.

She was trembling and her small hands were strong for such a little naked clawless thing. They twisted in my fur, but not hard enough to hurt. Can still feel the way they held on to me. Tightly. Her breath tickled the hairs in my ears; I flicked first one, then the other. She giggled, quietly. Put her face into my neck, blew hot breaths into my fur. Spoke to me. Can't remember what she said. Must have been crushing her knees, though I tried to be still. She'd stopped shaking now, gripped my fur like I was in danger of falling and only she could save me from slipping over a cliff edge. Through both our coats I could feel the quick beating of her heart. The hot pulse of a small living thing. Couple of mouthfuls for me, no more.

Her father waved at her. He liked using his hands. His voice was loud and his dark eyebrows were drawn together. They hung over his face like the threat of a landslide. The girl took her face out of my fur. Wide eyes, mouth pulled taut. You can see it in the picture. A hunted look. Her hands are hidden in my fur, burrowing for warmth and comfort. The father went quiet behind his camera, told her what to do, where to look, to *please* smooth down her cloud of hair. She was quiet, did as he asked. I strained to find a comfortable position, the boy's hands bony underneath my shoulders as he tried to keep my weight off the girl's skinny lap. My tail squashed uncomfortably between the cold seats.

She brought me the photograph. Two days later, as we were preparing for the next move. Clang of falling metal, sudden shouts. Air heavy with dusty rain, hot sweet smell of used straw. The boy strolled across to my cage laughing to himself, pointed nose in the air, streaked jeans hanging from his scrawny frame, all angles and bones. Not particularly tempting. Not much to get stuck between your teeth on that one.

'Hey, Jerry. Photo of us and that little girl. She came with her mum to drop it off and say hello. God knows why. Told her she couldn't come in where the animals is kept. Said I'd show you, though.'

He waved it in front of my nose and its breeze stirred my whiskers. He chuckled to himself. Squinted again at the small square of glossy paper.

'Could have got a bit more of *my* face in though.'

He sighed and took the corner of the photograph between his teeth, as if testing its worth. Wandered off through rising dust and flying slivers of straw.

That photo lived taped to the side of my box for a while. It became curled and faded. Like me. I got a bigger cage when I grew so much I could wear the small one like a locket round my neck. The picture got lost while I was being transferred. I like remembering the hassle I caused them when I found out I wasn't going to be going back to my old cage, even though it bent my spine almost double. Could have done a proper mauling job, even clawless, but my knuckles were too stiff that day from the cold and I couldn't move quickly enough. So I got my new home. And I could still get gasps out of the little ones when I was in the ring, even though I wasn't allowed near them any more.

She's too old to go to the circus now. I'd have thought she wouldn't have that hunted look any more. That her hands had found something more dependable to hold on to than lion fur. But here I am. She needs something. Needs me, apparently. She's still not learned. Lion fur comes with teeth. Teeth whose only purpose is to rip. And tear. And kill.

LOST: Sausage, a brown cat
White whiskers
which are long
One white foot and
a white Belly
Reward for information

Mr Irving was a writer. Is a writer. My dad is a writer. Not a great one. Not up there with Joyce or Nabokov, two of his favourites, but someone who can string words together on a piece of paper in a way that can make him a reasonable living. He should have been a university lecturer. He spent most of his time preaching to us. About anything, everything. The way we did our hair, the way we sat at the dinner table, the type of friends we had, the kind of books we read, the finer points of my mother's cooking. I thought he would have jumped at the chance to instruct hundreds of sagging eighteen-year-olds in stale-aired auditoriums.

But there had been that short story. I never understood why he wrote it. It was so unlike any of his other work, which tended to be introspective, esoteric. This was a trite piece of fluff which needed

49

no effort from the reader, or from the writer himself for that matter. A story about a poor young boy who dreamed of being famous, of being more than his family said he could be, and who became the hottest dancer in town. I know. Like I said, I have never understood why he wrote it. And I suppose I never will, now.

I remember my mother reading an early draft, sitting with her legs curled up underneath her on the orange sofa in our living room when we all still lived together. Dad sat opposite and watched her read the whole thing. He did that sort of thing. He would give her the loose pages of his latest book, she would fold herself into the sofa to read and he would stare at her until she finished. They would sit like that, sometimes for hours. I wouldn't have been able to read with eyes on me like that, but whether she actually read the words or just let them drift through her mind like tumbleweed, she always told him she loved it when she had finished. She would place the sheaf of paper in her lap gently, smile at him. A faraway smile, as if she was somewhere else. Then she would tell him it was his best work yet.

'It's your best work yet, Ben. It really is.'

And that would be it. My dad would beam at her, retrieve the paper while kissing the top of my mum's head and disappear again upstairs to his study.

When dad gave her the story to read the same form was followed. The solemn handing over of the manuscript, the seating arrangements, the unswerving stare from my father. But as soon as my mother started reading I could tell something was different. A fretful look came into her face. Her eyebrows moved towards each other, ever so slightly. She pressed her lips together, her shoulders rose, just a little bit, and her cheeks glowed ever so slightly more pink than usual. She read for a time, then her eyes flicked towards my father's chair. She glanced quickly at him, but not at his face, not in his eyes. Who knows what might have happened. He might have shouted her into a corner of the sofa. He may have ripped the pages from her hands and set light to them in the kitchen sink. Or he may have just smiled at her; expectant, hungry. But she wasn't risking it. Her glance grazed the tip of his slippers and slid back to the printed pages in front of her. She carried on reading. My father carried on staring. And I sat watching them both over the top of my book.

I remember it being quiet, the sigh of turning pages the only sound. I could have sworn I could feel the world revolve slowly beneath us. I could hear the noise my father's thoughts made, as they danced through his mind, jumping and cavorting.

What would she say? What would he do?

By the time my mother raised her eyes from the pages my hands had dampened the cover of my book. But as soon as I saw that timid smile on her lips I knew her verdict would be the same.

'It's definitely your best work yet, Ben.'

He leaned forward in his chair.

'Do you like it?'

My heart seemed to seize up. He had never questioned her like this before. I wanted to be the prince in the book I was reading, living on a far distant planet, watering the single beautiful rose that grew there.

'Yes, Ben. I like it. I really like it. A lot.'

She paused, the smile hovering at one corner of her mouth a moment longer than it had at the other before it slid from her face. He didn't move.

'Shall I put dinner on? Ben?'

Dad jumped up from his chair to take the papers from her, gave her a quick, hard hug and ran upstairs. I think it was only then that my heart started beating again.

*

It was nonsense, the story. But it was made into a screenplay which was made into a successful film and in the end made Dad an enormous amount of money. Mr Ben Irving never needed to work again. And so he didn't. He was now free to allow his writing to retreat into ever deeper realms of arcana and obscurity without having to worry about putting bread on the table. He spent longer periods of time in his study when he was home. He no longer showed his writing to Mum.

I thought that if I did some writing too maybe he would be interested in it and talk to me sometimes. He seemed eager to read my attempts, but would list my many failings, rewriting my scribbles, moulding them into his own. That thing with the poem for example. Well, he was right, it wasn't great. He was just saving me from getting my hopes up, proving to me I wasn't a born writer. *Making sure you won't be disappointed*, he kept saying. I knew he was right but couldn't stop myself. It made me feel guilty. So I stopped showing him the words I wrote.

I took to writing at night under the covers, once Jess was asleep and mumbling to herself in the darkness. Little scraps of poems or snatches of dialogue from hastily-imagined characters. Every now and then I would stop to listen for footsteps, but I was never caught. Sometimes I would end up with a couple of pages of slanted and sly-looking handwriting, sometimes no more than a couple of lines. And every morning, before I dressed, I would remove the offending pages from my notebook, tear them up into small pieces and flush them down the toilet.

He kept asking me where my next masterpiece was. He called it that. Masterpiece. He would nudge me with his elbow and grin to show me he was only joking. I would grin back, then look at my feet. He was only joking, making sure I remembered there would only ever be one real writer in the family.

It was OK. I didn't mind.

Lost cat – MAZZY
Grey, short curly fur.
7 years old.
Cataract in one eye.
Please, please call if you see
him.

Jess is tucked up on the sofa in the living room, swaddled within so many blankets I'm sure she'll die of heat exhaustion before morning. She says she can't get warm. It is now nine minutes past four in the morning and I've been seeing how long I can keep my eyes open without blinking. Lying on my back, staring at the outlines of things in my room. I thought this might encourage me to sleep but all it does is make my eyes sting and water run into my ears.

Knuckles hasn't been home for two days now. It's not unusual for him to be gone for longer than this, so I'm not worrying.

Have you ever noticed that things which should be inanimate – chairs, spoons, manhole covers – move, ever so slightly, if you stare at them long enough? They pulse. As if inhaling and then exhaling tiny breaths. As if the smallest spark of life exists within those dense molecules.

Nothing seems still any more.

When I was maybe fifteen, sixteen, he loved to take me out to dinner. Just the two of us. I would spend an age shuffling through my wardrobe, rubbing fabrics between forefinger and thumb, as if through touch alone the clothes would communicate which should be worn. Which one would please him most. Four or five skirts or dresses would be tried on hurriedly, pulled off and then cast into a corner to cool slowly and be forgotten until my mother found them later that evening, smoothed them out and hung them away.

On these occasions my hair would never behave, the lipstick I smudged inexpertly on my lips would either make my face pallid and sickly or clownish, and my shoes would clash with whatever I had chosen to wear. But every time he saw me, newly minted, he would tell me I looked beautiful.

'You look beautiful, Marnie.'

I lived for those moments.

'I'm the luckiest father in the world. My girl, my own heart. Flesh of my flesh. Bone of my bone.'

And silently his great car would slide us to our destination, invariably hushed and dimly lit, invariably filled with wealthy-looking men and women enjoying meals which looked like precious works of art. The menu would appear in my trembling hands, so exotic, so full of promise.

'What are you going to have then, Marnie? The grouse looks good. You'd love that. Why don't you go for the grouse? Have it, you'll love it.'

I would have the grouse. Or the venison. Or the duck. Whatever he suggested. Rich meats in brown silky sauces. Soups dancing with whole prawns and crab claws. Soufflés dusted with icing sugar and delicate ringlets of lemon rind.

He would order the food, taking time over the wine, tracing the names with his finger and mouthing the words. He would always ask me if I was happy with his choice of wine. I would always tell him yes, I was happy. And I was. And once the food had been ordered, the wine swilled around his mouth, he would settle to companionable whispering, a rumbling monologue, the candlelight glowing on his cheeks, dancing in his dark eyes.

'Isn't this lovely, just the two of us? I'm the luckiest man in the world to have such a daughter.'

And I would feel the luckiest daughter in the world, with the best father, as if nothing could touch us here in this sacred circle of candlelight. All that had gone before – forgotten. Gone.

I listened to him talk about a new poem he was working on, about philosophy, about the identity of Jack the Ripper. Sometimes he would stop suddenly and look at me, hard. Then a brilliant smile would spread over his face.

'The other men here. They must be jealous of me. Being with such a beautiful young woman. They must think you're my girlfriend.'

His grin was luminous and he would take my hand in his and raise his glass to me before emptying the wine down his throat. I didn't mind him making believe I was his young girlfriend. Soft voices in the back of my mind whispered that fathers should not pretend they are their daughter's lovers. I dismissed them.

And I would smile and smile, taking tiny sips of golden wine which sparkled as if covered with sunlight. The wine would redden my cheeks. He would talk and I would listen, his voice rolling over me. I would listen to his explanations of how the universe began, an enormous explosion from nothingness. I would listen as he talked of Jesus, who had not died on the cross but had married, had children and escaped to France. I would listen as he quoted Stevie Smith or Shakespeare, eyes closed, emotions chasing each other across his face like the shadows of clouds over fields:

> Be not afeard. The isle is full of noises,
> sounds and sweet airs that give delight but hurt not.

Be not afeard. And for a few short hours, I wasn't.

More and more now I think of the times when he wasn't in hospital, but my last visit there, it must have been about four months ago, stays with me. I had been asked by one of the ward nurses to attend Dad's case conference before he was discharged. I didn't want to go to the hospital, to delve into the details of his paranoia, his delusions, his sudden violence. But none of the excuses I made in my head made me feel any less guilty so I had a word with myself and went. After waiting for forty-five minutes in a long lemon-scented corridor, polished to a deep shine by the constant shuffling of slippers, I was directed into a small room and seated amongst a scrum of junior doctors, social workers, housing workers and a consultant psychiatrist who sat cross-legged on his chair.

'What do you want to tell us, then?'

This, barked in my direction by the psychiatrist. I was confused, but launched into what I expected to be a long description of Dad's behaviour. I was cut short.

'We *know* he is ill. We *all* know he is ill. Don't we?'

Silence and the weight of what felt like a hundred pairs of eyes on me. My face burned. That was sarcasm in his voice. I couldn't believe it.

'Yes, but I thought you wanted to know from a family member whether he's any different . . .'

I tried to explain that I was asked to come, that I didn't really understand what it was he wanted, but he wasn't interested, chewed on the arm of his glasses and glared at me. One of the older male nurses came to my rescue and started talking medication, dosage, housing options with the rest of the group. I tried to listen, but the blood booming in my ears made it hard to hear their words and I had to concentrate to stop hot tears spilling onto my cheeks. The talking stopped and suddenly everyone in the room was looking at me. I opened my mouth, but the psychiatrist spoke over me.

'Thanks for coming. You've been a great help. The ward's got your number if they need to call you.'

I got up, gathered my coat and bag and squeezed past the others. I pulled on the door. It didn't open.

'Give it a push.'

The young housing officer smiled up at me. I tried to grin my thanks back, pushed on the door and fell out into the gleaming corridor.

Once outside the consulting room I stopped to gather myself. I leaned against the wall, raised my eyes to the white ceiling, tried to slow my racing heart. Breathe in breathe out. Follow the yellow and brown curlicues on their cheery way across the peeling wall border. Up and round, gentle lines curving over curving under, changing direction, tangling with each other. It worked. Round and round. Up and down. Backwards and forwards. I began to feel more together. Swirls and vortices. Playful and arching and dipping and slow.

'You a social worker?'

Up and over and round and down.

'You a social worker?'

I dragged my eyes from the wall and found myself staring at a square, lightly-bristled chin, and up into eyes so dark they were almost black. The young man stood close. Looked down at me, puzzled.

'No.'

He made no move. I cleared my throat, aware that the noise I had made previously might not have resembled human speech.

'Sorry, no, I'm not a social worker.'

I tried a smile. He stood in front of me, impassive, unyielding as a rock. I would move away from him, slide along the wall. But he might think that was rude, and there was never any telling how he would react to that. I knew. I stretched the smile into a grin.

'I'm actually a writer – for my sins.'

I laughed softly, inviting him to share the feeble joke, asking him to release me. *Please, I mean you no harm, I just want to go home, I've had enough.* He frowned slightly. It seemed to take some effort, as if he was concentrating on understanding words being spoken in a language he had only recently learned.

'Why you laughing?'

Oh.

'I was just laughing at the joke? It was just a silly little joke.'

I looked at him, open-mouthed. Then glanced down the corridor, back to his face and to the floor. Apologise, I thought.

'Sorry. It wasn't very funny.'

He stared.

'Don't get it.'

Now it was my turn to stare. His eyes were like black holes.

'You said it was a joke.'

I nodded, pressed myself closer to the wall. He leaned closer. He smelled strongly of cigarettes.

'It's a joke but I don't get it. Say it again.'

I opened and closed my mouth like a landed fish.

'Sure. OK. I said "I'm a writer – for my sins". It's just taking the Mickey.'

Stare.

'Taking the Mickey out of myself, you know – not you – out of the fact I call myself a writer.'

Stare.

'Because, you know, it's a bit. Silly. Sort of.'

No number of yellow or red or purple curls on the wall could slow my heartbeat now. He shook his dreadlocks at me, stepped away and sighed.

'Don't know why you think it's silly.'

His gaze slid beyond my head towards the picture of puppies in a pink basket which hung above me. His lower lip hung slack, the tips of straight, white teeth just visible. He sighed noisily, seeming suddenly sad and tired and lost.

'Don't get it. I'm only young.'

He turned and started a slow shuffle back towards the dorms, holding loosely balled fists raised in front of him like a toy robot. His scuffed slippers dragged along the shining floor.

'I'm only young.'

And he was gone.

Dylan was waiting outside for me, propped against the side of the car, arms and legs folded. He hadn't wanted to come in with me, said places like this made him nervous. He'd offered me a lift without being asked though, and waited the hour-and-a-half I was gone. He opened the passenger side door without a word and gave my shoulder a little squeeze as I passed him.

'Survived?' he said, as he pulled out of the car park.

'Just'.

He said no more. Turned on the radio, quietly, and let me sit without talking. I stared straight ahead at the road in front and massaged my knuckles.

Some people know exactly what to do. The whens, the wheres, the hows. It comes to them, effortlessly. The quiet he created for me in the car; he just knew. How did he do that? I have trouble knowing what people mean when they say 'Hello'. But somehow he decoded me, made me a little space for myself and drove me home. And when I got home he saw me to my front door, kissed me on the forehead and went away, without giving me a chance to ask him in. I hadn't wanted to ask him in.

He knew that.

Lost CAT Please HELP
Male, answers to 'JAY JAY'
<u>Black</u> with a white nose, one
<u>white</u> cheek, and
four white paws.
He is new to the area & escaped from
our house
<u>He will be SCARED and not know the
area</u>
If you see him please phone.
Thank you so much for your help

The music is muted, which is a blessing with the low level headache grumbling around the base of my skull. My fingers are stiff, the throbbing in my knuckle joints not having been relieved by a large quantity of painkillers. I shall try out the analgesic properties of alcohol instead.

Shiulie and I are among a scattered few drinkers in The Bugle tonight. A man we call the Stick Insect sits in his usual corner by the fruit machine, thin to the point of being ethereal, tall to the point of being, well, extremely tall. (Dad was right – I've no way with words, none at all). The Arguing Couple swing on barstools, tipping back and then forwards, shaking their fingers in each other's red faces. Later they will kiss away the angry words. One day one of them will tip too far. And then there is my friend. She is trying to persuade herself that the job she recently applied for was never for her anyway.

'I mean it would be a lot more stressful for one thing, wouldn't it? I can deal with a hell of a lot, but I'd rather stay away from locked wards. My bottom line is *never* work in a place where the patients eat the furniture.'

She takes another mouthful of neat vodka with the final ice cube, holds the alcohol for a moment then swallows while ferreting the ice away in the corner of her cheek. She sucks at it thoughtfully.

'St Edmund's is OK. For now.'

'You said you hated it.'

She crunches and peers into the bottom of her glass. Which is empty. Again.

'You said if you didn't get out in the next month you'd end up eating your own furniture.'

She frowns, sighs and turns away from me to glare down the length of the bar. The Arguing Man is waving his remaining half pint at The Arguing Woman, who looks to be on the verge of tears. Again.

''Scuse me? Hello?'

She waves a ten pound note at the girl behind the bar, who stops fiddling with the CD player and ambles over to us with a half-smile.

'Vodka, please. Marn? And a Corona for my friend.'

The girl turns and goes for the drinks. Shiulie leans towards me. 'I don't *hate* it. I just fancy a bit of a change, that's all.'

She notices my raised eyebrows before I can lower them safely.

'Oh, for fuck's sake, I don't know. I'm bloody sick of it all, the whole buggering lot of it.'

Our drinks arrive, Shiulie pays. She swills the vodka round and round, staring into the glass like a fortune-teller. I take a swig of beer, knocking my front teeth hard on the bottle neck. The teenaged barmaid looks up and smirks. Shiulie winces.

'Careful. You're always doing that.'

'I know. I'm clumsy at the moment. My hands are a bit rubbish.'

She peers at my inflamed knuckles.

'You should get a doctor to look at those. A body doctor.'

She smiles and puts her hand on my knee. The coolness of her palm reaches my skin through the thin fabric of my skirt. I look at the back of her hand lying in my lap, brown and graceful like a cat.

'We'll be OK, you know?'

I look up at her face. The lights of the fruit machine reflect, flashing, in her eyes.

'I will get a better job and find a bloke who isn't a complete arse-munching tosser and I won't have to eat any furniture or work with furniture-eating patients, and you . . . you'll be OK too,' she ends, rather feebly. She squeezes my knee. I try a smile on, cover her hand with my own. I've never noticed before that the freckles on the back of my hands are the same colour as my friend's smooth skin. As if I am an incomplete version of her, as if my skin has yet to join up, to find the other parts of itself and become whole.

'I know, Shiu. I know.'

She grins at me.

'So, where's this buggery bollocks fella then, eh? He's almost thirty-five seconds late. Most unusual.'

*

Dylan has loved to talk about the 'underwater realm' for as long as I've known him. It was not the 'ocean', never just the 'sea'. The underwater realm. *His* underwater realm, the way he sometimes talked of it. I took to calling him Cousteau. Hardly original, I grant you, but then I've never been one for startlingly new ideas. Dad was right about that too.

Dylan is rarely far from water, seems somehow dried and slightly shrivelled if kept away from it for too long, like a piece of seaweed or a sponge. He should come with a user's manual, one with a health warning on the front: 'Keep away from dry land'. I always imagined deep sea to be a place of cold and silence and thick blue darkness. But on first meeting him he told me that his favourite sound – he would often ask questions like 'What's your favourite sound?' or 'What do you think space smells like?' – was parrotfish grazing on coral.

I laughed. I had not known, I said, that parrotfish were noisy eaters. Nor that parrotfish even existed. I laughed again. He smiled, but didn't laugh. I stopped laughing.

'Serious?'

He nodded as he swallowed the last of his pint. Without spilling a drop by the way. No mean feat, I thought.

'Yup.'

'Wow. Weird.'

'Weird indeed. The underwater realm is, in fact, a very noisy place. If you've not been there you'd never guess. It's not something you hear about.'

My turn to nod while drinking, but unfortunately not as successfully. A drop of beer ended up hanging delicately from my chin. I wiped it away with a fingertip, while pretending I was doing no such thing.

'I mean, if you've never been diving you couldn't imagine the noise.'

I could not imagine the noise. What was it like?

'It's hard to put into words. These parrotfish, they're so beautiful, like rainbows. They have tough beaks to strip weed from coral and rocks.'

His eyes looked through me towards the underwater realm.

'Sound travels better underwater than through air – something to do with density – I won't bore you. Diving on a reef surrounded by these huge, slow fish, tugging at the rocks like floating cows, the sound is like grass being ripped up, loudly, at the roots. But it's everywhere – crystallised – and inside your head. Amazing.'

He beamed at me and I longed suddenly to be below the waves somewhere, deep and blue, floating with the gentle fish and the forgetful rocks. His eyes gleamed, phosphorescent in the dim lights and for a moment it was as though his entire being – body, hair, eyes – had been leached of colour but glowed, from long years spent underwater far from the light, like a soft-bodied, half-formed creature of the deep, naked and tremulous. His hair was silver, cropped short as velvet. It had turned palest grey when he was only seventeen, as if jealous of the blanching of the rest of his body and determined to fit in.

He kept us rapt with stories of eel gardens and shoals of trembling ghostly cuttlefish suspended like bead curtains, motionless in the water but disappearing at the slightest disturbance. Of free diving, its purity, its freedom. The long, slow breaths at the surface preparing for the dive. The calming of the heart, the slowing of its pulse to seventy, to sixty beats a minute and less. The jack-knifing of the body and the powerful first thrust downwards. The measured strokes to the bottom and then the lazy euphoria of joining the pugnacious damselfish and the dancing arms of anemones, basking underwater for minutes at a time.

'Relaxation, that's the thing. You've just got to relax and enjoy the experience.'

Then the insistence for the surface as cells are starved of oxygen, the way air has never tasted so good. The body feeling at first heavy all over, then muscles singing with new energy.

That night I tried holding my breath in the bath. I breathed deeply for a few seconds before dunking my head. Tried to empty my mind, slow my body, as my puckered fingers gripped the slippery, white edges of the tub. But when I surfaced, spluttering and wiping my eyes, my watch had logged only forty-seven seconds. I put free diving from my mind, dried myself and went to bed.

I dreamed that night of swimming with Dylan in a moonlight-filled ocean with the jewelled fish. We ate kelp sandwiches which we found under the rocks.

'They're good for you. They help you breathe underwater,' he told me.

And we swam and swam until I realised that I had been under for more than forty-seven seconds and that I would be late for my wedding. I turned to tell Dylan, but he had begun to drop down, deeper and deeper, waving at me and opening his mouth to let go great clouds of silver bubbles. I yearned to follow him but knew that if I did my wedding day would be ruined and I hadn't even bought a dress yet. While I hesitated among the creeping starfish he dropped from sight into the depths, and I woke up.

And here he is now, in this pub. I sense him before I see him; a sort of reverse sonic boom precedes him. He looms at us out of the thick fug of cigarette smoke, like a windjammer sailing out of sea mist. His hull comes to rest mere centimetres from my knees.

'Marnie. Babe.'

His voice rumbles through my legs. A grin springs unbidden to my face.

'Hey you.'

I am scooped up and hugged fiercely. Dylan holds me tight, tighter. I decide then that I would marry this man for his hug alone if he were not already wed.

He drops me back onto the seat as he might a puppy and rubs his hands together.

'Drinks', he says, and it is a statement not a question. With only a cursory glance at the table and then at the glasses in our hands he turns and heads towards the bar to charm the barmaid into surreptitiously doubling the vodka measures for no extra cost. Over his shoulder he calls to me.

'Come and help me with the drinks.'

I trot after him. He orders at the bar.

'Where's Ruth tonight?'

He snorts.

'My good lady wife is out at one of her personal development workshops. "Potty Training your Inner Child", or some such. Bless her.'

He props his elbow on the bar's damp surface, props his chin on the ball of his hand, taps his finger tips along his jaw bone. The movement makes the muscles and tendons under his skin dance and tremble, in turn animating a tattoo I had never noticed before. A pair of black eyes framed by flowing mane, so huge it looks electrified, and teeth. Teeth bared and twitching at me.

'Do you like him? Got him done couple of weeks ago. Ruthie nearly killed me.'

He grins over the tops of his fingers. Bares his teeth at me and growls.

'Grrr.'

My heart judders gently. Ruth, I think, is a lucky woman. The stylised lion ripples under Dylan's white-furred skin, outlined in heavy black ink.

'He's . . . nice.'

Dylan pulls a face.

'Nice. For a writer, Marnie, you certainly have a way with words.'

'I'm not a writer, Dylan, I'm a copywriter. There's a difference.'

He leans closer.

'Bull. Shit,' he says, and winks at me.

I watch the translucent hairs on Dylan's arm move over the lines of the tattoo, as if they ache to clothe the naked creature painted there. Something makes me want to reach out and touch it.

I surprise myself by asking a question, a question which has just popped into my mind.

'Why?'

The question is actually nothing to do with the lion tattoo, but Dylan takes it as such. As would any normal person.

'Well, I kind of thought it was obvious. Leo? Me? You know?'

The black mane furls around the beast's head like a war banner, the eyes pull together in a furious grimace, pouring scorn and defiance. Rampant, ferocious.

Maybe I should get a tattoo. I've wanted to for years, maybe it's about time. A protective talisman. A guardian, like a dragon. Or a dolphin. Let's face it, an amoeba would probably do it.

The lion's mane ripples at me.

'Marnie?'

I look up and Dylan is staring at me. His eyes are wide. They seem suddenly very close and high above me, but it is only as I straighten that I realise my face has been almost level with the surface of the bar and my nose almost touching Dylan's forearm.

I am about to apologise, or make some excuse, or both, but am saved by a question.

'How is she? Shiu. Is it time for us to hire a hitman yet, get that bastard Will taken out? Reason I ask is that I saw him in town last week with some blonde girl.'

I rub at the back of my neck.

'She's OK. I mean she's better than she was, but she's wanting to jack everything in, start again.'

'I'm sure.'

He nods at the bar top, then looks at me.

'You've not cooked up some fantastically evil revenge yet? You writerly types, I'm sure you could come up with something particularly nasty.'

On anyone else I'd called that facial expression 'leering', but I won't allow myself to where Dylan is concerned. I had hoped to just forget about Will but I grin, lean in close.

'Of course I have. It's nefarious in the extreme, but you'll have to wait and see.'

Dylan nods, satisfied, and Shiulie is calling us back. I place my glass carefully on the table. Shiulie turns bemused eyes on me. I edge a few more centimetres away from an equally bemused-looking Dylan.

'Marnie. You OK? It's just that from over here you looked like you were doing a line off the bar or something.'

She laughs as she settles herself more comfortably on the low stool, flings her hair over a shoulder, but her eyes search out mine, hold them for a little too long. She is concerned. He is concerned. I need to get out of here.

My cat Bubba is missing
And I need him back.
He is grey tabby with a green collar.
Please call if you have him.
Please send him home.

Now he's gone too: Mr Knuckles. Four days it's been. I shouldn't be upset, he's only a squatter. It's not like he's managed to claw his way into my heart in the time he's been hanging around demanding food and making me sneeze. But I was used to his morning scowls and fighting with him over the armchair. Bastard.

'Well he was probably stressed too.'

Jess is pulling at her eyelashes. Delicately pinching a dark hair between thumb and forefinger she yanks, hard, then holds the lash up to her eyes. Scrutinises. Holds her hand out over the rug and rubs her fingers lightly together to rid herself of the offending hair. She is pulling out her eyelashes. One by one.

This shocks me. A vague feeling nudges me, that I should stop her hand as it rises towards her face to pluck out another lash. That I should stop what she is doing to her face. A cloud passes across my heart as I watch her. But pass it does, and I shake it off.

'What do you mean, "stressed out"? How can a cat be stressed out? I mean, obviously, if it's being strung up by its tail on a washing line – Jessica – *that's* pretty stressful, but Knuckles is a well-loved cat.'

Jess's hand stops halfway to her face.

'What? I was trying to get that cat *down*. Anyway, I was only seven. Loved? Knuckles?'

She snorts at me.

'OK, maybe not "loved" exactly, but he's healthy, he's well taken care of. He gets fed, watered, talked to. I don't torture him. Yet.'

I mean the last as a joke. Jess doesn't laugh. She squashes her nose against her face with the back of her thumb.

'Cats get stressed by *loads* of things.'

She rolls her eyes and sighs extravagantly. She's doing this more and more these days.

'A death in the family. A loss.'

Another of my sister's crazy theories.

'Jess. Knuckles doesn't live with Dad, he lives with me . . .'

I can't believe I'm actually having this conversation. She's not listening, and carries on.

'Or it could be any change to the family. A baby. A new family member. Stuff like that. I was reading about it. One of your ancient magazines. Why on earth don't you get rid of them? You shouldn't hoard. It's bad for the soul.'

And with this she turns back to the TV, plucks another hair from her eyelid. I slip further down into the chair, tuck my legs underneath me. I can't seem to get comfortable any more. A cushion is bullying my lower back, so I extract it and throw it onto the floor.

Light from the screen flickers against my sister's cheek, in her eyes. She hunches her shoulders against my words, as if they are barbed and threaten to tear her skin.

'You'll have to go and look for him, Marn. Stick a poster up. You're a writer, you could think of something witty yet heartbreaking, you know. We could put a photo of him on it. Do you actually have one? We can put it up tomorrow morning, yeah? We've got to do something. You can't just sit around here moping about it.'

'I wasn't aware I *was* moping.'

My voice drops.

'And I'm not a writer.'

'Don't be stupid, of course you are. I just thought that as you're not having much luck finding Dad you could try with something smaller, try and ease yourself into trying to find him. A plan, I think.'

She really did just compare looking for the cat with trying to find our father. I search her face, but find no hint of cruelty or mischief. A glance at my watch reassures me that it's too late to check in with the police to see if they have any news. They would have let me know if they had heard anything. I'll call them tomorrow.

I extract one of my notebooks from where it huddles between the chair cushions. I have many, all stashed in semi-secret places throughout the flat. I feel like an alcoholic trying to hide bottles of spirits from my family. I find myself drawn to stationery shops, fondling suede and leather-bound books containing handmade paper, elastic-secured journalist pads, reams of coloured sheets. I will buy one, slip it into my bag with a furtive look, as if expecting to be caught purchasing some delicious yet illicit substance. And on returning home I will secrete the book, unopened, into a bottom drawer or under a pile of books. Or, as in this case, under a cushion. Occasionally – very occasionally – I will pull one out and open it, savouring the new paper smell, and point the tip of a pen to its clean page. The pen will hover uncertainly, unsure of how it has found itself in so unusual a situation: *Ladies and gentlemen. Unaccustomed as I am to writing anything other than vacuum cleaner manuals, catalogue copy and cheques . . .* I may write my name to see what it looks like:

Marnie

But it won't look like my name. It won't attach itself to me. It won't rub up against my shins, twine itself around my ankles, mark me as its territory. And usually I will put the pad away. But sometimes, sometimes, I may try to write something else:

The wind shuffles the sunlight in the branches above my head.
The bones of my fingers glow through my skin.

After a line or two I will stop. I always stop. There is no point carrying on. I know this. I will stash my book away again, lay it back down to sleep.

But now I've been given a job. This I can do. My pen floats for only a second over the page (which is the colour of old ivory and peppered with flattened iris petals) before I have a few lines fully describing my predicament.

Please help me find Mr Knuckles, a short-haired ginger tom.
No idea about his age, but he's older than he thinks/acts.
He's slightly cracked, enjoys tormenting small children and never did
me any good, but I'm feeling guilty now he's gone.
Please call if you have any news. Or don't.
I don't really care.

There are moments that are unlike any other. That's not very clear, is it? All moments, of course, are different to those which go before, those which come after. What I mean is that, sometimes you take the world at face value, you enjoy the sunshine, you play with the kittens. But sometimes neither sunshine nor kittens nor even the wide wide sea is enough to make you feel that the world is not against you.

Still, I'm garbling the words, mixing them up so they come out of my mouth in the wrong order, with the wrong meanings. Let me explain.

There are moments when you look at the stars and see only the darkness which surrounds them.

When a tender hand leaves your skin scored by claw marks.

When food turns to ash in your mouth.

When even tears feel like a betrayal.

These moments find me more and more often. The shutters letting in the light are being inched closed, day by day, and I am too tired to wedge them open. Soon I will be left sitting in darkness. My hands empty. Alone.

It's at moments like these that Roget comes to my rescue. Only the words can calm me, the lists of words, like strings of pearls, some rough, some smooth, but all soothing. I will take my copy from underneath my bed, stroke the torn cover back into place, settle it on my lap and let it fall open at any page. And I will read silently to myself, mouthing the words, for as long as it takes to slow the beating of my heart. Names of flowers. Synonyms for 'prevaricate'. Verbs describing forward motion. It doesn't matter. All I need is the words.

Jess caught me at it only last week. She stood in the doorway, mouth agape, as she watched me reading aloud. I didn't even try to think of an excuse, just shut the book and asked her if she fancied a cup of tea.

I think she thinks I'm losing my mind.

When Dad was writing the house had to be silent. He would disappear into his room and not come out, sometimes for days. Mum would take him food. I would sit on the landing and watch the closed door, hoping for a hint of whatever magic was happening in there. I was never allowed in, but one day I noticed his door was open just a crack and a strip of light slunk from the room and lay on the landing carpet. I could hear a low voice from within. Mum was downstairs in the kitchen. Who was he talking to? I edged closer. I held my breath so that my heart started pounding in my ears and put my face up to the slit in the door. I could see paper stacked in great blocks on his desk, on the floor. He sat there, hands cradling his chin, eyes fixed on the windowsill. He was talking quietly. I couldn't make out his words. I followed his gaze to the window. There was no one there. I looked back at him and yes, he was still talking. I craned my neck forward, took a deeper breath. Still no face at the window.

I glanced back and suddenly I was looking into his eyes. He must have turned towards me as I was trying to catch a glimpse of who he was talking to, alerted perhaps by my raucous heart. He didn't blink. I didn't speak. After a few moments of opening and closing my mouth without letting either breath or sound past my teeth, I shut my mouth, stood back. Dad turned back to his desk and put his head in his hands again.

'Go away'.

To this day I don't know whether those words actually left his lips, or whether I just imagined them.

I backed away, away down the hall thinking he saw me, there was no air. He was there, he saw me, I thought, until I bumped into my bedroom door. I slid down to the floor, my dress pushed up my thighs by the wood. I sat there for a while. And I sat for a while longer. The slash of light from the open door of my father's room thinned and disappeared. I sat in the dark until my mother called me down to dinner.

I never asked him who he had been talking to.

I'll curl my tail round, tightly, and I can just about squeeze into the gap between the car and the wall. Hardly comfortable, but don't want to get tripped over. Wouldn't want wailing and groaning and people running around in terror. Not that I could terrify many these days. Used to be strong. Used to have scary teeth, she'd say. Then she'd laugh, stick her tongue out at me, run round the garden. Dare me to catch her and make a meal of her if I was such a scary big old lion. Oh little thing. She didn't know it but I could have. Could have easily.

I remember the day we left. I was six years old, bundled into mum's car, boxes under my feet, a bag on my lap, squeezed between the cat's basket and my sister's car seat where she slept, ruddy-cheeked and unaware.

Why are we taking the cat?

Looking between the front seats towards the house where he stood.

Why are we taking the cat? It's his cat.

Crying.

No, he wasn't crying. He was just standing on his own, watching. Watching us go. Watching us leave. With his cat.

He will be lonely. Why are we taking his cat?

I had always been scared of the cat. Of the way it stayed at a distance, of the way it would stare at me from where it crouched underneath the dining table. I was curious too. And my fear mingled with my curiosity mixed to form what some would have called cruelty. One day I took it into my head to take the cat for a walk. On a lead, like I'd seen people taking dogs for walks in the park. I wanted to take the cat for a walk in the park and see what it was like to hold a small living creature at the end of a line. To hold something captive, to make it do what I wanted it to do. But I had no lead. So I found some wool in my mother's crochet basket. There were plenty of colours to choose from and I chose yellow, a happy colour, a colour that made me feel a little bit braver, because I could see the cat watching me and it looked like it could read my mind.

I coaxed it from under the dining room table by dangling one end of the ball of wool and while it was batting it from paw to paw I slipped a loop around its shadow-soft throat. Immediately

the cat spooked at the strange constriction and the line tight-
ened. Suddenly the cat was a fury, squirming, hissing, contorting
itself in its efforts to escape the throttling line, jumping away
from me but unable to escape what held it. It was strong. I was
surprised how strong. But I held on, gazing at the bizarre dance.
I was afraid, but there was also a deep thrill stirring in my stomach.
I knew it was wrong, the pounding of blood in my head told me
so. My heart raced, and my cheeks burned.

After a while the cat must have realised struggling was useless
and crouched low, ears flat against its head, growling deep in its
throat and watching me with wide yellow eyes. I let the line go
slack, and the moment the cat felt the tension lessen it shot down
the hallway, dragging the ball of wool out of my hands. I stood
and considered my next move. I had to untangle the cat now,
somehow, or it might strangle itself, I could see that. So I found
my mother's nail scissors, curved like a pair of tiny blunt scimi-
tars, in the knitting basket and trotted after the animal. I found
it by the front door. I managed to cut the cat loose, but not before
it had scored the backs of my hands and forearms with needle-
sharp claws. It huddled by the door, flattened itself, as if trying
to squeeze underneath. I pulled open the door, apologising to it
under my breath, and let the cat out into the winter air. It disappeared around the corner and I stood and looked at the red
lines running down the back of my arm.

Mid-February, the pavements deep in snow, the cat had stayed
away. It had long fur but my parents were worried about it freezing
to death. So Dad hunted for it all night. He left, dinnerless, in
the evening with a large rubber torch, returning in the early hours
of the morning, grey-eyed, exhausted, the lines between his eyes
etched deep. My mother argued with him that there was no point
searching for a cat, he may as well try hunting for a bubble in
bathwater. But he ignored her and went out again the next evening.

For two more nights he searched but the cat returned by itself, scratching at the door one morning to be let in as if nothing had happened. From then on it kept clear of me, vigilant for attacks. I never tried to touch it.

I thought of the lines between my father's eyebrows and the wool and the frightened cat on the morning of our leaving, as the car stuttered into life and pulled us away from the house. He still stood by the open door, watching as Mum backed the car from the drive. He looked as though he were being sucked away from us, away and down into a tunnel.

My eyes were hot but dry. And the cat, locked in the car with its former tormentor, cried and cried.

Pollux has got himself lost again and we're
worried about him. He's black and white
with orange eyes.
Reward for any information.
Call on . . .

'Hello love, how are you?'

Mum's voice bubbles up towards me through the receiver. The felt-tip pen I was clutching in the same hand that I picked the phone up with has given me a black slash across my cheek. I imagine it looking rakish, punk. But I probably just look like someone who has answered the phone with a pen in the same hand. I try to make my voice sound light.

'Hi Mum. I'm OK.'

What else do you say? What do you say when your father has disappeared, when your little sister is curled up on your sofa, back arched against the world, and hasn't moved for the past eight hours? Best keep my feelings to myself. Best not to worry her.

'You're not to worry about anything, alright? Everything will work out.'

Really?

'Yes.'

A moment of silence.

'Is Jessica with you? She said she'd be back yesterday but she wasn't, so I assumed she'd come over to yours to stay for a bit.'

'She's here. She's fine. She's watching telly.'

'Good, that's a relief. I knew you'd take care of her. Right, well, I've got to go. Give me a call sometime, won't you?'

'Of course I will. Mum I . . .'

'I'll speak to you later, love, I've really got to go now.'

More silence.

'I just wanted to make sure you were both alright. OK?'

'OK.'

'Love to your sister. Oh, and do tell her to stop biting her nails, she's driving me mad. She'll listen to you. Take care.'

She's gone. I struggle to contain the urge to call her back, beg her to come over and tuck me up in bed, read me a story. Instead, I shall pull my hair away from my face, knot it tight behind my head. Slightly too tight, so that the drag on my temples distracts me.

I spent this morning wandering the streets aimlessly like a ball of tumbleweed, tangled and jumbled. Peering into dark shop fronts, dodging dogs and prams, running my fingers over the bunches of flowers standing tall in their buckets outside the florist's on the corner. I bought a small bunch of jewelled anemones, carried them upside down to keep them fresh for longer. I dropped my bag in the road. I sat and drank strong milky coffee in a café, watched the passers-by weave around each other like river eddies around rocks. I watched them through my pale reflection, concentrated on focusing my eyes beyond the ghosts of my hair, my eyes. I left a clutch of cold coins on the table with the mug stains and walked home.

I thought this break from work would do me good. Everyone did. Now I'm not so sure. Time seems to have sped up, leaving me panting and confused in its wake. The golden light of early evening is slanting into the room already. I feel like the day has been stolen from me, and no tracks remain to give a hint of who the thief was, or where they have taken it.

Jess is eating flat squares of processed cheese from the packet, peeling each one from the rest, rolling it into a tube and then sucking it into her mouth. She's reading my first attempt at a heart-wrenching poster pleading for information on the cat.

'Mum sends her love.'

'Yeah?'

'Yeah. She asked how you were. I told her you were OK.'

'OK.'

She peels off another shiny yellow square.

'You staying tonight?'

She looks up at me.

'Can I? I'm staying at Roo's tomorrow, I'll be out of your hair first thing in the morning.'

'Of course.'

Another cheese roll disappears.

'This is a piss take, yeah? You're not really going to put this up.'

I had actually been hoping to. I thought it might bring a little light relief to a street apparently in mourning for the loss of legions of feline friends.

'I mean, this looks like you don't even want him back, like you don't give a shit.'

With her greasy hands she crumples the page into a ball and hurls it at me. It hits my knee and falls to the floor. Where it will probably stay for a couple of days before I can summon the energy to throw it into the bin. She is right. I don't really care.

'Do a proper one. I'll put them up for you.'

Again I search for a notebook. The pen waits over the virgin paper. What to say about him? What to say about him that is truthful but not inflammatory?

Missing.

Yes, definitely that. Definitely gone. Not sure for how long now, but longer than is usual.

Missing from Jamaica Road.

Maybe a photo would get results. People work better with visual clues.

Missing from Jamaica Road since mid-October.

Or 'lost'. No, you can't be lost *from* something. Can you?
'Jess. "Missing" or "lost"?'
'What?'
'Never mind.'
Missing it is. What else? Sex: male. Temper: foul. Fur: short. Colour: ginger-striped. Eyes: orange. Name: Mr Knuckles, but doesn't answer to it. So not much point putting that in but everyone else has names in. I'll try that.

Missing from Jamaica Road, cat called Mr Knuckles.
Male, with short, ginger hair. Orange eyes.
Scar behind right ear.
Please call with any information.

I read it out to Jess. She grunts.
'I'll take that to mean you don't want to change anything. OK,

I'll get this copied tomorrow and you can put some up around the place. Also get some stuck through doors. People take more notice when something lands on their doormat.'

And I suddenly remember the envelope I found in my father's house the last time I went, the purple italics spelling his name smiling up at me from his doormat. Mr Ben Irving Esq. I'd brought it home with me that day, I don't know why, clutching it so tightly in my hand that the creases are now indelible. He'll kill me.

'Back in a sec.'

In my bedroom I delve through the piles of paper that litter the floor, sneezing as dust rises. Old bills, receipts, lists and more lists. Here it is. Still creased, spotted with water stains. Part of the flap torn. I bend the envelope gently and it resists me. There is more than paper inside. I turn it over. Thick black words at the bottom: *Do Not Bend*.

I cut my thumb running it under the flap to open the envelope, the pain quick and sharp, shake the thin paper to empty it. A cardboard framed photograph of a young, green-eyed woman falls out onto my bed. I look back into the envelope. Empty. Nothing else. The green eyes look up at me from the frame on my duvet. She can't be more than twenty-two, twenty-three. Copper-haired. White blouse, silver crucifix around her neck. In her left hand she holds a scroll of paper. I pry the envelope open again in the hope that some hint of what this is will have appeared within. Still nothing. Her eyes are wide open, eyebrows slightly raised, as if surprised at not seeing who she expected after the long gloom inside of the envelope. Her mouth is slightly open. She could be about to say something. She doesn't. Who the hell are you?

'Marnie! Want me to do the vegetables?'

I push the photograph back into the envelope, slip the envelope under my pillow. In the kitchen I find Jess crying over blood-red slices of onion.

*

'Stretch your fingers here. Curl your thumb round the wood a bit more. That's it. Now: this is called the fret board. Wait a minute, move your arm down a little.'

He laughs softly.

'It'll be easier to hold it when you're bigger. I'll buy you a guitar of your own.'

And he did, when I was sixteen. A guitar which was all warm honeyed wood and cold steel; which thrummed deep chords at me, answering when I put my mouth close to the strings and hummed at them.

But here I am only six, the year we left with his cat, and I am sitting cross-legged beside my father on his floor cushion, so huge and green to me it seems like sitting on a small hill in the centre of the room my mum called 'your father's study'. 'Your father's study'. I didn't know what someone would do in a study, but it sounded grown-up, forbidding. The door was almost always closed when I got home from school and we were never allowed in.

This evening something must be different. It might be that dinner pleased him more than usual. It could be that the wine he'd opened was a little bit more expensive, or that the hairstyle my mother wore did not drive him into a fury. I don't know. And I don't care. What I do know is that I have somehow been given permission to enter my father's strange and exotic den. I find myself holding air in my lungs too long and then breathing out very slowly, dizzying myself with lack of oxygen so as not to disturb anything. The rows and rows of books jammed into their shelves so only their creased spines show. The wide black desk. The silver picture frames holding me and my sister and my mother shiny and frozen and smiling. The smell of leather and aftershave.

All his things sleep; a shallow, dreamless slumber. But I feel as if my presence disturbs the room itself; I feel it shifting uncomfortably, trying to throw me off balance, the floor tilting, the windows skewing their outlines around the twilight which spills into the room. I will have to stay still and quiet. Just one of my thoughtless breaths could waken the books, tarnish the frames, blow the pages from his desk, ruin days, weeks of his work. He would banish me from his side and never speak to me again. If I am quiet, if I am still, the room might just decide to put up with me for this one evening.

His arm around my shoulders warms me. The cushion lurches underneath us as he shifts his weight and I have to clench my leg muscles to stop myself rolling down the side of the hillock, but I do it silently, without moving, without making it obvious. If I make a fuss, move around too much, he might get bored of me. He might get angry. He might send me away.

So I am as still as I can be, and he has no reason to ask me to leave. Instead he settles the guitar on my lap and places my fingers on the strings to form a G. My hands are too small though. I have to give up.

'Don't worry. I'll play something.'

He takes the instrument from me, slowly, gently, making sure that the lifting guitar doesn't hit me under the chin as it rises up and over my head. I catch a glimpse of my face in its polished back as it ascends: a blur of dark hair, wide eyes. Then he leans back against the legs of the heavy desk and begins to play. He strums a simple tune, the chords thrilling, slightly melancholy. He sings a song about someone called 'Mr Tambourine Man'. His voice rises and falls. Sometimes he closes his eyes, sometimes he looks at me. My heart swells. I smile at him. But not a big smile, not anything that might upset him. Not anything that might disturb him. He might get bored of me. He might get angry. He might send me away.

Mittens has gone missing.
PLEASE, if you see
a black cat
With short hair
And red collar
And white socks
Contact me on ...

I'm convinced that if I think hard enough, scour the dusty corners of my mind which seem to collect so much junk, I'll pick up on a detail of my father's house which will give me a clue as to what happened to him.

Thursday, last week, I visited him – not particularly concerned that he hadn't been in touch for the past three days – but determined to get the visit out of the way before the weekend so I didn't have the guilt hanging over me. Though this sly intention in itself made me feel guilty. There is no winning, it seems.

I stepped up to the green door and rang the bell. I could hear it echoing down the hallway and through the white kitchen. As I waited for the approaching shadow through the textured glass I rubbed the underside of the small white shell I keep in my coat pocket, its silky surface perfectly moulded to my cold fingers. Moments of silence. I rang again, pressing the button for as long as I dared and putting my nose right up to the glass. My hot breath blossomed on the pane and I wiped it off with my sleeve, careful not to smear it, to leave a mark. There was no movement, no sound from inside. I stepped back, looked up at the first floor windows. Then, crouching, I flipped open the letter box, squinted through the cold breeze which blew from the slot and called out. No movement, no sound. I felt eyes on my back and turned, still crouching, expecting to see him standing a little way down the street watching my attempts to rouse him. But there was no one there. And still no sound from inside.

I decided to use the spare key and unfolded my now stiff knees. I'd never let myself into my dad's house before. Normally I'd breathe a silent sigh of relief if he didn't answer his door. I'd congratulate myself on another duty done and leave, thankful not to have to deal with either his bizarre conversation or his accusatory glances. But this time, for some reason, I let myself in.

There was a slight tang in the air as I closed the door softly behind me. Lemon air freshener. I hate the stuff and can't understand why he fills his air with microscopic choking chemical droplets. My foot crunched over a large unopened envelope, and I bent to retrieve it. The address was handwritten, a looping, skydiving script in thick purple ink: 'Mr Ben Irving Esq.'. I can remember thinking, I've never really known what an 'Esquire' is. I can remember thinking, what a beautiful shade of purple. I can remember wondering why the place was silent.

The kitchen entrance was a rectangle of sunlight at the end of the hallway and I had to squint against the light after the darkness of the passage. No one there. I called out to him, my voice thin and high in the long corridor. There was no answer. Once in the kitchen

I peered through the window into the tiny concrete garden. A magpie was pulling at the stone eye of the sculpted rabbit which squatted under the ivy-covered fence. My sister had given it to him as a birthday present some years back. He had smiled, run his fingers over its humped back, its oversized ears.

The far wall in my father's study is dominated by a window, wide and tall and spilling light. Clustering around it are hundreds of photographs. I knew I should be looking for dad but I was drawn, as I had been so often before, towards the pictures. Cabal-like groups of suited men. Hills blanketed in purple heather. Unfamiliar faces, some open, some closed. And tucked away in a corner are childhood pictures of myself and Jess. Side-by-side, washed, brushed and gleaming at the camera from the first sofa my parents bought. Jess's grin reveals the gap in her front teeth that she was so proud of. She was able to wedge a drinking straw there and waggle it around with her tongue. Another image of her paddling in the sea in a bathing costume covered in seashells. One of me, eyes wide, mouth open as if saying something. I'd forgotten this photograph. It was in the circus. The lion cub. Look at my eyes, a rabbit in headlights. Or should it be deer in headlights? The angle of a stranger's elbow by my head, the tweed hem of a coat at my side. And the lion cub, balanced on my lap by a pair of disembodied hands over which hovers a scythe-like nose. I remember now: that the cub was heavy on my knees, I thought it might crush the breath out of me. All around me people were leaving after the show. My father took photographs. I had wanted to touch the cub, but had been afraid when it was brought close. This writhing creature which tried feebly and in vain to squirm away from the hands which held it had frightened me, but I stayed quiet and held on to its hot fur. Neither of us wanted to be there. Neither of us had much choice in the matter. The cub must have been as bewildered as I was at the noise, the movement, the lights. I can remember a pang of pity for it, and I think I put my mouth close to its ear and whispered to it:

'Run away with me.'

But maybe I didn't. Maybe I just sat still and tried to smile for the camera.

It was a long time ago.

*

I reached up and unhooked the frame from the wall. Handwritten words the colour of dried blood stuttered across the wooden backing:

Marnie. Aged 5. 1984.

The slope of the short phrases, the heavy fall of the full stop after the number 4 drew stinging water into my eyes. I put the photo back and returned to the hallway.

The house was empty. No one in the living room, no one in the bathroom, no one in the study. The bedroom door was closed. I looked down at my hands. I still held the letter, and it was shaking. Such beautiful, archaic handwriting, who could possibly write like that these days? I hesitated for a moment with my hand on the cold bedroom door knob. And I knew he wouldn't be there. I knew he wouldn't be sitting on the bed, right arm draped over the heavy curves of his guitar, left fingers stretching to span the vibrating metal strings. I knew he wouldn't be dozing, half-covered by a thin blanket, the rise of his hip swelling the wool. I knew he wouldn't be standing by the window, staring out at the low clouds, running his fingers over his lips as he muttered to himself. I knew he wouldn't be there. And he wasn't.

Something in me ripped open on that day, the day I knew he had gone. My seams were torn apart. I felt at once splayed and vulnerable, sensitive parts exposed like a shucked oyster, yet at the same time profoundly numb. I didn't cry. I didn't panic. My sister called to him through the night. And Mum said nothing. And I didn't cry.

*

How do you go about looking for a missing parent? Where do you start? Should you, in fact, start at all? Even if you *are* in the right frame of mind to make rational decisions, like what liquid should get poured on cereal in the morning (don't ask), which shoes go on which feet, that sort of thing. What do you do if you spend your days shaking and blank-minded from lack of sleep, and waking with heart knocking against your ribs in the deep blue hours of the night? What, exactly, should you do?

After my first phone call to the police, despite their kind but firm insistence that there was not much they could offer me by way of assistance, I felt lighter. I clung to the idea that these people would take the burden from me. They would track him down. They would release the bloodhounds, noses twitching and full of the scent of one of his shoes, one of his ties. They would question concerned neighbours door-to-door until they found him huddled in the corner of an alleyway, confused, grubby, but unharmed. That is what the police are for, I reasoned.

I don't know where I get these ideas from.

As the days have gone by, the words of the kindly operator and the blank indifference of the desk sergeant have begun to sink through the fog of my mind and make an impression. It seems she was right. That they are powerless to help. That there is nothing they can do. That it is up to me, after all.

I have tried, even though I don't know what to do, where to start. Jess expects me to do something. Do I try calling his old friends? I know that he has lost touch with them all. I don't think he has been in contact with anyone other than Jess and me for two years or more. Do I call his psychiatrist? He has missed all appointments at the hospital for the past eighteen months, brags about this fact. So I doubt Dr Grant would have any news. Even if he did he wouldn't be able to tell me. Confidentiality.

So then, what? Do I go out, pound the streets, try to scent him on the air? Is that what I should do?

Try not to worry. No news is good news. If something had happened to him you would have heard.

What kind of advice is that?

Why is there not a guide, a manual? A single point of reference for questions of this nature. I'm not asking for a pill to take to make everything better. I'm not asking for a wand to wave to bring him back. Just a little advice. Some good, constructive, kindly-meant, trustworthy advice for the lost. For the abandoned. For strays who really need it.

*

My father's first suicide attempt failed. They all did, as far as I know, but the first really captured my imagination. All I heard at the time – I would have been about thirteen – were snatches of telephone conversations, and a few hushed words from my mother, brow creased, sheened with hurt. A bluebell wood. Dad's new car. A length of hose pipe. Something went wrong and he didn't die. I filled in the gaps, my teenage imagination stitching together the scraps and tatters of a story into a series of scenes, a film which ran over and over in my mind for years. I'll tell it as I remember it, shall I Dad? You never told me what happened, so I'll tell you how I saw it.

The warm smell of leather fills the inside of your new car as you drive carefully off the track and into the woods. A new car every two years, trade up to the next model, trade up and trash the old, drive slowly so you don't scratch it, mind those low branches. It all gleams: the dashboard, the aluminium buttons on the stereo, the windscreen. Even the case of your spectacles (spectacles, never glasses) sitting on the passenger seat looks brand new.

You have organised everything, all the details are taken care of. And these are:

remote spot, one
length of hosepipe, one
duct tape, roll of (extra wide just to make sure)
1990 Chateau Margaux (an ethereal, sensuous nose, violets, cedar, black fruit, roses, spices, tobacco; multi-faceted, self-assured, with a voluptuous palate of velvety tannins, raisins, black tea), bottle of

You arrive at a particularly thick patch of woodland, the car can go no further and you are a long way from the footpath. You turn the key in the ignition and the engine dies. Open the door and step out into the leafy gloom. It is high summer and you look up towards the sun. The sky is barely visible through the leaves. You can hear the beetles whispering among the rotten branches, the worms mumbling below the bluebells. You know that the honeyed elephant ears and delicate frills of fungi which adorn the fallen logs are listening to your thoughts. Soon it will be quiet, you tell yourself, soon they will have nothing more to listen to.

You take off your jacket, open the wine, sniff the bottle neck with eyes closed and then take a long swallow. Straight from the bottle, leaning against the cooling bonnet of the car. This is unusual behaviour for you, swigging from a bottle. Usually so fastidious, so alert to the delicacies and complexities of etiquette. Even when eating alone you eat your pears with a knife, peeling the skin off before slicing through the grainy flesh.

You watch the leaves flutter in the slight breeze. You smell the damp earth.

Now the hose is put in place, taped securely. The car is expensive, German, efficient, there will be no leaks of fresh air, the seals will do their job. After a few minutes you stand back to look at the car. You bend and pick up the half-empty wine bottle, take another pull at its neck then prop it against a tree.

It is quiet now. The birds make no sound. You look up again at the branches. You see their black eyes watching. Watching you.

You climb into the car. You make yourself comfortable by sliding the chair back so you can stretch out your long legs. You slam the sounds of forest out of the car. You check for air holes in the tape, carefully. There are none.

You turn the key in the ignition, the car starts easily. A hot gust against your cheek. You lean your head back against the headrest, breathe in the smell of new leather, quickly becoming thick and acrid.

The car hums, breathes out and out and out.

You breathe in. And out. And in again. You begin to cough. The trees swim in front of you, darken.

You open your eyes. It is quiet. You cough again. You try the key. The car engine coughs with you, stutters.

Stops.

What has happened? What has gone wrong? You prepared for every eventuality.

You let your hands fall into your lap and sit in the thick atmosphere for a few moments. Then you try the key in the ignition again, and for the few moments the car continues to run your eyes rove over the digital displays, the trip computer. The petrol gauge. Which shows empty. The car is out of petrol. How ridiculous. You have to smile to yourself. All that preparation. All the small details. All for nothing because you lost sight of what was most basic, most important.

You fumble the door open and the birdsong tumbles in. You notice the wine bottle propped against a tree trunk. You hadn't finished the wine. What a waste.

Was that how it was? I suppose I'll just have to wait. Wait until you come back and tell me how it was. Because I don't understand it. I don't understand at all.

TIBBS MY LOVELY CAT IS
MISSING.
HE IS TORTOISESHELL,
LONG-HAIRED AND FAT.
HE WAS A STRAY WHEN I
FOUND HIM.
PLEASE CALL IF YOU KNOW WHERE HE IS.

I read these words out to Jess as she stares morosely at her breakfast, standing with the small of my back pressed to the cold edge
of the kitchen sink.

'What the hell's happening around here? Where have they all
gone?'

She shrugs, bounces the flat of her knife against her toast.

'If he's a stray how do they know his name? And *why* should
we ring if we see it? Maybe he'd rather stay stray. Strayed. Whatever.'

She is in a facetious mood, sucking on a lock of hair as she
sits at the kitchen table. The A4 sheet of paper, now coffee stained,
dropped onto the doormat this morning. Each letter is pain-
stakingly outlined in black biro. Capitals which begin almost two

centimetres high on the left-hand side of the page have, by the time they reach the right margin, shrunk to tiny scrawls, as if they have fallen off a cliff and are tumbling further and further into the abyss. I flap the paper in front of my eyes and the draught stirs my hair.

'Maybe he just wants a change. Maybe he's run away from home. I don't know.'

She leans back in her chair, cranes her neck to stare at the ceiling.

'Everyone's got something to run away from.'

I can't help but argue, even though I don't have the energy.

'I don't.'

She doesn't move, but I can feel a mental eyebrow raising. She's been talking to herself, not me, and is now silent again. Pulls the damp hair from her mouth and begins to twirl it around a finger. The skin around her nails is ragged. She must have been chewing that too. I want to take her red fingers and run them under the cool water from the tap, dry them with a soft towel. I want to make it all better. Her toast has been left untouched.

'You're not hungry?'

She shrugs, her eyes scanning her thumb for areas of skin or nail she may have missed. The sight of her gnawing her cuticles is painful.

'Please don't.'

'What?'

'You know. Don't do that to your fingers. They look so sore. Can't you chew gum instead, or something?'

She doesn't grace this with a reply. Smirks at her hand as the tip of her thumb again disappears into her mouth. I try another approach, one that I've known to work in the past.

'They *look* terrible.'

Jess pushes her mug away and stands up.

'I'll get out of your face then, shall I? Maybe Roo will have a bit more time for me. See you later.'

She stalks out of the kitchen, slams the door. It shudders on its hinges for a few moments.

I turn away and stare through the window. The lamp posts are swathed in more missing cat posters, which seem to be sprouting on them like growths. Fragile white fungi on leafless trees. The air inside the kitchen is suddenly choking. I need to be outside.

I slip quickly down the stairs. Doing my jacket up hurriedly as the front door swings open I catch a tiny piece of skin from my neck in the zip. The quick pain hits me at the same time as the cold air, laden with the smells of wood smoke and damp rubber.

I walk down the street, through clouds of my own hot breath. I hadn't realised how many animals are now missing. I pause in front of one of the posters. More scrawled, desperate words, a blurred stripy face, a notched ear.

'Jasper.' I read the name to myself out loud.

The next shows a kitten on its back, grappling with a piece of string suspended by an invisible hand, mouth agape, tiny claws, fangs reaching, reaching.

'Mango.'

I smooth a torn corner of Mango's notice back against the cold iron post. It flaps mischievously back at me in the wind. I smooth it back again, try to tuck it under the peeling tape. It comes loose again. This scrap, this bold fragment is defeating me and I find myself breathing heavily, a stinging and a weight in my throat, behind my eyes. I squeeze them closed for a moment, lean my forehead against the cold lamp post.

'They'll be fine. Start worrying about yourself.'

The voice is low behind me. A hint of some kind of accent

maybe. The words pronounced slowly, carefully, as if they were unfamiliar, the vowels rolling uncontrolled around a mouth unused to speech.

I've heard this voice before.

I take another second before I open my eyes, but keep my forehead pressed against the metal. Suddenly I have developed a headache, which is pushing itself up the back of my neck. It's strange, but I don't feel the need to see who's speaking. Somehow I'm content. Somehow I'm content just to listen to this voice.

'Stupid buggers,' it says.

A snort, loud, then a sound somewhere between a whine and a yowl. Wet sounds now, as of great jaws being smacked together. I lift my head. I turn.

And there she goes. Bet she hasn't run that fast since she was small. Did try to be careful. Even tried being helpful, told her not to worry about those stupid little bastards. And what do I get for it? A silent shriek. Fingers pulling hair. And the sight of her arse disappearing round the corner. Bloody disappointed, to tell you the truth. Would have thought she'd recognise me. Even after all these years.

So. What am I supposed to do now? Chase her? Bowl her over before she reaches the house, roll her in the dirt, make my demands with my claws? Can't run that quickly any more, even if I felt inclined to. Tell you the truth nothing I'd like more. Cuff some sense into her. Incredible how a little pain can focus the mind. Too old for this now, all this sneaking around, tailing her, hiding in the shadows.

Got to make her listen. She did this. She's the only one who can help me.

Missing cat: Mr Bojangles.
Tabby and white male.
Please contact me on . . .

Stop. Just stop now. Breathe. Now I see that if I don't get some sleep soon I'm going to lose my mind totally. The backs of my eyes sting again and I squeeze my eyelids together, hard. A long, loud sniff. I don't care who heard. My grandmother used to be driven almost to the brink of tears by my constant sniffing as a child. I hated blowing my nose. It felt wet and messy so I kept my mucus to myself. Nana, hands wringing, would press tissues, pieces of toilet roll, stiff cotton handkerchiefs into my hands or tuck them into any pocket she could find in my clothing. 'Please!' she would whisper desperately, before hurrying away to resume some mysterious chore.

Where am I? End of the street, past my house. I need to sit down. My usual retreat, the hilly park beyond the rows of terraced houses (but it was real, so real), isn't far now. Not stopping to look behind me, I labour up the grassy rise, puffing great hot breaths in front of me which warm my cheeks until they throb. I feel better as I reach the top. I kneel on the damp ground, then lie down and roll over, stretching out on my back. As I reach my arms over my head and away from my feet the bottom edge of my jacket pulls upwards, exposing a sliver of stomach to the cold air. I feel vulnerable lying here like this, staring through the thick black pylon wires which thrum overhead.

Think of something else. Anything else. My grandmother. Why did I just think of her? I've not thought of her for years. My father's mother. She was always a mystery to me as a child. She lived in 'the country'. Every year Dad would tell my sister and I that we were going to visit Nan, in the country. She lived on what she called a farm, though it consisted only of a small flock of squabbling hens, two vicious goats and a hairy black pig with human eyes, all housed in a yard with a few leaning outbuildings crouching over her cottage. The chickens were allowed within the damp, low-ceilinged house. I could never quite square my father's fastidiousness at home with his allowances for these odd-smelling, bad-tempered creatures scratching around, pecking crumbs from the kitchen table, settling on jackets and cardigans, chairs, tables and often my grandmother's lap. After hours of driving, my father often talking non-stop for the entire journey, Jess and I would spill from the leather sweatiness of the car into the cottage, have rock cakes pressed into our damp hands, Nan's bristly lips pressed to our foreheads and, after eating, would be shooed into the field to 'play with the animals'. The goats would stand a way off on bales of straw and glare at us until we threw the remnants of our rock cakes at them and scampered away to climb the apple trees. Within seconds our knees would be scratched and bleeding, but high up in the boughs of the sheltering trees we would pull the small, unripe fruit from their twigs and tell each other stories about how these tough little apples were poisonous enough to kill a little girl, no, to kill a lion, no, no, to kill a whole elephant. Then we'd dare each other to take a bite. By the time our eyes were watering with the sourness we would be surrounded by raucous goats. We'd pelt them with apples and shriek with laughter when our tiny missiles hit their target.

After a day left to our own devices Jess and I would creep back to the house. Dad would already have left. Soup would be steaming in huge flat bowls, always an indeterminate colour, always an indeterminate taste After a sleepy, wordless dinner we were clapped up the narrow stairs to our room. Two cot beds. A large mirror over a dark chest of drawers. A painting opposite of the moon behind bare branches which always fascinated me. We always left the door open just a crack as Jess was afraid of the dark. I would climb onto the bed and manoeuvre my way underneath the sheet and rough blankets, sometimes still fully clothed. Often the light expired of its own free will.

Breathe.

It seemed so real.

I remember one particular night. As soon as my eyes closed I heard a quiet, regular thumping coming closer, closer. It sounded like footsteps climbing the stairs. I forced myself to open my eyes and glanced down the gloomy corridor through the open bedroom door. A squat shape stood at the far end of the landing. I was too afraid to look away. And then the shape moved. The black pig trotted past, slowed as it reached our doorway to snuffle at Jess's shoes, pushing them further into the room with its pin cushion of a nose. It then resumed its tiptoe journey down the corridor, trotters as dainty as a ballerina's point shoes, dark belly slung between its legs and swinging from side to side like a full hammock. I closed my eyes and fell instantly asleep.

I had a dream that night that I still remember. Me in a white-feathered dress. Me with ballet shoes bound tightly onto my feet. Me dancing slowly, slowly in a forest, the trees so dense I couldn't see the sky. My feet getting heavier and heavier. Then I was dancing in thick sucking mud and soon I couldn't lift my feet from the quagmire, could only shuffle from side to side, trying to recall the music that had played in my head a moment before. The feathers fell one by one from my dress, landing like a snowdrift at my feet. They sank into the mud and as I trampled them I began to weep.

I woke to the cold wetness of the pillow. It surprised me. Lost, I am lost. I stared into the blackness for images of comfort. Nothing came. Tried to remember what my own bed felt like, its size, its smell. Especially its smell.

I missed the pig.

*

I sit up and sweep the hair back from my forehead, rub my aching knuckles. The sky is already darkening.

Walking down the knoll my legs are stiff, reluctant. I slow as I near the bottom and the end of the row of narrow houses. Breathe the cold air deep into me. This is fine. Nothing is wrong. I'll just walk home, go inside, have a bath. Be not afeard.

I relax as I walk, pull my shoulders down from where they have been hovering just underneath my ears. Nearing my house I see a huddled shape at the bottom of the path. Someone's fallen over. Maybe it's a drunk, passed out in my doorway. No. No, it's not. I walk past the first paving stone of my path. Ignore the strangely sweet smell of warm breath. I leave the path and walk over the flower bed where a few miserable flowers cluster, walk over the small front lawn, towards the door, there's the door. There's the door to my house. Red. For some reason I can't get the key into the lock, its clattering booms through my head. I can barely even see the key now, it blurs and swims. I feel as though a hand is crushing my windpipe. I can't hear anything but my breathing. It roars.

I drop to my knees, this time on the hard stones. The shock of the sudden pain clears my head. OK, so I thought I heard something as I stumbled over the flower bed: 'Have a word with yourself, girl, you know it's me.' Now, we have to talk about this. No, not *we*. There is no we. I mean *me*. Me talk. I have to talk about this. To myself. Talk to *myself*. That's what he, it, said to me: *Have a word with yourself, girl*. But isn't that a sure sign of madness, talking to yourself? Do I take the advice of a lunatic part of my mind or not? Two options as I see it. Ignore. It'll disappear, go away. Ignore him. He'll. Just go away and leave me alone. Concentrate on the smell of leaves in the air, autumn always smells like that, wet leaves and petrol pumps. But I can't just ignore it. That would be denial. You hear it a lot: 'You're in denial.' How can you argue against that accusation? 'No, I'm not.' 'There you go: you're denying it.' Or else. I could look at him, long and hard. It. Face up to it. Long and hard. Examine it. Something won't be right, there will be a tiny detail that's wrong or it will be translucent like a ghost and my brain will catch on and say 'You see, it's not real after all, that couldn't possibly be real, normal.' As if having a full-grown lion sitting at the bottom of the path talking to me could ever be normal.

OK then. Let's have a look at you.

I swivel on my knees, pressing them harder into the stone, hoping the pain will bring me back to the real world. My hands are flat on the cold slab. It's there. It's still there. *His eyes.* Start at the bottom. *His eyes.* His feet. Paws. So big. Like plates. *Dinner plates*, that's good, real stuff, just keep thinking of the real stuff. Mine have a red stripe running around the lip. Tiny cracks spidering outwards from the centre, barely visible. One has a small chip on its edge. Something's not right about those paws though. Where his claws should be sheathed are thick bulbous knobs. *He told me once what they had done to him.* No he didn't. Just look. It's sitting like a Sphinx, lengthening its neck upwards, raising its head and then lowering its chin so the pink tongue can reach the chest to rasp and clean, down and down and down again. Steam is curling around his tongue in the cold air. *It used to be warm on my cheek, lifting the hairs around my face.* His mane is so long the fur covers all but his paws and the front of his thick forelegs. It's golden and white, and auburn and black, black around the fringes. *I used to bury my hands deep, deep in that fur, feel the thick pulse under my fingers.* His chin is grizzled, bearded. The black slash of his thin lips, an upturned wishbone underneath the mottled pink and black nose. Wiry, white whiskers sprouting from a black-dotted muzzle. A faint parting of fur down one side of his nose, pale skin visible; it looks like a scar. He shakes his massive head. The long slope of his sandy body against the path, so heavy against the earth, so solid. The muscled thighs, the vague undulation of ribcage beneath tight, yellow pelt.

His eyes. But he's not looking at me, he's contemplating his left paw now. His tongue covers it like a rag as he licks it, snorting and muttering quietly to himself. I can't make out what he's . . . saying. He lays his enormous head down on his paws, lowering it slowly as if its fragile weight must be handled carefully.

'. . . only came because she . . .'

His words rumble through my chest, though he's speaking softly. Muttering to himself.

'. . . never even . . .'

A grumpy old woman.

'. . . wasn't like I had any choice . . .'

He snorts into his great paws, shakes his head. Lifts it up from where it rests, opens his mouth and yawns, hugely. That massive tongue again, furred, pink, reaching from a cavernous throat. I stare into his golden eyes, as if searching for the remnants of my exhausted mind among the ripples and eddies of a river. If I look hard enough, deeply enough, it will be there. He will disappear, and everything will be alright.

And I'm so caught up in my detailed examination, my scrupulous doubting inspection, that they've drawn level with me before I notice. A pink tricycle, its owner poised and eyeing me warily, seriously, beyond the gate, from beneath a Barbie cycle helmet. Me. A crazy woman kneeling on a cold path, hands gripping the jagged edges of the paving stone so hard her knuckles are pearly white, staring at the ground a few feet in front of her. I smile at the girl, she must be about four, five. And instead of the shriek of terror, the dampening of the eyes I expect, I get a smile in return. We stay that way for a while, eyes locked and smiling, until a shepherding hand on the tasselled handlebar tugs gently and she's gone.

See? All in my mind. They saw nothing. Nothing there.

I hear a low humming. A tune. He's humming now. Singing quietly into his beard, eyelids drooping. He's singing to himself.

What's happening to me?

Suddenly a saucer-like ear turns backwards to catch some sound too soft for my hearing. And he's quiet again, waiting. Perfect. Even his flanks seem to have stopped moving in time to his rasping breaths. The other ear turns now until both are pointing away from me. I look over his rump to see a small black cat standing as if petrified a couple of feet away, all its senses straining in our direction. Its tail bottlebrushes, inflating as if with pumped air, and its eyes are wide, staring. The lion lifts its great head unhurriedly and looks over its shoulder towards the cat. His gaze is like the sweep of a lighthouse beam. As his eyes fall on the animal (so small it looks, dwarfed by this great beast) the black cat leaps into the air, all four legs ramrod straight beneath it as if an electric shock has thrown it from the earth. It lands and is off down the road, has disappeared within a heartbeat.

'It saw you. That cat saw you . . .'

He turns his eyes towards me.

Don't. Don't look at me like that with those eyes. Your eyes. Are golden, kohl-rimmed and shining.

Jericho.

You've come back.

LOST CAT–CLARA
Bluey grey female cat,
with flea collar.
Missing a bit of her left ear.
Call us on . . .

'Don't call me Daddy.'

I'd stopped in mid-sentence. His quiet order had broken it in two. I looked at him; the book open on my lap, my finger resting on the picture of a crocodile, tears like water-filled balloons hanging from its jaws.

'Call me Ben, not Daddy. I don't want you to call me Daddy anymore. Or Dad. OK?'

I nodded without understanding. He smiled and turned back to the page.

'Go on. What's the next word?'

I had no idea what the next word was. It blurred and swam before my eyes. He prompted me.

'Cro-. Go on.'

'Cro-co. Dile. Cro-co-dile.'

'That's right. Crocodile. And look. Why do you think he's crying?'

I looked at the glossy drawing. I couldn't imagine why this creature could be sad. It lounged in a turquoise pool, snowy lilies adorning its scaly skin, palm trees tossing their leaves in the breeze. The sky was blue and the sun shone. It looked perfect. I could imagine stroking that knuckled cheek. Smoothing away the tears as I lay on the beast's back and floated in that quiet pool.

'I don't know.'

But he'd lost interest.

'Density. It's all a matter of frequency, you see. For example, if I knew what frequency the molecules of that wall were vibrating at . . . you see everything vibrates, all molecules, at different frequencies and if they, or molecules, didn't, vibrate that is, we wouldn't exist, I could walk straight through it. Did you know that? I'll show you one day. Would you like that? Of course you would. See me just walk up to a wall and disappear through it.'

He talked like this for a while. I tried to listen, to understand, but the words ran into one another, slipped from my grasp. Finally he was satisfied that I understood and left me alone on the sofa. I curled my legs beneath me and lay down, resting my head in the hollow where he had sat. It was warm against my cheek. I closed my eyes and fell asleep. I was six years old.

I was woken some time later by hot breath stirring the hair around my face. I giggled, but kept my eyes closed, guessing who it was.

'I knew you'd come,' I whispered.

Something soft and warm touched my ear, blew the milky-smelling breath into it, then moved down my cheek to push gently against my neck. I opened my eyes.

'Hello,' said a low voice from beneath a pair of huge golden eyes.

'Hello,' I said.

'Want to come outside and play?'

'OK.'

I jumped up, but in my haste to get outside somehow didn't manage to unfold both legs from underneath me quickly enough to land on my feet. One hand flailed for a grip on something, anything as I pitched forward off the edge of the sofa. It found thick fur and gripped hard. This stopped my forehead from meeting the corner of the glass coffee table, but I still crashed to the floor with a squeal. Dad came running in from the kitchen, the pungent odour of frying garlic and onions behind him. His face wore a look like a storm cloud. I scrabbled back against the sofa but didn't try to stand up.

'What's going on? What happened?'

He ran to where I sprawled and kneeled over me. Thwack. He slapped me across the top of my head, hard.

'Did you hurt yourself?'

Thwack. Again. My hair fell into my eyes as my head rocked forwards.

'Tell me! Are you alright?'

Thwack, thwack.

'I worry about you. You *must* be careful. Did you fall? You mustn't hurt yourself, alright? You mustn't. Promise you'll be careful.'

He folded me in his arms and kissed the top of my head. He held me and I squeezed the tears back down into a hard knot in my throat.

'OK?'

I nodded. I didn't want him to be sad. I tried a smile on. It worked. He sighed, squeezed my shoulders, rocked back on his heels and stood up. Then he was gone. I swallowed the knot deeper.

'Come on, outside. Last one to the apple tree's It!'

I turned to see the dark end of a rope-like tail disappearing out of the sliding door to the garden. And rubbing my nose with the back of my hand I followed it out into the sunshine.

Scamper is a lost black cat. He is a
neutured male with very long black
fur that looks brown
in the sunlight. Scamper might
have jumped into someone's car, or
have been picked up by someone
with good intentions. He
likes to explore and plays in
the mud, so he looks messy from
time to time. Scamper is fat and
cute, with a belly that swishes back
and forth when he scampers across
a room. He has a thin tail that is
crimped at the end, and a large deep
meow when he gets annoyed. He
was last seen wearing a purple
collar with ID tags. We are checking
daily with the cat shelter. We
miss him greatly.

Let me touch you.
    Help me. Please. Help me.

What the hell am I meant to do now? What? I mean, just look at her. Crouching as if I've got her trapped just for a taste of her flesh. Eyes open, wide open, but closed to me. Wake up! Need you here, now, with me. Was always there for you, always. You listening to me? Can you hear me? Should I roar my frustration in your face? Always with you when you wanted me. Came without you needing to call, felt the pinpricks in your fingertips and knew. Came to you. Always came. At night, when you were too scared of the dark to unwind the blankets from your sweating body and breathe fresh air. When you hid from your parents in the broom cupboard with the spiders. When you pretended to run away, leaving a scrawled note on the blackboard in your room: I have run away. *I have gone to the woods. Do not worry about me I will be OK I wont come back. Bye. Marnie.*

Was always with you. Always.

Now it's your turn.

Ptolemy – Gone Missing
Male Burmese cat
Honey colour
Blue eyes
Please call if you see him

I never knew why. A whim. A flash of inspiration. He slammed unannounced into Jess' and my bedroom a couple of years after our parents split up. A couple of months before my ninth birthday. I heard heavy steps coming towards me up the stairs.

'What the hell is this all about?'

He was holding my latest school report so tightly it was bent into a V-shape by the pressure of his thumb. I could feel the blood drain from my temples and head straight for my heart, which started hammering against the inside of my ribcage.

'Answer me!'

His voice filled the room, squeezed me into the corner against my bed. I said nothing. He took a step into the room, another. His lips were pressed so hard together that they were rimmed with white, trembling. I dropped my gaze, unable to meet his eyes.

'How dare you. You have no respect for me. You have no respect for your mother. You have no respect for yourself. What is this? What did you get in maths?'

I was surprised he could hear my whispered 'B'.

'Is that all I'm worth? You are going to end up cleaning toilets. Is that what you want?'

I had no idea what I wanted. His rage had shoved all my thoughts aside and all I could do was stare at the blank white page my mind had suddenly become. I could feel the familiar knot in my throat grow. I shrank farther against the bed, curling up on its edge, hanging my head as low as it would go. Maybe if I curled up tight enough, stayed still and silent, he would forget I was even here and leave me alone.

'Is it?'

A tiny moan escaped my mouth, too small to be heard against the white noise of my father's anger.

'I'm talking to you.'

He was always talking to me. I had no choice but to answer.

'No.'

The effort of speaking squeezed tears down my cheeks. I hid my face behind my clenched fists so he couldn't see me crying.

'I didn't hear you.'

'I said "No".'

He glared at me for a moment. I was disrespectful. I didn't love him or my mother. I wouldn't care if they were dead. I moaned again, deep in my throat, at the thought of my dead parents. I was bad, so bad, he was right. I deserved this, all of this. They couldn't possibly love me. I deserved to be alone.

I'm not sure how long he talked at me, but my legs had pins and needles and my fingers were numb by the time I noticed a change in his tone. Suddenly he was conversational, almost conspiratorial, as if he was letting me in on some wonderful private joke.

'I'm taking you out of school. After the holidays you're not going back. I'll get your mother to organise you going to the local comprehensive. You can say goodbye to your friends tonight. Go downstairs and call them, tell them you're not going to see them again.'

I was so stunned I actually dared look him in the eye. What was he talking about?

'You obviously don't care about your education. Go on. Call them. Call, what's her name? Eve.'

I nodded.

'Call Eve then, and I want to hear you say that you won't be seeing her again. Off you go.'

'But . . .'

'But? But what? Get downstairs. I want you down there in five minutes.'

He turned and left. Then reappeared at my doorway. He was smiling.

'OK love? Just a quick phone call and it'll all be over.'

As if he had asked me to phone a bookshop and ask if they had a particular paperback in stock. Nothing more important than that.

I didn't move. My hands were cradling my head, and I felt that if I let go it might fall from my shoulders. I couldn't move. I tried to concentrate on my breathing, tried to calm my heart. Tried not to think what this actually meant. Whether he was serious. I sat against the edge of my bed. I squeezed my eyes closed.

From downstairs I heard the doorbell ring. Quiet, then the sudden rumble of raised voices. My parents arguing. I guessed that this meant Dad's threat was in earnest, and that Mum had been told.

After a few moments a warm breeze on my arm made me open them again. He nudged at my shoulder and I reached back and grasped a handful of rough fur. Held tight.

WHERE is Buffy the Mouse Slayer?
Lost cat, please help.
She is brown and cream
And very friendly.
If you have seen her
Please call me.

I knew it. I bloody knew it. All those times Mum told me to stop worrying, to stop being silly, to stop thinking about it. That I'm not like him, that I'd never be like him. But I was right. I was right all along. I've lost my mind.

Will I be as bad as him? Surely not. I can't be. Maybe I'm just overtired. Completely and utterly exhausted. They say that when you're so tired you can't think, when you're so tired you no longer need sleep, you see things, things which aren't there. Hallucinate. I'm sure I heard that somewhere. So maybe this is just a waking dream, a type of daydream. Just a very realistic one.

Or maybe not.

What if it's true? That I've gone, you know. Mad. I can't go through life like that. Should I tell someone that I've lost my mind? Probably. And would they lock me up if I did? Probably. And, bearing all this in mind, should I just try and ignore it, pretend it hasn't happened?

I thought that when you went crazy your entire world dissolved; the sky blossomed clouds of purple and orange; passers-by wore the heads of owls, zebras; toasters spoke back. My *dad*, for example. When he was really bad he knew that the world was ending, that legions of white-suited men were around every corner simply awaiting the sign to pounce and drag him away. At times like these he would be unable to speak, his entire world contracted to this tiny hard nugget of terror. When I was little I thought he was seeing invisible monsters, which scared him so much he lost his voice. Maybe he was.

But I never thought that madness could be so selective. I mean, here I am and the rest of my world is exactly as it was before. My hair is still brown. The sky is still grey. I don't believe armies of men are spying on me. I understand the English language and my kitchen appliances behave just as they always have. The only sign of my lunacy is a large lion sitting by my armchair. He wants to talk to me.

OK then. Let's talk.

'So. Why, why are you here? I mean, what are you doing back?'

He snorts, and the fringe of mane semi-concealing his glowing eyes flicks up above his head in the sudden gust.

'You *are* here, aren't you? I mean, you're not just in my mind?'

'Why the hell are you asking me? How should I know?'

I have no words for this.

'I just meant.'

Seriously, I have no words for this. Who would?

I'm sitting cross-legged on the sheepskin rug trying to roll a cigarette. I found a couple of old papers in my kitchen drawer, a new box of matches under the sink and a twist of old, dry tobacco in my sister's jeans pocket. I gave up smoking almost two years ago. Now seems the perfect time to start again.

'Look, let's say I actually believe you're sitting there. Glaring at me. You've come from. You've obviously come from . . .'

'Nothing obvious about it.'

His eyes strafe my face. Napalm flames blossom from a forest canopy. Amber strands of stale tobacco keep falling from my shaking fingers. I'll never get them out of the dreadlocked pelt of this sheepskin.

An hour or so ago I managed to get my front door key into its lock and stumble through the doorway into the hall, backwards, keeping my eyes on him all the time. I have no idea how long I'd been staring at his eyes. He rose from the cold slabs, unfolding his great limbs, and stretched his front legs along the ground. Then followed me inside, up the stairs, blowing loudly as if each step were an effort. Once inside my flat he folded himself into the corner by the chair. He didn't look around.

'What I mean is, you've come to . . .'

'I was brought here. Against my will.'

The wide waxy leaves of the cheese plant tremble slightly.

'You brought me. *You* did this.'

I can feel my eyebrows pulling together. I don't understand. I didn't do anything.

'You don't understand. Do you? *You* did this.'

Best I don't say anything. The words which make it past my lips are facile, unable to carry the weight I feel pressing on my chest. Everything I say makes him angrier.

'You. Did. This.'

I pull into myself, appalled at the noise. Concentrate on the tiny stone at my centre. The hard little pebble which feels nothing.

'You're going to shut up now, aren't you? Try not to piss me off any more than you already have. Don't make the nasty lion angry. It's a bit bloody late for that!'

If I had hackles I'm sure they would rise at the sound of his voice. I feel it rolling through the floorboards and up through my thigh bones.

'No. No, I'm not.'

Talk to him calmly, reason with him. Speak to him as if he's an old friend, recently rediscovered. We're catching up, that's all.

'So. Where were you born?'

I have no idea why I ask this. The lion turns from me, licks a haunch once, twice, and sighs. He shrugs. At least, I think it's a shrug. His shoulders move backwards and he shakes his head slightly. His tufted tail twitches, but he doesn't answer me.

'Was it . . . Africa?'

I feel stupid as soon as this is out of my mouth. Jericho evidently thinks me as stupid as I feel. He snorts, closes his eyes, lays his white chin on his paws.

'Born in the Midlands. Brought up in the circus. You know that. You remember.'

'I didn't. I thought you might have been, you know, brought over from your original, from where you're from. Africa.'

I pause. Bite my lip, which is becoming sore from the constant chewing.

'I mean, that *is* where lions are from, isn't it?'

'How should I bloody well know? I've never bloody been, have I? All I knew was the inside of cages and the circus ring. How the hell would I know about *Africa?*'

He hisses the last word, as if blaming the entire continent for his lifetime of humiliation and pain.

'They took my claws.'

He stretches his paws to show me his swollen knuckles and raises himself slowly from the floor to stand over me. This is harder than I thought it was going to be. Though I had never really thought about the possibility of having to calm down an adult lion. An adult lion who talks. An adult lion who talks and is very angry with me. In my own flat.

'Look at me. You. Look.'

Random thoughts pile on top of one another in my head, a defence mechanism I learned in early childhood and which now takes over. What exactly are hackles? How would I raise them if I had them?

'Don't *do* that.'

'Don't do what? I wasn't . . .'

'You used to do that with *him*. Disappear somewhere in your head. I need you here.'

Maybe you need to have fur to have hackles. Maybe Jess would know. I'll ask her when I see her.

Jericho lets go a booming grunt, rolls heavily onto his side and closes his eyes. He seems to give up easily, like me.

I want to say I am mad. Finally. Lack of sleep, trauma, stress. But this creature is so – here. The slide of his muscles over bone and under hide. The glisten of saliva strung between two yellow canines as he yawns. His breathing swelling his ribcage, again and again.

What is this? What has happened?

What have I done?

'Tone' where are you? Chocolate
Burmese five-year old male cat.
Striking blue eyes. Very clever.
Needs lots of love. Last seen 3 days
ago. If you have info please call me.

I drifted off to sleep last night sitting at the kitchen table. I've just woken up. The clock on the oven tells me it is 5.17 a.m. My fingers are stiff from being curled around a mug all night. The hot chocolate is cold, covered with a thick, rubbery skin. I don't even remember making it. My feet are icy. My forehead is ridged from resting on the kitchen table. Nothing moves. Just the hands of the clock.

I stagger to the bathroom where I stop and stare at myself in the mirror. Apart from being monochrome in the darkness my face looks no different. I thought it might be obvious, be written in my hair, my eyes, in the turn of my lips, that I was now a crazy woman. But no.

Still, I have the feeling that at any moment my reflection will walk away and leave me staring at the empty glass. It wouldn't surprise me. Nothing much surprises me any more.

I don't know where he's gone. He may be asleep in the hallway. He may have left. He may never have been here. I don't know. I don't care. I'm taking my deranged self back to bed.

Knuckles are killing me. Cold.
     Get me out of here. Will hound your every step until
you let me go. Let me go.

We can't find our cat Footie
Footie is white and black
all over
And is fat and
Likes to play and run after
things.
We'd be grateful for any
information.

'And finally . . .'

This always the best bit, the 'And finally'. The local 'human interest' story designed to entertain, amuse, pull on the old heart strings or, if it's really good, all three. The eleven-year-old boy dying of leukaemia whose younger siblings are doing a sponsored abseil for his charity; or the horse who saved its owner from a gang of thugs during a night-time raid on a stud farm; or the children's *gamelan* orchestra who are finalists in the world *gamelan* championships; or . . .

'The mystery of the missing cats.'

Or the mystery of the missing cats.

Holy crap, as Shiulie would say. I know this one. I fumble with the remote to turn the volume up, sidle closer to the television, *you'll hurt your eyes you'll hurt your eyes* running through my head.

'. . . local residents continue to be mystified by the disappearance of many of their beloved pets. Every day brings another story of loss and heartache . . .'

Slow pan down a street. A street like many others. Different only in the huge number of A4-sized pieces of paper stuck to lamp posts, railings, shoved under the windscreen wipers of parked cars. Then a close up of a grainy black and white photocopied photograph of a cat's face, head tilted slightly to one side, staring out with wide eyes. A pan down the picture to the words beneath:

Dennis has GONE. He is black
with yellow eyes.
Please call if you have information on his
whereabouts, we are REALLY
WORRIED.

The reporter's commanding voice again.

'We caught up with local resident Archie Battle, whose award-winning Siamese, Queen Niobe Starburst, went missing two days ago . . .'

I know this I know this I know this.

'Well, er, I don't know. She's a house cat, never goes out. Never. She loves people, so, um, I don't know. Um.'

Cut to concerned, nodding reporter.

'And what did the police have to say about it?'

Archie.

'Well, um, I thought at first there'd been a burglary, you know, a break-in. But the police said there was no sign, nothing, no broken glass, or fingerprints, or anything. It doesn't look like there's been a break-in. Um. So. Er.'

The man is distraught, his double chin trembling as he speaks, his eyes moist as they dart from camera to invisible questioner. Concerned reporter's face.

'Do you have any idea where the cats may have gone?'

Cut back to Archie, who has just blown his nose and is stuffing a handkerchief into his breast pocket.

'I just, um, I just don't know. There's talk it could be to do with the travellers.'

God God God. My fingers seem to have found themselves stroking the old man's flickering glass face. I put my hand back in my lap, clasp it with the other to stop it shaking.

'Residents say that the strange disappearances started about four weeks ago, coincidentally about the time a group of so-called New Age Travellers arrived in a nearby field.'

Ah, well there you are then, an obvious explanation, nothing too odd about that is there? A scene now of a group of large trucks and vans in a field. Colourful flags. Complicated-looking outdoor cooking arrangements. Dogs gambolling good-naturedly with frizzy-haired children.

'We spoke to Jemima Button, a spokesperson for the group, to see what they had to say.'

Cut to a very skinny very pale young woman with eyes the colour of a stormy sea and a ring on every finger. She leans against her violet painted ambulance and smiles patiently.

'Well it's typical we're blamed for the cats going missing, isn't it? We get blamed for just about everything that goes wrong when we're around. But look at our dogs.'

Back to the dogs and kids.

'We keep dogs, not cats, yeah? Why would we take cats?'

To feed the dogs with?

'I mean, we're not exactly going to steal cats to feed our dogs with, are we? Much simpler to buy dog food. Not to mention less messy.'

She laughs uneasily. The reporter laughs too and the camera turns once more to concentrate on her dark fringe.

OK, she has a point. I was grasping, I realise that.

'And so, as the traumatised local population searches for their lost feline friends . . .'

I sag back from the TV. Why has it taken me so long to realise what's been happening?

'. . . on the helpline number at the bottom of the screen now, where advisors are waiting to take your calls . . .'

He couldn't. Could he?

'. . . scattered showers and occasional sunny spells throughout the day. So that's all from us. Have a peaceful evening.'

Thanks, but I can't imagine ever having peace again, evening, morning, whenever.

Where the hell is he?

FIVER is lost.
Small brown and white cat.
Three legs. Please help.

'The cats.'

Sitting on my front doorstep in sunshine which struggles to warm me, I pick at the soggy label on my beer bottle. Some wild beast cavorts with a deer on its crinkled surface. It's not even noon but I shall drink it anyway. It might even do my addled brain some good – you never know – and I'm willing to try anything right now. I also thought that with a beer inside me I might be able to approach the subject of the missing neighbourhood cats. Now, watching the lion roll around on the front lawn, I'm not so sure.

Jericho is lying on his side, one massive paw flapping idly at a fly which frets around his upside-down head. It dive-bombs his nose; he snaps at it and the sound is of a great trap slamming shut. The fly appears from underneath his elbow and resumes it's eddying flight.

'Jericho?'

'Hmm?'

'I said, the cats.'

'What cats?'

'The cats from around here. Next door's cat. My cat. Mr Knuckles.'

'What about them?'

'Where are they?'

'Hmm . . . ?'

'I said, where have the cats gone?'

'Don't know.'

'But they've all disappeared. All of them. Just gone. Run off . . . or something.'

He stops batting at the fly for a moment. It lands on a sandy ear, which whiplashes it into a nearby bush.

'How should I know? Cowards.'

As he says this he twists his head along the ground to look at me, picking up fallen leaves in his tangled mane. Searchlights, those eyes.

'I just . . . I thought you might . . . don't know. Doesn't matter.'

He stares.

'You think I've done something.'

I hesitate for only a fraction of a second.

'No I don't.'

'Yes you do.'

'I don't. I just thought, well, you might have picked something up, know something, you know, with you being a cat and everything . . .'

He snorts into his mane, flicks his ears.

'Me being a *what?*'

What have I said now? It wasn't meant to be like this.

'A cat. You're a cat. A bloody big one, but a cat nonetheless.'

'Comparing me to those runts? You're saying we've something in common?'

'But you do. I thought. That's why they call lions and tigers and things like you "Big Cats".'

Another dismissive snort.

'Isn't it?'

I don't say anything for a while, try not to stare at him.

'You think I've killed them. *Eaten* them.'

My brain is still trying to make sense of all this. Any kind of sense would do. I'm not fussy.

'Surely you can see how this looks? I mean you turn up and suddenly all the local cats have scarpered. And I mean *all* of them. You can't see the lamp posts anymore, they're covered in missing cat posters. I *saw* the way that black cat reacted to you when you followed me to the house. And I . . .'

He's obviously not interested. I sigh. Drum my fingers on the stone step.

'But I don't think you've eaten them. I saw the way that cat tore off down the street. They're probably all too quick for you, run off before you even get a good look at them.'

He narrows his eyes at me, as if squinting through bars.

'And anyway, you couldn't eat them. I mean, they're obviously scared of you, but you couldn't actually *do* anything to them. Physically, I mean.'

Not a flicker from those eyes.

'You couldn't. Can't.'

Nothing.

'Can you?'

He's looking at me as if I had crawled out from beneath his enormous paws. He's obviously decided the question doesn't warrant a reply. He seems to be scanning my face, but I feel him inside my head. Don't.

'Anyway . . .'

And he's humming to himself again. I've heard the tune before, but can't place it.

'That tune.'

'You used to sing it. Sometimes in the garden, underneath the bushes. Sometimes under your covers. I'd lie on your cold feet. Always cold, you were. Always bloody cold. You'd sing quietly so only I could hear. A song just for me.'

And he stretches a muscled foreleg along the ground to touch the toe of my shoe.

'You'd wriggle your toes to tickle me. Remember?'

I remember.

'You'd plait my mane. In the dark. You couldn't see anything. Jess would ask what you were doing? Remember?'

Yes, I remember.

'You'd wake in the morning at the foot of the bed and your Mum would ask why you couldn't sleep normally. Remember?'

'Yes.'

'Well then.'

'"Well then" what?'

He doesn't answer, has shut his eyes away under those heavy lids and is breathing heavily. His paw is touching my shoe, just.

I remember the touch of that coarse mane. I flatten my hand against the pitted cement, caterpillar my fingers towards Jericho's foot. I stop, fingertip hovering a centimetre from the fur. What if my hand goes straight through? What if it doesn't?

'Just "Well then". And I *can* feel your hand. Whiskers on the ground, vibrations sort of thing. What *are* you doing?'

> Wotsit where are you?
> Please call if you see a long-haired
> Tabby cat, with a blue collar and bell
> Call me at home or on my mobile, any time day or night.

A girl called Gemma in my class at school also had a friend only she could see, jealously guarded and whispered about only during our mumbled morning prayers. Smiff was a tiny creature (male, female, I never knew and it didn't matter) who lived in the laundry basket in her bathroom. It had big ears and played with the bubbles when she had a bath. If you weren't nice to Gemma, Smiff would cut your head off and eat it with ketchup and jam. This sounded pretty disgusting to me, but then you never could account for the tastes of your imaginary friend.

Gemma sometimes came to school with red marks on her wrist or on her shoulder, occasionally a cut above an eye or along her jaw. She was clumsy, she told me. She fell over a lot at home, bumped into things. But Jericho said he found it odd, as she was always the best at gym in our class, would sail over the horse in fearless somersaults, twirl and tumble, never falling once and landing

135

perfectly on the trampoline, placing her feet exactly during ballet classes.

She lived on her own with her mum. Her dad had risen with the sun one misty morning, opened the door and disappeared into the fog. He had left Gemma's mum for the lady who walked their two greyhounds.

I never went to Gemma's house. I imagined it must have wooden floors polished to a high shine and treacherous as ice on a lake, because that would explain why she was always falling over and hurting herself. I imagined her sliding, graceful as an ice skater, down a long draughty corridor with its mirror-like floor. A long-nosed hound darting out in front of her to play, and Gem, unable to stop on the slippery surface, trying to avoid it. Clattering head-first into the edge of an open door. The silent flailing of arms. The heavy, jolting sit. The hand raised to the slow-blooming redness spreading along her cheekbone. The tender questioning pink of the dog's nose at her ear: *Why are you crying? Why are you crying?*

I didn't entirely believe in Smiff. How could someone live in a laundry basket?

I talked to Jericho about it one afternoon after school, as we leant against the rough white garden wall, his solid rump, my skinny back, while I picked at a scab on my knee. He yawned, hugely.

'I'd have *his* head off.'

'Do you think he exists then?'

'No.'

And that was the end of the subject. He made me laugh by curling his huge tongue up over his nose and going cross-eyed at the same time. I tried to copy the feat, and held the position for so long I felt dizzy. Soon Mum called me inside for dinner, but Jericho stayed outside. I watched him for a while through the window as he tried to catch the bees and the fat blue flies which zizzed around his head in the low evening light.

Lost Siamese cat – Pepo
(pronounced Pea Poe) is a
13-year-old spayed Siamese Brown Seal
Point Cat. She managed to get out
Sunday evening, Sept 21 near
Jamaica Road. She is very
affectionate, and docile, a 24/7
house cat. She may be close. If you
know her whereabouts please call
us. REWARD offered.

Spiderman. Could be Superman. Possibly Hulk. No. No, it's not raining, won't be Hulk. I know. Batman. I bet it's Batman today. A stampede of footsteps as a small rhino approaches beyond the door, flings it open.

'Hey.'

'Hi Ravi. You OK?'

'Yeah.'

'Your sister home?'

'She's my *half*-sister.'

I try not to let my smile slip.

'You're absolutely right. Half-sister. She about?'

'Yeah.'

Clattering from inside. Shiulie's voice now.

'Marn, come in! Living room!'

Ravi's not moved from the doorway.

'Can I come in and see her?'

'OK. But you've got to say the secret password.'

The secret password. Of course. I was hoping he might forget it for today. I'll have to play along for a while.

'OK. Is it . . . Hulk?'

'Nope.'

'Is it . . . Spiderman?'

'Nope.'

Time to get inside, my feet are going numb.

'I know. What about . . . Batman!'

'Nope.'

Oh.

'OK, I give up. What's the password?'

He frowns.

'No, you've got to guess!'

'OK, then. Um. Is it Superman?'

He rolls his olive eyes. Creeps his fingers to the plastic toggles of his duffle coat to pull aside the opening and reveals . . .

'Ah, of course! That's . . . what is it?'

'Jason. The Red Ranger.'

I am no clearer. I need to get inside. But Ravi demands I know the full story before I can enter.

'He's the leader of the Power Rangers. Everyone knows that.'

Of course.

'I'm going to get my Blade Blaster!'

He turns, canters down the corridor and disappears around

the corner. I step over the threshold and close the door softly behind me.

'Marn? Where the hell are you? Get in here. Ravi get off me, you spaz!'

A yelp. A thud.

'Mum! Shiulie called me a spaz!'

Shiulie is sitting cross-legged on the floor of the living room, swathed in yards of orange and red fabric dotted with thousands of tiny mirrors. She looks like she is drowning in a fiery sea.

'D'you like it? Good colour, eh?'

She holds a length of sari up to her face.

'I call it "Madras Meltdown".'

She bursts into laughter, while Ravi crouches at the shore of the sari's folds, pink-faced and thunder-fisted in his Power Ranger pyjamas. He swings his face from his sister's to mine and glares.

'Marnie, Shiu's a bollicks. She called me a spaz.'

Shiulie gives a delicate snort and gathers an armful of cloth to her chest.

'Well, don't mind her,' I say feebly.

The boy drags the corners of his mouth down, rummages half-heartedly in a nostril with the tip of a finger. His eyelashes lower to shutter his eyes. I always fix on the beauty of those eyes. Some would call them hazel. They're really the colour of copper-veined slate, warmed in the sun, hot against the spread palms of the hand. Eight years old and already he has an older woman in love with him. He drops to all fours and hangs his head towards the floor.

'Marn, look, give me a hand with . . . Rav, *please* move. Hold this Marnie. *Ravi*.'

Ravi acts as though he's not heard her. Coils into himself a little tighter.

'Ravi, if you don't get off that corner I swear I'm going to . . . Marnie, just shove him out of the way would you?'

The boy crawls into the far corner of the room, sits on his haunches in the shadow of the enormous TV. His eyebrows are pulled together tight, but a tiny smile flickers over his lips briefly. He's staring at the doorway.

My arms are full of material, my chin is buried in it. It smells of the metallic glints and thread which are woven in the warp and the weft of it. When I close my eyes it smells cold.

'Marnie, God's blood woman, you look like shite. You alright? Look, forget that, just dump it over there. There, no, here. OK. Sit. Chai?'

Her fingers dance over my sleeve. Pluck at the enamelled button on my cuff. Smooth their backs over my cheek briefly and fall to her side.

'I'll make it. Nice and strong, sweet-sweet.'

She mimics her mother perfectly, winks and leaves for the kitchen.

God's blood.

Shiulie will be able to help me. I know she will. She has to. I follow her into the kitchen where I find her trying to decide whether I will be more amused by the mug with a Kiwi bird saying 'I like to rock the party!', or the one emblazoned with a complicated prescription drug name which sounds like it may be something to do with haemorrhoids.

'Shiulie.'

'Hmm?'

She decides it's a Kiwi day and throws a handful of spices into a small pot of water on the stove. I'm not entirely sure how to start. *Today I upset Jess, again, went for a walk and, oh yes, there's suddenly a talking lion in my flat which no one else can see.* Or maybe it should be more subtle: *Um, does it necessarily mean you've got mental health problems if you hallucinate?* Or possibly I should just come straight out with it, get straight to the point: *Shiulie. I've*

lost my mind. Give me drugs and lock me up. It'll be safer for everyone.
These all work within the confines of my head, but I can't seem
to force the words past my teeth. I feel suddenly ridiculous. And
find myself laughing. At nothing in particular.

'What's up, Marn?'

I stare at my shoes on the lino. The curve of the toe fits
perfectly with the brown pattern. How odd.

'Sweet fancy Moses what is wrong with you today?'

I look back up at her face, open and close my mouth a couple
of times. I must look like a fish.

'Have you spoken to Dylan, recently? He's been trying to call
you. Marnie?'

'Yes. I mean, no. I've not spoken to him. I will.'

Shiulie eyes me.

'OK. While you work your way up to telling me what's in your
head, I think you should know that I've made a big decision. Sit,
sit down. OK. You remember we were having that big life choice
discussion the other day? I told you I'd never really wanted to be
a doctor? That I'm good at it, but it's not me? Well, I've decided
what I want to do.'

She stops and looks at me expectantly, her eyes wide and
brown.

'What do you want to do?'

She opens her mouth but pauses for effect. I've always thought
she should be an actress.

'I'm going to open a bookshop. A little ramshackle one, with
piles of rare second-hand books all over the place and I'll get a
cat and it'll live in the shop and hunt mice. I won't have any
kind of filing system, it'll be like a lucky dip. What do you
think?'

I'm not sure what to think.

'And I'll grow old doing it and when I'm ancient and bent I'll smell of cat pee and small children will be afraid of me, but book enthusiasts will visit from all over the world to sample my literary delicacies. After *him* I've decided to become celibate and love books and cats instead.'

She stops, mouth open. Pulls her lovely eyebrows together.

'Though not in the same way, of course.'

I nod. I smile. I nod and smile.

'Well, that sounds . . . nice.'

Shiulie's frown deepens.

'No – I mean – it's just a bit of a surprise, that's all. It's not really what I expected.'

She sits down at the kitchen table opposite me, places both hands on the tabletop and looks at them as if they were a rare species of small animal she has just discovered lurking behind the skirting board.

'I could carry on with the head shrinkage. I know I'm good, and I do care. But after what's happened I need to do something I really love. Something for me. And that something for me is books. And art. Put them together and you get books about art. Being my own boss, Marn. I want to do some courses, see how to go about things.'

She smiles crookedly, snorts at a thought.

'My parents will never forgive me, though.'

Her smile leaves her. She looks suddenly tired and smaller.

'The thing with him, Will, really sucked the joy out of it all. I just can't deal with the stress any more.'

She rubs at the tender flesh between thumb and forefinger.

'And I need to find something I'm passionate about again. Do you understand?'

I do understand. I understand exactly.

'I do. I know.'

'I can't listen to people's tragedies again and again and not be able to help them properly, you know? What can I do if a young woman comes to me with severe depression, and the main reason she's depressed is that she's living on her own in a shitty, cockroach-infested bedsit with three kids under the age of five and she can't feed or clothe them properly?'

She is staring at the patch of skin she is rubbing red, spitting the words from her mouth now.

'I can't re-house her. I can give her pills, listen to her, shake my head at the sight of the cuts she's carved into her thigh with nail scissors, but I can't give her the thing she really needs. I feel bloody goddamn fucking helpless.'

She has raised her voice and looks surprised at herself. She smoothes a lock of hair behind her ear and sighs. Gives me a lopsided grin. Gets up to make the tea.

I watch her back, supple beneath a sage-green shirt. Her long hair flows down it, shines in the harsh kitchen light. I know she has been working long thankless hours. I know she is often tired, drinks too much to relax in the evenings and at the weekend. I also know the problems with her husband have shattered her, though you wouldn't know it, she hides it so well. But I didn't know it would lead to this.

'Come on, you. Back into the living room and you can tell me what you were going to tell me.'

My friend smiles. I try to smile back.

'I'll be fine. Don't worry. Come on, take your buggery tea and get next door.'

She shoos me back into the living room. Ravi has not moved.

'Ravi, what the hell are you doing? Marnie, sit down, sit. Right, what's up?'

She is looking at me intently. You can tell me, I'm a doctor. But I can't tell her now. She's exhausted, she's had enough. Yearns to cast away everything silting up her life. So I can't tell her that her friend has lost her father, lost her mind, is talking to invisible animals. I can't tell her that I wake in the small blue hours of the morning and feel I am spinning apart. She would have yet another hopeless case, would fret at not being able to return my father, to restore my sleep, my health. My mind. And secretly she would resent me for adding to her caseload. She would be sympathetic, listen, try and help, but she would be drowning inside, desperate to get away from my demands.

'Talk to me.'

Still, she tries to help.

A wave of exhaustion pushes me further into the depths of the overstuffed armchair. I thought that this, here, these lives, would bring me back to myself. That the slap of reality would banish the crawl and prick of crazed thoughts against the nape of my neck. That talk of weather, football, clothes would steady my mind. That a cup of tea, that legendary weapon against sorrow, trauma, fear, would scare the beasts from my door.

I was wrong.

I look up from my shoes to Ravi, who's still crouched by the TV, and realise that if I were his age I could get away with it. *Shiulie there's a lion in my bedroom, his breath smells funny, he won't go away, he keeps telling me it's all my fault. He frightens me. I think he might hurt me.*

I look at Shiulie and her face swims through my tears. My eyes must be sparkling.

'I'm just tired, Shiu, it's nothing in particular.'

She is looking at me. I wish she would stop.

'It is. It is something in particular. That bloody bully of a father of yours for a start. It's OK. You talk to me when you're ready. Did you try those pills for sleeping?'

I nod, mutely. It's a lying nod. I can't bring myself to lie to her out loud.

'You just need a little time, a rest. If he comes back he comes back. If he doesn't, well, maybe that's for the best, no?'

She blows on the frothed surface of her spicy Chai.

'Marnie, he terrorised you. Let him go.'

What was I thinking? She'd stroke my face, kiss me and then probably have me sectioned if I told her about the things I've been seeing, hearing. Doing.

'Anyway, at least you don't need to worry about work for a while. That Leo; gem of a boss, sorting you out so much time off, eh?'

'He is. I'll go back soon, though. I can't bear just sitting around doing nothing all the time.'

'Good. Moping about the bloody house isn't what you need.'

She rakes her fingers through her hair. Ravi is still staring into space. Motionless apart from his fingers which weave around and around each other in front of his face. I've never seen him so quiet.

D raft lifting hair on my back. Wind finding its way underneath the front door into the corridor. Rich smells filling my mouth with water. Hungry. Hot. Tired.

Mostly hungry.

Boy sitting there. Eyes like a deer. Brown and soft and warm. An option, I suppose. Always that option. If she doesn't listen, that is. Then we'll see. Yes. Marks in his soft flesh. I may not have claws but I can still do damage. Considerable damage. Not smooth, clean damage but jagged and torn and ripped damage. Nice, messy damage.

She'd take notice of that. She'd listen to me then.

Male bobtail cat with yellow collar –
Joe is an orange coloured male
American short hair/Manx mix cat.
He was last seen on 07/10. Very
loving. He is meant to have
surgery this week. Please help us
find Joe. One of the bells on his
collar is larger than the others.

I walk home and my shoes are too loud in the dusk. I feel I might wake some slumbering beast unless I tiptoe. This is surely what the cracks in the pavement are for: alarms for legions of nameless dozing creatures. A carelessly placed heel, a scuffed toe, and red eyes blink open in the dark. Long-dead claws stretching their unused cartilage clench and dig and make their way to the surface.

I'll deal with this on my own. I was foolish to think that Shiulie would be able to help me. She would be too close. I can't burden her with this – she would worry even more than she does already. She would try to help me out of the pit I find myself in.

Would end up grinding her teeth in frustration at her inability to make a difference.

She made me Chai, sweet-sweet, and we sat and chatted. We didn't talk. We chatted, about inconsequential things, while the little boy kept to himself in the corner. We ate ginger biscuits. We hugged. I even managed to squeeze out an exhausted tear or two, and Shiulie held me for a while, wiped my face dry, commented that many fathers were indeed the devil's own work and that I was best off without him. I smiled and nodded at her, hugged her back and left, the light from the open doorway remaining until I had turned the corner.

Once I'm home there will be the inevitable phone message from Leo, asking about how much longer I will be off work. I will delete the message, not reply.

I can deal with this. The way I've always dealt with things. Alone.

The smells of autumn are amplified at night. Damp leaves and tar. Wood smoke again, though I can't imagine that any of these houses have open fires. I slow down between the pools of light which hang from each street lamp, preferring to remain unseen in the shadows, then hurry through the sudden showers of brightness. It's like trying to stay dry by running through the spray from broken guttering.

My sister was always afraid of the dark. The spilling forth of slick, dark bodies, the scurrying of countless clawed feet, haunted her imagination. Even after a whispered bedtime story from my mother, head bent low, hair brushing Jess's face, our bedroom door had to be kept ajar to allow fingers of light from the corridor to reassure her until she slept, lying on her front, hands clasped beneath her. She slept in the oddest positions: on her back, head flung over the edge of the bed and hair touching the ground as if in ecstatic abandon; curled on her side, snailed in on herself with pillow clasped tightly over her face. Sometimes I would look over towards her and think I should move her slightly, allow her some breathing room. But my feet refused to touch the floor. You never knew what would reach out from under you, grasp your ankle and pull you down.

But I was not really scared by the dark when I was a child. A strange thing, that. I say strange, because most other things frightened me. Being in crowds of people. Muzzled dogs. The shapes of some clouds. Speaking my mind.

I'm concentrating on light-pool dodging while tucking the end of my scarf into my collar to keep the draft from my neck, so I don't see the broken paving slab jutting from the ground in front of me. My foot is jarred to a stop and I stumble, almost fall. It is late, no one else is around, but I still feel the colour rise to my cheeks. And my feet have dragged themselves over cracks too numerous to count now. I can't stop myself checking over my shoulder.

My oh my, what big teeth you've got.

All the better to eat you with.

LOST MY BOY – Thomas
the Tomcat
Skinny grey mackerel-striped
five-years-old, great fun and
very loving
Please help us find him.

The birth of a new baby. A cause for joy in any household, you would have thought. And so it was with the arrival of little Jessica. My grandmother – Mum's mum – had come to stay for two weeks and the house was full of food and flowers and cards. Mum stayed upstairs in the bedroom most of the time, whispering and cooing into the tiny marzipan ears of her puffy, squinting newborn. I hid in the shadows, sliding from corner to corner, trying to attract my Nana's attention when I could. I was six years old and I wanted some of the chocolate-dipped biscuits which had appeared overnight in a beribboned basket.

The Friday afternoon after Nana arrived my dad left the house. He did not return until early Saturday morning, and had a woman in tow. The woman was the strangest looking creature I had ever seen.

'Is she a pirate?' I whispered into Mum's hip.

She didn't answer, so I supposed she might be.

We stood in the hall; clouds gathering around Dad's head, Mum wide-eyed and heart-stopped, the pirate woman lounging unconcerned by the door, a huge duffel bag slumped at her feet.

The woman's hair was a cloud of bright red ringlets pulled back and cascading over her shoulders and down her back. Thick black lines were drawn around her eyes. She wore a purple frock coat with regiments of gold buttons and tight black trousers underneath. Her ears were pierced a number of times with heavy-looking gold hoops which matched the gold braid on her flat black thigh-length boots. I looked for a cutlass or dagger stuck in her belt. I couldn't see anything. I wondered how such a small woman could carry such a huge bag. But if she was a pirate she would be terribly strong so that made sense.

Mum stood next to me, tensed like a deer. The baby was asleep in its white lace-frilled cot in my parents' bedroom. Nan was in the garden tending the camellias.

'This is Marina. Marina is an astrologer. She has some news for me.'

We were silent. Marina the Astrologer smiled at us. I didn't know what an astrologer was, but thought it must be something to do with the high seas.

'Nice house. Can I stick my stuff somewhere?'

'Upstairs, second on the left. You can have that room,' said Dad.

Mum's frown deepened.

'But that's where Mum's sleeping? Ben, what is . . .'

But he'd turned and walked away into the living room.

'Upstairs Marnie, to your room,' she said quietly and went

after him. Turned back to where I was dithering on the bottom stair.

'And don't come down until I call you.'

She was gone. I tramped upstairs and stopped on the landing outside my bedroom door. I could hear things being moved around in the small room next door. I imagined Marina unpacking all manner of strange and wonderful things; crystal balls, curved daggers, long black capes, monkey skulls.

That evening Nana was packed off to stay with one of my mum's friends. No real argument was put up against it. She left with wide bemused eyes and many backward glances, clutching her little tapestry suitcase. Mum patted me on the head and told me not to worry, it would all be alright, as she gazed after the shuffling figure of her mother, who was being ushered into a taxi. I had no idea what was happening and why Nan was going, but, as Mum had asked, I didn't worry. I didn't give the matter even a passing thought. Because I was the happiest girl in the world. A couple of hours earlier Marina had produced from the depths of her gigantic duffel bag a plastic-shrouded bundle of gauzy white fabric and golden embroidery. It was a costume, a fairy dress. It was for me, and came complete with star-tipped wand and a tinsel tiara. Sequins dotted the full skirt, pink flowers were sewn onto the bodice and the puffed sleeves were cuffed with white lace. I had never seen anything so beautiful. I wore it all weekend, weeping and whining when asked to take it off for bed. Marina never spoke to me, just rubbed my cheek as she walked past, produced boiled sweets from the many folds of her voluminous clothes. I was still convinced she was a pirate. Dad was hardly to be seen and Mum spent all her time in the kitchen, standing at the cooker stirring and stirring the contents of saucepans and pots, pale face taught and a tiny bewildered smile fixed on her face.

I was so tired from being delighted with my new dress that I fell asleep almost instantly each night, only hearing for a few moments the raised voices from the living room below.

After two days Dad seemed to forget there had ever been a problem. Marina the Astrologer went back to wherever she had come from, duffel bag slung easily over her shoulder, red hair piled like a frothy helmet on her head. She turned back once at the bottom of the street, winked at me and disappeared around the corner. I loved her with all my heart then and wished she wouldn't go. Nana came back to the house later that day and was welcomed with outstretched arms and a beaming smile by Dad, a shy kiss on her dry cheek from Mum. Nana barely spoke for the three remaining days she was with us. And Mum said to me, 'You see? It was all OK after all.'

And I thought it was.

But it wasn't, was it? It really was not.

It was years later when I found out what had happened. Dad had been contacted, Mum said, by Marina, who had bad news about the new baby. She never told me who this woman was, or how she had known Dad. The news had been that the child, Jess, was not his. A spirit guide, or an angel – he had been vague about the details – had told her that she must break the news. Dad had gone to meet with this woman, this pirate, and believed the story instantly. After all, the spirits could not be argued with. He had brought her home, thrown Nan out and spent the weekend studying the alignment of the stars with his new confidante. And then one morning my Dad had risen, asked Marina to leave and hugged my Mum, who by now was red-eyed with crying and lack of sleep. She accepted his embrace silently, as she did all his moods and actions. Pressed a smile into his shoulder. Disappeared into the kitchen to make breakfast for Marina before she left.

As far as I know the incident was never spoken of after that. It was more than likely my dad forgot it completely. He never brought up the subject of Jess's spirit-contested paternity again.

The white fairy dress hung for years in my cupboard, the tiara and wand in a paper bag looped over the neck of the wire coat hanger, until one day they were bundled up again in plastic and given away to the little girl of one of our neighbours. I like to think she spent days in it spinning round in front of a mirror watching the sunlight bounce off the glittering sequins as I had done all those years ago.

> Ginger, male cat nearly twelve
> and of small build. House cat – not
> streetwise, and timid. Lost in
> Stewart Drive. Wearing leopard-print
> collar with tag. Called
> 'Charlie'.

The concrete paving stone was heavy. I couldn't even move the broken corner piece. I scrabbled at the brave weeds which poked from beneath, pulling them aside, picking out the pebbles, to get a better grip. Jericho sat in a flowerbed next to the path and yawned, whining quietly and then licking his chops.

'You could give me a hand.'

He bent his head and sniffed the verge delicately. Sneezed as a thistle pricked his tender nose.

'I could *not* give you a hand.'

He glowered at the broken paving stone.

'It's boring. Let's go chase cats.'

I stopped my delving and looked up at him. I could feel a patch of dried earth pulling at the skin on my cheek.

'This was *your* idea! Find out what's underneath, you said, what's under there that makes it bad luck to step on the cracks.'

I turned back to the tiny hole I had created.

'Your stupid idea,' I mumbled into it.

We'd been running down the path outside the house, racing each other, and again I hadn't been as careful as I should have been in avoiding The Cracks of Doom. One paving stone was split, a sneaky corner raised above the level of the rest, pushed up by the tireless strength of a light-seeking dandelion. The concrete had snagged my careless, scuffed toe and I had been hurled earthwards, scraping both knees and the heel of my right hand.

Sitting on the path in my thin cotton summer dress, I sobbed silently, eyes squeezed closed, while Jericho stood over me and licked my hair, my cheek, my bloody knees, growling softly so my whole body shook with it. His tongue removed the worst of the grit embedded in my flesh. Normally I would limp home, hold my wounded palms up to Mum for sympathy, hugs and plasters. But I was staying with Dad. I couldn't let him see me like this. Anything could happen.

Jericho had railed against the creatures which must have been responsible for my injuries, those living beneath the cracks in the pavement. He suggested we dig to find them, under the broken slab, and confront them once and for all. The idea terrified yet thrilled me, so I started scraping away the dirt and pebbles from around the corner of the stone to try and loosen it.

What would they be like? I thought that they must be very small – this, I felt was obvious – and possibly green, because all evil things are green. Or blue. They would have little black eyes and long dirty fingernails and sharp yellow teeth. They would be bald. Jericho favoured the theory that they would be blind like moles, with large noses and an excellent sense of smell. Either way, we would find out and I would lift the stone and Jericho would pounce on them before they could disappear into the ground – he could be very quick – and kill them all with swift snaps of his jaws.

Only now this plan seemed more and more unlikely, as my fingertips were becoming sore with work which wasn't yielding spectacular results and Jericho's attention had drifted. He no longer seemed to want to dish out retribution to the under-the-pavement dwellers. I tried to use a stick to scrape deeper but it broke. I wailed in frustration and sat back on my heels. Jericho stretched and ambled over to me from the pile of dry dog poo he had been examining and peered into the shallow depression I had made. It was evident that the stone would not budge.

'Come on, leave them buggers for now. We'll get them another time.'

I scowled at him, rubbed my nose with the back of a grimy hand.

'But we've got to get rid of them. What if they do it again?'

'Well, we'll prepare and we'll be ready for them next time.'

He narrowed his eyes at me.

'They'd just better watch out.'

So I picked myself up, dusted off the creased seat of my dress and, with one backward glance at the mocking paving slab, trotted after my friend.

The pavement people could wait for now. We would be back.

> My cat, May, is lost. She is grey
> with blue eyes. Very friendly.
> I'm worried and need her back.

Lying here now, my cheek cradled by one of Jess's fluffy, powder-puff cushions that she bought me in return for letting her stay over so often, I suddenly can't get an image of him out of my mind. Emerging gasping from the warm Adriatic sea many summers ago, hands clutching at his nose and mouth to sweep away the stinging water. The sun was setting. The other tourists had returned to their hotel rooms and apartments and stone villas as the shadows reached across the beach to the whispering shoreline. I sat on my towel on the rocks watching his frantic search, while Jess terrified herself with the next in a long line of H.P. Lovecraft novels we had swiped from Dad's bookshelves. The occasional yelp from her.

'Marn! Listen . . .'

She would read me a particularly graphic passage, describing subterranean passages of unimaginable depths, creatures spawned from the unknowable recesses of a troubled mind; jackal-headed monsters, tentacled aliens, ancient gods long-forgotten but soon to wreak a terrible revenge on humankind. Alternate worlds only visible through clockwork contraptions specifically designed to show the horrors which surround us. I think Jess thought that by sharing these terrors with me it would lessen her nightmares. It never seemed to though. She would shake me awake in the still blue hours of the night, imagining lurking horrors on the threshold of the en suite bathroom.

The sun touched the horizon and I hugged my cardigan closer around my shoulders in the cooling air.

Dad dived under again. He was searching for a ring. His ring. A simple gold signet ring he wore on the little finger of his right hand. It bore a crest he designed himself, a stag crowned by three stars engraved on its flat yellow surface.

'What do you think of that, then?' he had asked me after driving fifty miles in the snow last February to show us his latest cause for excitement, and grinning like a boy whose wildest Christmas present dreams had just come true. 'Wonderful, isn't it?'

The heat of the day and the warmth of the sea had loosened the ring and during one of his faltering swims – he was never a strong swimmer – it had slipped off his finger and was now hidden in the sand. He had been looking for it now for just over two hours. Jess and I were hungry. I was unable to see why this tiny thing warranted such a frenzied search. A new ring could always be made. And two hours was a long time to search for anything which wasn't your own flesh and blood, I felt. These were thoughts, though, which I would never share with him. I watched as he swept his arms about in the water and knew he would never find it. It was gone, to lie patiently in the sand until someone stumbled across it, maybe a year, maybe ten years, maybe thousands from now.

I loved him at that moment and it hurt my heart to look at his brown body, the droplets of seawater clinging to his hair, to his curled eyelashes like tear drops above those brown eyes. I wanted to take him home and take care of him, sweep the lines from his high forehead as finger-dug letters in the sand are smoothed away by waves. I wanted to turn myself into a mermaid so I could find his beloved ring and make it all better. I watched him, and didn't know whether the cold drops falling onto my skinny chest from my chin were seawater or tears.

He emerged finally, bent to retrieve his towel and walked away into the trees without a word. I grabbed my things, kicked Jess out of her horrified reverie and followed him back towards the hotel. Entering the foyer we just caught sight of him entering the lift, and the doors closing behind him.

That evening at dinner in the hotel restaurant he bolted down his bowl of soup, announced that he was not giving up the search, told us to get ourselves to bed and disappeared. We were both used to our father running off suddenly on his missions. We finished our food alone while discussing Lovecraft's latest story in frenzied whispers.

Back in our room I watched from the balcony as a dark shape moved slowly across the beach, pausing every now and then before moving off again. A restless shadow, a forlorn ghost.

The crickets purred in the bushes and the scent of pine was everywhere. An insistent whine at my ear. I shook my head fiercely and slapped the sound away.

I could foresee another sleepless night ahead.

That was years ago. I would have been about seventeen, I think. Jess eleven. Long ago. So many things lost and never found. Was that the mantra of his life?

Is it becoming mine?

*

I must have dozed off because when I open my eyes the room is dusky, deeply shadowed. Strangely quiet. Though I hear the breaths, the rasping sounds coming from the black corner of the room opposite the sofa where I lie. A slight wheeze as each breath is taken in. A rattle as it escapes. I look up at the ceiling and breathe loudly, timing my inhalations with the breaths I can plainly hear are not mine. After about a minute of indulging myself in this pointless exercise I try to get up, but my hair is trapped under my arm, the fingers of which are now prickling with the blood that is rushing back into their tips. I struggle to heave myself into a semi-upright position.

'See? You forgot about me once. I wasn't there was I?'

What?

'On that beach. I wasn't with you. You'd forgotten about me, just like I said you would. You forgot about me that time, you can do it again. Can't you?'

What did I forget?

'Sleep well? No bad dreams? Not feeling guilty at all?'

Guilty?

I squint at the talking corner. The shadows hide whatever lurks there.

'Go away.'

A loud, wet snort.

'Well, that's what I'm trying to do, isn't it? What I'm trying to get into your thin little eggshell skull. If you'll let me I'll be on my way, get out of your hair, all that sort of thing.'

This again.

'Yes. This again. This is your fault.'

My fault. As a child a vague fear of impending retribution would crouch on my shoulder, whisper in my ear *it's your fault, it's your fault, all your fault*. And this even before my father started shouting me into corners of the house, telling me that I was the one who should be in a straightjacket, that he was able to hear my traitorous dreams through the wall as I slept.

'I'm talking about now, not then. It's not about him. It's about you. Idiot.'

I can only gape at him. Suddenly he has leapt onto the low coffee table which trembles under his weight. His paws clutch at the edge, twisted knuckles flexing, flexing. He thrusts his golden eyes towards me.

'Alright. I'll try and make it simple. You called me here. No one else. You. Something's happened. I don't know what, but something happened, so you called me. Couldn't think of anyone else. So you called me. See? Not that difficult to understand. A five-year-old could grasp it.'

A five-year-old. I was five.

He sneers, snarls at me, lifting his top lip high above long yellowed incisors and a faint rumble starts in his throat.

'I . . .'

'What, idiot? You what? You didn't do this? If I hear that one more time . . .'

A rush of tears behind my eyes threatens to spill down my cheeks. I will not cry.

'I didn't. I really didn't do anything. I promise you. Please believe me, I didn't *do* anything. I don't know what you are. I don't. I'm having trouble sleeping and, and you're just some . . . figment, a figment of my . . .'

What happens next leaves me too shocked to even cry out. With incredible speed the lion is off the table, has cuffed me down onto the floor and is standing over me, teeth bared and inches from my nose. A blast of hot, stale, meaty breath hits me in the face and I gasp, gag, squeeze my eyes shut and try to hold my breath. One massive paw rests on my chest. The weight makes it hard for me to breathe. I open my eyes. Thick whiskers dot his lips and chin. Suddenly I feel a sharp point on my breast bone, two, three. The pressure on my chest increases.

'Please . . .'

I whine this one word then can say no more. My lungs will not take air. I close my eyes. I will wake up now I will wake up now I will.

'Call me a bloody figment, would you? A dream? A bloody daydream? Is that what I am?'

The weight on me is huge, is crushing. I will surely break in two, this weight driving through me, past me into the floor underneath.

'This a dream, is it? This all some bloody nightmare? You going to wake up in a minute, scratch the sleep from your eyes and I'll be gone, will I? Your nightmare, am I?'

The weight on me. The noise thrumming through my ears, my head, my body.

'I'll show you what a nightmare is.'

A sharp pain flashes through my chest and the weight falls from me. Air is dragged into my lungs with no effort from me, great gagging, heaving breaths which tear into me. My heart is hammering in my temples, in my throat, in my stomach. The room is silent except for my ragged breathing. And, of course, the occasional whimper which manages to escape my throat, though I try to be quiet.

After what feels like an age I roll onto my side on the floor, rest a moment and open my eyes. Tears spill from my eyes and onto the rug. I can't see him. I get up from the floor using a chair arm for support. My legs feel as weak as a new-born foal's, are threatening to fold underneath me. I put my hand to my throat. Nothing here. No one else in the room. Just me. I lower myself into the armchair, rest my elbows on my knees and sit with my hands encircling my throat. No one else here. I rock, ever so slightly, back and forth. It comforts me. No one. Else. Here.

After a few more painful breaths, I make a conscious effort to relax my shoulders. I am alone. I get up, but I'm not sure what for. I sit down again. I burst into tears, but the tears seem to dry up after a couple of sobs. I try to cry again, but the tears won't come now. Something is lodged in my throat, in my heart. I am dammed up. I am damned.

My mouth feels dry and I get up to go to the kitchen. As I pass the mirror in the hall I glance at my reflection. The sight makes me stop. I move closer, and raise my hands to the outer edges of my collarbones, trace their sweep down to my sternum. Where my fingers find five small red marks etched into my skin. Five red marks spaced across the width of my chest. Five perfect blood-red circular impressions each about the diameter of a match head. They are simple. They are beautiful.

I button my shirt to my throat.

Then, fully dressed, I walk up to my bedroom, climb into bed, pull the heavy duvet over my head and am asleep.

S he was asking for it. Bloody asking for it. You saw that. If she's going to play games with me she's got to expect to be slapped down. Hard.

I never meant to hurt her. Not really. It's just she just makes me so angry. She's probably laughing at me. Playing, pretending she doesn't know what she's done. All she has to do is reverse it. Not too much to ask. Then I can be out of her hair, she can be off my mind.

Asking for it, she was. Just asking for it.

I was sure the violence would work. Has done before. She responds to a raised voice, a raised hand. Sharp teeth. But I'm wondering now. What if the marks I gave her didn't do the job?

Would she keep me here out of spite? She could. She could. Just to really piss me off. Have a laugh.

No. She was never spiteful. Sweet-tempered, really. Quiet, shy. Used to shrink away from you if you brushed past her suddenly. Shrink away into a corner, into the dark.

She was quiet away from me. So quiet. So afraid. So desperate to please him all the time. Never believed me that he wasn't worth the effort. Would never be worth the effort. Got beaten back time and time again. Poor little mite. She'd run to me, bury herself in my side and gulp back her tears. Poor little sod. Little thing. My little thing.

She was still asking for it, mind. I can tell. I can always tell. Though I'm not as sharp as I was once. OK, I *used* to be able to tell, every time, no mistaking it. Could it really be she's telling the truth? Is it possible she doesn't know what she's done? Maybe. Maybe.

And if she doesn't know, if she really has no idea what she's done? What then?

What the hell are we going to do?

Tigger-Boo has gone missing!
Please help us find him, he is black with yellow eyes
And loves to play.

I'm not answering the phone today. I'm not even getting out of bed. The sun is almost at its highest point but I've piled the pillows round my head to muffle all sound, and though I'm beginning to sweat I'm staying swaddled. I have a vague memory of overheating when I was much younger, hiding under the bedclothes despite knowing I was protected by a beast which would never allow harm to find me. And no one now will find me here.

I put my hand on my breastbone, feel the tiny circles which dot my skin. They will disappear soon enough, but I should probably wear something high-necked for a few days.

Despite the amount of cotton and wadding between my head and the bedside table, I can still hear the phone. It has demanded my attention twice already this morning. At each shrill ring I've started to reach for it but stopped myself and huddled down further into my nest, guilt lining my stomach and making my mouth taste bitter. I watched it from the one eye not blindfolded

167

by the covers, willing it to stop. Which, of course, it did eventually. I lay and stared at it, as if expecting it to rise up and come scuttling sideways towards me crab-like and threatening. But it just crouched there and eventually I fell asleep again.

This time the phone's ring drags me out of a dream which tastes of cold steel and sawdust. I watch it for ten rings then launch myself from the echoes of strange lullabies and pick up the receiver. I almost drop it from my sweat-oiled palms but finally wrestle it to my ear.

''llo?'

Nothing. I cough to clear my throat.

'Hello?'

It's then I realise that the corner of the pillow is muffling whoever is at the other end of the line. I punch it down beneath my chin and repeat the question. At last, a voice.

'Marnie? You can hear me OK, yes? OK. You OK? OK.'

It's Shiulie's mum. Unusual.

'Marnie, could you do me a favour? Take Ravi for a few hours today? Shiulie told me you are not at work. I've got to go and get my feet done, and that Georgie is sick and there's no one else. Could you, sweetheart?'

No, sorry, I would rather eat the very receiver in my hand. I would rather boil my feet, stick pins in my eyes. I will stay here and smother myself in covers, dive back into the musty depths, muffle myself to the world, fill my ears with wool, tie a scarf about my eyes and rock myself back to sleep. Forget about you, forget about little Ravi and his ailing babysitter. Forget about myself. Forget about him. Don't ask me again. Don't ask

'Sure, no problem. I'll be round in about half an hour.'

*

'Zoom, zoom,
    the zoo, the zoo,
    the poo-zoo,
    the poo-poo!'

He has a mean sense of rhythm, I can't deny it. And it never fails to amaze me how even the most innocent things can be translated by children into poo jokes. Or poo songs. Ravi is shrieking gleefully now, hopping at my side, swinging heavily on my hand when he trips as I try to hold him up and keep his knees from the unforgiving tarmac. He whoops once, twice, unclamps his fingers from my hand and wheels away from me, circling the lamp post and then trying to hop back, grinning from ear to ear. He stops at my side, squawks loudly and grabs my knees. I can't help an idiot grin spreading over my face. He lets go and tears away again down the road, arms outstretched. He reminds me of a tiny fish, darting here and there without reason, weightless and carefree.

Today, underneath his everyday clothes, he is Batman, ready to fly to my rescue should a rampaging rhinoceros or tiger become over-excited and decide to eat me. Apparently there are dangers at the zoo, dangers I should be taking much more seriously than I am. I have tried to explain that the towering walls, electric wire and moats should protect us both from the slavering beasts; that the fangs and claws and hooves will be unable to reach us, but Ravi just looks at me and rolls his eyes, as if to say *Look, only last week I did battle with a polar bear. I know what I'm talking about and you don't.*

Ravi is small but strong, and drags me towards the great gates of the zoo like an untrained mastiff puppy. Hops up and down with impatience while I buy tickets. He is so excited that once we are inside, he is totally unable to decide which way he wants to go first, seems to fling different parts of his body in different directions at the same time. He finally makes a decision and I amble after him as he jogs to the wolf enclosure, hangs from the wire railings and tries to get his head through the gaps. The skinny grey creatures seem to be asleep in a distant pile, so we walk on. We visit enclosure after enclosure, him galloping ahead and stopping every now and then to check on my frustratingly slow progress, then trotting back to gather me up and herd me towards the next cage or pit or pool.

Very soon it is past three o'clock and I'm wondering where the time has gone and what I've missed, as my mind has not been entirely on this zoo trip. But we've stuffed ourselves with burgers and ice cream and somehow I've managed to steer us around the lion enclosure, which for most people would be the highlight of the visit. I haven't meant to. It just happened.

I lingered in the reptile house, convincing Ravi that I'd been hypnotised by a hooded, swaying snake and lumbered around the darkened corridors like a zombie. He shrieked with delighted terror. We squashed our noses up against the glass walls of slow-worm and iguana tanks, requested, ever so politely, that the chameleons please change out of their mossy green and reward us with orange stripes, or purple dots, or at least a fiery red belly. But they only swivelled their golf ball eyes, each in a different direction, and plucked flies out of the air with tongues like wetted leather strops. Ravi soon got bored of the darkness and the slow animals that lurked there and dragged me back into the sunlight.

We laughed at the monkeys, who laughed back at us, chattering and teasing and hurling themselves head over heels through the air in heart-stopping displays of fearlessness.

We watched the seals play with their fish, slipping through the water like quicksilver.

We speculated how the giraffes might reach food left for them on the ground, until they demonstrated a delicate, shuffling splits for us.

We gawped in awe at the armour-plated rhinoceros pouting behind its double horns, left in a hurry when it turned its tiny piglet eyes on us, pawed the dusty ground.

We asked the okapi who were its mother and father: the zebra and the gazelle or the giraffe and the horse?

We wondered what the smart penguins wore to bed when they took their dinner jackets off.

We were soaked by an elephant's bath water, sent squealing with laughter from the high fence, pelting down the wide walkways until we found ourselves at the eastern corner of the lion enclosure. Where I slowed and stalled. Ravi ran back to me, puzzled but grinning, tried to pull me along with his enthusiasm.

Mine had dried up, shrivelled.

I could put it off no longer, though. The lion's den beckoned.

A wide dry moat separates us from the grassy hillock which rises from the centre of the enclosure. Rocks and old logs dot the artificial landscape, large bushes surround the patch of land and a stream empties into a large pool.

I don't see anything moving.

'Where are the lions, Marnie?' Ravi whispers. The mere possibility of the animals' proximity seems to have quieted him. A kind of awed watchfulness descends on us as we stand at the edge of the enclosure and wait. Are there pairs of eyes in the bushes, watching us waiting for them? Does our scent reach them on the sharp breeze which brings goosebumps to my arms? Are pawfuls of knife-like claws being sharpened, readied on those old mossy logs?

A lioness emerges below us, sleek and iron-muscled. She has slipped from an outcropping of boulders like a lengthening shadow at dusk and stands, ears swivelling, belly heaving as she samples the cold air.

She takes my breath away. Ravi is unmoving beside me. We do not speak.

Does she dream of the chase across the dusty plains, as dogs do, legs kicking and twitching as she sleeps in her man-made shelter after a bellyful of goat or heifer? Does she yearn for herds of sooted wildebeest, knots of skittish gazelle? Does she remember the panic of the stampede, the blind leaping frenzy, the slide and scream of the weak, the old, the injured that she has picked out, rounded up? Or does she dream of the only live beasts she sees now? Two legs, two arms, slow. An unchallenging catch, easy to swallow and without thick, furred hide to get in the way of the sweet flesh.

Ravi gives a little squeal and pulls his hand from mine.

'You're hurting!'

He rubs his knuckles.

'Oh, God, sweetheart, I'm so sorry. I didn't mean to squeeze so hard.'

I kneel down in front of him, so quickly I jar my bones.

'I didn't mean to hurt your hand, Ravi.'

My fingers stroke dark fringe out of his accusing eyes.

'It's just that I'm scared of the lions.'

I stop. An unexpected, but familiar, stinging behind my eyes. I realise that what I have just said is true.

Ravi clasps his hands together and gives me a stern look.

'Don't worry, Marnie. I won't let them get you.'

I look at his dark eyes, so serious. I pull him towards me, hug him hard to my chest so he won't see the tears falling down my cheeks.

After a moment he wriggles squealing out of my arms, cocks two fingers at the sleepy lioness and fires once, twice, three times.

'Peeyow, peeyow, peeyow!'

She shakes her head as the bullets fly past and lodge in the tree trunk behind her. Ravi looks at me.

'Warning shots,' he says.

'Good idea.'

The warning shots, though, only seem to have attracted another lion. A young male strolls out of the bushes, sneezes, drags a huge paw over his nose and licks it a couple of times. He walks up to the lioness, head butts her gently and rubs his forehead against her cheek. Then they stop their nuzzling and look up towards the walkway where my little hero and I stand watching them. They stare back, golden eyes narrowed and unblinking. Two pairs of black nostrils flare delicately, tasting the air. Then the lions turn as one and disappear noiselessly back into the bushes.

Ravi takes my hand and, gently, leads me away.

See the way they were looking at me? See that? The scowling? The looking-down-the-noseness of them? They smelled me over the people, saw me hiding. They don't know anything, with their skulking in bushes, their fresh meat slung over the wall by stinking humans, their lying in the sun, not a care in the world. Not a bleeding care. Bastards.

Pretty female, though. Feisty, nice eyes. Wouldn't mind a bit of that myself, wouldn't mind a bit of a scrap for her. Not at all. I'd show him. I'd take a few cuffs and gouges for a couple of minutes of her haunches. And I'd leave him gutted in a pool of his own red by the side of that little lake.

If I had my claws, of course. If I had my claws.

I buy Ravi a soft toy crocodile. The interior of the zoo shop is dark, the walls draped with plastic vines. Piped bird and monkey calls ricochet from wall to wall, mingling with the wails of small children disappointed in their ambition to own every single piece of merchandise on display.

Ravi is fascinated by the rows of teeth in his new pet's grinning jaws. He had wandered down the aisles, canyons of fake fur, inspecting the animals carefully, methodically, wondering aloud whether the monkey was too big to fit in his school bag, or whether polar bears really have eyes that small. His face crumpled into a grin, though, when he saw the crocodile.

'He'll protect me when I'm sleeping, won't he?'

'Of course he will, mate. He'll always protect you. He's on your side.'

Ravi strokes the long green tail. His eyes widen.

'Yeah. He's on *my* side.'

He puts his face close to those teeth and whispers something. Then holds the crocodile's face up to his own ear and squints as he tries to make out the words.

'He says his name's Smoothie.'

'Why Smoothie?'

More intent listening.

'He says it's cos he's got really smooth fur.'

Another pause, concentrating on words not meant for me.

'And he says he's on my side.'

Ravi grins and tucks his new friend under his arm. They wander outside to have a look at the curl-horned goats, and I follow. I find myself pleased, can almost feel my heart swell under my skin. It's good he has someone on his side.

Because we all need someone to watch our back.

Ravi chats to Smoothie all the way home on the bus, holding the toy up to the greasy window and pointing out to him his favourite swing in the park, the local cinema, his school. The crocodile now knows his way around the neighbourhood almost as well as I do. He rushes inside to introduce his mum to Smoothie, almost bowling her over in the corridor, covering her belly with crocodile kisses. She tuts at me for spending money on him and offers me dinner, as she always does. I decline, saying I've had a wonderful time with Ravi, but should go. This she refuses. So I tell her that I have to get to bed early to try and get some sleep, as I've not been sleeping very well lately. This she agrees to, but reluctantly, and only when I promise I will dine with them some time later in the week. I'm sure Shiulie has told her as much as she knows of my current problems. So, with my ribs still aching from the strength of her hug, I came home.

I've been lying on the sofa, wondering whether to phone my own mother but somehow can't find the energy to pick up the receiver. She'll probably be out anyway. Theatre, dinner, cinema. Tate members' evening, something cultural, something social. She will smile at people, listen intently to conversations, laugh quietly, covering her mouth with her hand. She's sociable, in a quiet way, and is out most evenings. When she is with people she concentrates on them completely, as if she is afraid that at any moment they may just disappear – poof! – in a little cloud of smoke and she will never see them again. So she watches faces with the intensity of a surgeon performing a complicated operation, stores up the sound of their voices, their little stories, the details of their families, trying to imprint these moments firmly on her mind so that if the worst happens she will always have this final solid memory of them.

Sometimes when I am with her and we aren't talking, maybe just sitting together reading as we used to do, I will catch her staring off into the distance. I wonder whether she is replaying her most recent moments with her friends, with her daughters, trying to keep the memory fresh and bright and alive.

It's funny, but I don't really remember her from my childhood: she always seemed to be on the periphery of our lives. This is strange because it's not technically true, of course. It was our mother who brought us up, fed us, clothed us, bathed us, hurried and scurried us off to school, tucked us in bed at night. She did all this quietly, efficiently, and usually with a secret, faraway smile on her face, as if she was somewhere else, thinking of something else. She loved us, loves us still, but she was always elsewhere. Waiting for him. She spent her days poised at the brink of the next crisis, muscles tensed, perfectly poised like a high diver on the highest diving platform. She moved through the house, through the garden, through our lives, keeping to the edges, careful not to disturb the slumbering beast lest she rouse him to anger.

But try as she might, tiptoe and hide and whisper as she might, there was no telling when or how the eruption would come. A book cover might one day suddenly be the wrong colour. The cat may have looked at him for a second too long. I might have brushed a lock of hair from my forehead with the wrong finger. Just the wrong way. Then thunder clouds would bank, the room filling with his dark, roiling thoughts, and she would stop, trembling, in the darker recesses of the house until the bad weather had passed.

I'm sure at one point she must have tried to understand, even tried to help in some way. But then she simply gave in and let it happen, unquestioningly. After all, why try to understand the whys and whens of a lightning strike? Analysis of that sort was a luxury afforded to others, not to her. Did she feel there was no choice? Or did she just love him so much she felt it didn't matter? I've never asked her. I'm not sure I ever will.

She has been quiet since Dad's disappearance, won't mention it. The few times I've tried to talk to her about it she sidesteps neatly and retreats to some corner of her own imagining. Maybe she now feels lightened, free. And maybe that's just how I should feel. Maybe I should not be seeking out that old anger, the thunder that split our days so unpredictably and so often. Maybe I should let him go too.

Woo the Kung Fu cat is gone and is
probably OK, but if you see a fat
white cat please contact me.

A sudden noise jolts me awake and I spill some water from my glass. A voice – my voice – sounding as if I'm speaking from the bottom of a dry well. A low tone. Another voice.

'Hey, Marnie.'

It's Dylan.

'It's Dylan. Obviously. You there?'

A moment of silence.

'I just wanted to say 'bye. Jon's asked me to go on a diving trip, last minute, and I'm going, for two weeks. We're off to Honduras, how good is that? I wasn't going to go – after what I promised Ruthie and everything – but she persuaded me, said it would do me good.'

A chuckling snort.

'Get that, eh? God I love that woman. So, anyway, 'bye. You take care of yourself, OK?'

OK.

'Marnie? You sure you're not there? I'm sure I can hear some heavy breathing or grunting or snoring or something, you naughty baggage.'

Another snort. I can't help but smile.

'OK sod you then. 'Bye babe.'

A crackle and a click and a tone and the machine clicks off.

'Bye babe. 'Bye Dylan.

Missing cat, reward if found – Kitten
is long haired, large light grey-black
tabby, long bushy tail. He was last
seen on Oct 4th. He may have
wandered too far, got lost, maybe
adopted or transported by
mistake. Please call with any
information or possible sightings.
Substantial reward offered.

Sunny late autumn is raucous with children. They squeal and shriek in nearby gardens. Open windows broadcast arguments, radio music, the clattering of pans at dinner time. Our good weather lives spill over the edges, their outlines blurring with others. So different to the coming colder months when we cocoon ourselves, wrap our walls around us and descend into chilly silence.

I'm lying on my front on the hill behind our street. It's not even a hill really, more of a grassy slope, one which hasn't yet been covered in shoulder-to-shoulder houses. Pylon wires vibrate above me. My face against the cool green, my fingers rummaging in the earth, spears of grass finding their way a little way up one nostril until I sneeze. Snail's-eye view. So much more interesting than bird's-eye view. A worm cast nestling against the fleshy stem of a thistle. Slivers of stone hiding from the clouds. A dandelion lifting its gentle spikes of light to the wind.

And me. Hiding from myself.

But he's found me. Somehow I know this, though it's been some days since I saw him last. I feel him panting up the hill now, his great head swinging from side to side with the effort, tongue drooping from the side of his jaws. The top of his yellow mane appears above the gentle rise of the hillock and I watch him from beneath a curtain of hair. I knew he'd find me. I also knew he'd find the walk a problem. I intend to use this against him.

'Nice walk?'

He doesn't grace this with a reply, or even look at me as he throws himself at my side. It takes him a while to catch his breath. When he does he bares the tips of his teeth and glares at his feet.

'Bugger off.'

I turn onto my back and stare at the thick black wires hanging above me. If I fell off the world now all I would need to do is stretch out my arms and catch at them as I passed, and I would be saved. Safe. In the cat's cradle of pylon wires.

'What are you doing?'

What does it look like I'm doing?

'Nothing.'

He snorts into his paws, where he has lowered his muzzle.

'Actually I was wishing myself off the face of the planet. That OK, is it? You not planning on trying to disembowel me again if I give you the wrong answer, are you?'

He is silent.

'I mean, if it'll make it easier I'll pull up my T-shirt and lie really still. Look. I won't even scream.'

He does not move.

'Oh, just try not to get too much blood on my jeans, I'd like to leave them to Jess. She's always wanted them.'

A tiny shudder ripples through Jericho's great frame.

'Be quiet. Just. Be. Quiet.'

Then a deep sigh, as he closes his eyes.

He is close. Why so close? Maybe he's going to lunge at me again. I feel I should get up, walk away. Save my neck. Save myself. But I'm too tired. I'll just lie here and wait. Watch the clouds. He seems to have exhausted himself. Crazily, I feel like reaching out to him again. And what if he took my hand off? Honestly? I can't say I care. At least then I would be able to feel something again.

I reach out and grasp a handful of mane. He doesn't pull away.

'So what are you doing? Why did you climb all the way up here? Just to snort me to death?'

'Came to see what *you're* doing. Not feeling like running away screaming?'

'I never screamed.'

'Wanted to.'

'I didn't.'

Jericho doesn't reply. He settles his head on his paws more comfortably. He does this slowly, and my hand remains clutching his fur. Maybe he wouldn't mind if I put my arms around him. Maybe he would set his head on my belly, and I would feel the strings of his great throat rumble through my body. I move my fingers deeper in to where it is warmer, close my fist a little tighter. He doesn't move, breathes deeply, steadily. I would bury my face in his shoulder, feel the swell of muscle against my cheek, if I thought he would stand for it. And now everything in me cries out towards him. Help me. Please.

He does not move. And low, so low I cannot hear it, can only feel the slightest tremor through the very tips of my fingers, he begins to purr.

*

And I am the doziest old puss around. Lying in the grass with her. With Marnie. Lying here in the sunshine. Warm above me. Cold below me. She smells young and soft and tender. Her hand in my fur. Holding me here. Holding me. It's warm. It's.

Have you seen Bingo? Bingo is an elderly,
deaf, thin black cat. We
returned from holiday to find her
missing. She was last seen by our
cat-feeder on Monday morning.
Please check anywhere she could
have got herself trapped in your garden?
If you can give us any help or
news please phone us . . .

It's strange but I don't even remember clearly what he was like during the past weeks or months. Years ago, yes. I can bring to mind childhood memories of him as easily as tracing the lines on my palm. I can recall the tone of his voice when I was seven years old, see the darkness in his eyes as he looks at me from the well of all those years past. Smell the aftershave on his jacket from his rare hugs when I was ten, just before he was sent away to hospital. But ask me what he was wearing on the last day I saw him and I will look at you blankly. Ask me what we spoke about recently and my mind will skid and falter and slip back to a holiday in France when I was nine and he talked to me about the mermaids he had met during that morning's swim in the clear blue Atlantic.

It's as if he is someone I last saw many, many years ago. As if he disappeared for good when I was a teenager and the past months and years never really happened. As if I have sent another part of myself to see him while the piece that keeps memories stays at home with its hands over its ears, humming to itself and rocking back and forth, back and forth.

As I grew up I avoided him whenever I could. I would often not answer the phone, fearing my father's voice – cold, alien – on the other end. Fearing another tale of his own bloodletting to release the demons. Fearing the fingers of guilt which would come at every story of his pain, and which have never loosened their spidered grip on my heart.

I would appear on his doorstep most weeks, gripping my courage between my teeth, to knock at his door, to sit with him, to listen to him. 'How's Vivien?' he would ask sometimes, enquiring after my mother's health with no great conviction. I do remember the taste of copper which filled the back of my throat while I sat across the table from him. The painful throb of the vein in my right temple while he kept me fixed with his dark eyes. I can remember the hardness of the chair beneath me. But not what we talked about. Not what he talked about.

I'll not call the police again for a while. I'll wait for them to call me. I'll take their advice. They'll contact me, I'm sure. Soon.

There's a part of her inside me. Again. Deep, just below the ribcage. In my guts. I feel her small hand clutching. It holds fast. It sits, hard and warm, the bones of an animal in my belly. I could heave it up, push it away. I'd be lighter for it. I'd be able to concentrate on what I need to do. I'd be able to concentrate on escape.

But something in me wants this. Something creeps and squirms. Demands. Makes me crazy. I'd forgotten, you see. Forgotten what it feels like to have someone believe in you. To call you forth. To make you real. To stick flesh on your bones, tie sinew and veins between them. Swell the dark marrow, set to work the dark, secret creatures that live inside. Forgotten what it's like to have someone believe. Because where would I be without her? Not here, that's for damn sure. Not dragging my old bones around. Not wearing out my voice with repeated argument. Not surrendering to her warm arms. Not here. Not here at all.

I'd forgotten how breakable she feels. Is. Like the mimosa plant, folds into itself when touched. We saw it once. In a huge hothouse made of glass it was, full of plants from every corner of the globe. Full of towering trees. The metal on the floor too hot to walk on. I kept to the cooler earth between the trees. She was fascinated by one plant, couldn't take her eyes off it. I couldn't see why she was so bothered. The uniformed man told her she could touch it, gently, if she wanted. Of course, she just stood staring at it until I got bored and pushed my nose against it. It shrank immediately, retracted its leaves like tiny umbrellas. Almost jumped back out of its pot. Made the man jump too. He did this weird little laugh, said he hadn't noticed her touch it. Backed away to talk to some other people.

Still. She almost feels like mine again. My little thing. My little bit of a thing who called me to her, though she didn't know she was doing it. Every day I stay here the sun on my fur feels warmer, the grass softer. And she feels more mine. My Marnie. Her.

Have you seen my cat? She is:
Tortoise Shell and white.
Half of her face is ginger, on
left side. White paws. White breast
& Belly. Small & Skinny. Name Mrs
Nins. She is also very Shy of people
She very unlikely to approach. She
was last seen on monday in
Verulaneum Rd. If you have seen her
please let me know ASAP. As she is
missed very much!

Mr Ballantine drove the ice cream van that visited our street when we were children. When he first started coming his van, as many did, played *Green Sleeves*. We kids, conditioned after only a few early summer days to salivate like Pavlov's dogs at hearing the whimsical chimes echoing down our road, would hang on our parents' clothes begging and pleading for icy treats, resorting to tears when the less extreme tactics produced no results.

But come July the strains of *Green Sleeves* were heard no more in our neighbourhood. Mr Ballantine's van did not appear. For a couple of weeks parents were forced to buy ice cream at the shops, all the while wondering when the ice cream seller would be replaced, and the sooner the better.

Eventually, on one especially hazy summer afternoon, children came creeping out of their homes and from their gardens, again tempted by the chiming of the van. But this time we didn't run, pelting down the roads with coins clutched in our hot fists. Instead we stood and listened, and then the parents came out of the houses and stood and listened too. And we all stood and listened and looked at each other with raised eyebrows and cocked heads. We didn't recognise the tune. But when the van came to a jerky halt in its usual position at the end of the cul-de-sac we shook ourselves and bought ice creams anyway.

It only took a day or so before we came skipping down the street as we always had, trained now to associate our favourite summertime treats with the chimed chords of *Ace of Spades* or *Bat Out of Hell*.

After that I wondered if there was an ice cream van jingle shop, and imagined Mr Ballantine browsing the shelves and drawers of a dark and murky old room, thumbing through racks of heavy metal and lifting out his prize, a slow smile spreading across his wide face.

I always tried, but never quite persuaded my mother to buy me three ice creams.

'But they're not all for *me*,' I would wheedle.

'Well who exactly *are* they for then?'

'One's for me. The others 're for Jess and someone else.'

It never worked. She just thought I was being greedy. Mum would purse her lips and cross her arms.

'Marnie, I don't know how many times you're planning on trying this with me but it's not going to work. Here. Enough for you and your sister. Or you could always donate yours to this "someone else".'

I would look up at her, whining quietly through my pout.

'Off you go.'

I knew not to push it too far, or Dad would be called from his study.

There would be one '99 Flake for my sister and another for me, handed down to us from the van window by the thick-veined, hairless hands of Mr Ballantine. Huge though they were, those hands were used with the delicacy of a surgeon or a pastry chef. The grasping of the delicate tip of the wafer cone between forefinger and thumb; the gentle spiralling of the cornet below the nozzle, thick ribbons of ice cream piling softly on each other; the positioning of a powdery bar of Flake and its planting at just the right angle in the snowy mound.

Mr Ballantine never spoke. I didn't find it strange that he never spoke. That he asked for our orders with a widening of the eyes and a waggle of sprouting brindle brows (although after only a couple of days he knew exactly what each of our favourites were). Held out his fat paws for the amount of money indicated on the picture menu on the side of his van with a sausage-like finger. Nodded his thanks for the coins or notes. I liked it. I understood it. I thought it entirely natural for someone not to speak because they simply didn't want to. There were too many words spoken unnecessarily, I thought. Most were loud and hurtful too. How much more peaceful my life would be without having to speak, without having to make noise. Without people speaking to me. Shouting at me. Jericho and I could communicate just by thinking at each other, catching each others' thoughts drifting through the air, plucking them from where they floated.

That was it then. It was a sudden revelation. I would not talk again.

But when I got home – I had managed not speaking to Jess for the two or so minutes it took us to reach our front door and felt my heart swell with my achievement – it was only a few more minutes before the words were forced from me in answer to whether I would prefer beans or peas with dinner. I was disgusted, accused myself silently of being a coward, promised myself I'd try harder the next day. But by the time I woke in the morning all my fervent vows of silence had been forgotten.

Anyway, Jess and I would get a cone each and that would be that. I would retire to the grassy swell of land behind our house to share my spoils with the lion while Jess played with her friends out front. Jericho would always get half the Flake and the end of the cone. I would bite it off for him, scoop some ice cream into it and drop the miniature cornet onto his pleading, outstretched tongue, giggling at the delighted grumbles and growls he made as he crunched once, swallowed and licked his lips.

The following year *Green Sleeves* returned, and we knew without being told that Mr Ballantine was gone. I saw him only once after that. He was sitting motionless in a wheelchair, pushed by a woman with white hair and red boots, his face drooping like a sad mask, his right hand a clenched claw in his tartan lap. I imagined him singing his favourite tune to himself, inside his head:

> *And the last thing I see is my heart*
> *Still beating*
> *Still beating*
> *Breaking out of my body and flying away*
> *Like a bat out of hell.*

Balou – Cat Balou has gone –
She has grey short fur and a black
Ring around her tail and
Is quite shy

'Mmrrmph.'

'What?'

'Feels nice. Bit lower. Lower. Mm. Mrmph.'

My hand is up to the wrist in honeyed mane and beginning to ache, as Jericho hardly feels it unless I press hard. His flesh is warm and firm against my fingers. He smells of damp old dogs.

'Enough now I'm afraid. I've had it.'

I retrieve my hand from his fur, stretch my arms over my head. He mmrmphs again and lies still. Then, as I used to do years and years ago, I lie down as well, my head cradled in the hollow between his body and foreleg. My nape warms with his heat. And I never want to lift it from his side. I want to lie here, staring at the low grey sky, my head rising and falling with each of Jericho's breaths, for ever.

'And you'd find your Dad that way how exactly?'

'What do you mean?'

'Just lying there you're not going to solve anything, are you?'

The wind has picked up and is tormenting small branches on the trees. They thrash around as if seeking something safe to cling to. The sky is darkening. A darkling sky. A lovely word: darkling. My darkling, I love you . . .

'Are you listening to me?'

'Of course.'

'Well?'

I think of lightness, and of darkness growing.

'Maybe I should stop looking for him. Maybe I can't look for him and maybe I shouldn't.'

My head lurches suddenly from Jericho's side as he rolls and heaves himself to his feet. I have to move quickly to stop my head being squashed like a grape under him as he performs this delicate manoeuvre.

He turns, puts his face close to mine. His breath moves my hair.

'What. Do. You. Mean?'

I can't read his eyes.

'Just that there's nothing I can do.'

I try bullishness. But he doesn't blink.

'And me? What about me?'

He says it slowly, as if speaking to a very young child.

'What about you? What's it got to do with you?'

A blast of heat and noise in my face heralds his laughter. But he is not mirthful. There is derision tucked loosely into those sounds. He stops suddenly.

'Don't play that game. It's got everything to do with me and you know it. You want to keep me here? You want me to stay?'

I don't know. And I don't know what to say. I'm not even sure I know what Jericho is talking about, why he keeps bringing himself into conversations about my father. I take the easy option, the one I'm used to. I say nothing for a while.

He turns away. I look at the regal profile of his nose.

'I feel I've got to keep pinching myself hard. To make sure I'm not dreaming. To make sure this is, you know, really reality.'

Jericho runs his tongue over a long canine, carries on studying the clouds on the horizon.

'I could pinch you if you like. Pinch your nice juicy flesh.'

He turns to me and cocks his head to one side.

'Oh, actually I couldn't. What I *could* do, though, is rip a nice jagged hole in your nice juicy arm if you like.'

He wrinkles his nose and shows his top teeth. This gives the impression that he is grinning.

'That might bring you back to reality.'

He snorts and gets to his feet stiffly, twitching his tail from side to side and up and down as if conducting the scattering of my thoughts.

'Nice, juicy, tasty reality.'

He shuffles sideways, seeming as though he's trying not to fall over.

'Reality bloody bites back', I hear him mumble as he stretches his back legs, stiffening each in turn behind him, and begins a lumbering walk down the hill.

I look at my tasty, juicy arm. I lift it to my mouth and test my blunt teeth on it. Only gently, but still I manage to leave a faint oblong set of dents impressed into my skin. *Grr*, I say to myself. For some reason this makes me laugh, and I throw my head back, almost tipping over backwards. *Grr*. Well, if I am losing my mind at least I'm having a laugh doing it.

Jericho's voice sobers me.

'Hurry up. It's raining, I'm cold. I'm getting pissed off with this weather. No good for the joints. Let's get inside.'

I trail after him, wondering about the plains of Africa, images from the TV documentary slipping through my mind. Yellow dust. Yellow grass. Yellow cats. And clouds of black heat-frenzied flies clustering around bloody muzzles.

S aid she was sorry to take my claws, Irene did, but she had to protect herself and the paying public. There it was. Her eyes glittered when she said 'paying public'. I was young, only a baby. Would never have hurt her. Not then, anyway. They still brought out the pliers and the saw.

Felt dizzy when I woke up. Bloody feet throbbing in bandages, tongue dry, too big to fit in my mouth. Smoothness of each tooth. Tried to get up but fell over, feet couldn't take the weight of me. Wasn't the pain so much, just couldn't balance. I'd get up again, fall over, again, fall over. Each time. After a day sprawled in my cage I managed to stand without falling. Useless bloody feet. If I moved my weight back, to my wrists not my toes, I could shuffle around. But a couple of minutes of hobbling would get my feet too sore. I'd throw myself down, down in the straw.

She visited every day, inspected my bandages, whispered to me. The tears in her eyes: she was sorry. She meant it. She did. She'd scratch me behind my ears, I'd rumble at her. She'd promise to visit me the next day and then leave, slapping her boots with her crop. Sometimes she'd wave to Caesar, who stalked from one end of his cage to the other, over and over.

He saved her once. Nero'd grabbed her by the shoulder in

training. Good jaw lock, shaking his head, trying to pull her arm off at the socket. Caesar roared, jumped down from his platform. Fought the bugger off. Took a mouthful of fur with him too.

Nero had scars for a long time but Irene was only away for a few days. Straight back to training. Number of times she ended up in hospital? Mauled arm (six times); broken wrist (twice); dislocated shoulder (once); torn scalp (once); broken ribs (three times), broken collarbone (twice); mauled legs (five times); black eyes, broken nose, cuts, gashes, slashes. Take a lion's claws away, but it doesn't make him harmless. One day Jay asked her why she kept coming back.

'Irene, for God's sake, you're sixty-three years old. Haven't you had enough?'

She snorted through the broken teeth in her scarred face. Called him a ridiculous young man. Strode to Caesar's cage and led him out for another training session.

'These cats are my life, Jay,' she said, over a bandaged shoulder. 'I'm not going to stop just because Nero got a bit boisterous. So there it is.'

Brave woman, Irene. There it was.

Her famous trick was the Lion Swing. Swinging platform, suspended from the roof to carry her and Caesar far above the ring. I knew when they were swinging while I was back stage: the audience would be silent. Only sound would be the squeak of chain on shackle as they went back and forth, back and forth. When they were lowered to the ground Irene'd offer Caesar a bloody chunk of meat. She knelt in the sawdust in her deerskin trousers. Delicately hold the meat in her tiny, blunt teeth, vein throbbing in her neck. One time Caesar hesitated for just a moment before he took the food, careful not to rasp his fangs down her face. I could just make out his one quiet thought: *the throat, the throat.*

I asked Caesar if he enjoyed it, flying above the crowds in the air. When I was very young. He looked at me.

'Shut up.'

That's all he said.

He never talked much. Just walked up and down his cage. Head low, sunk between his shoulders. Sometimes he'd stop, just stare into space like he'd been amazed by an idea. Then he'd snort, shake his head. Go back to his pacing, pacing, pacing.

Hurt my feet just watching him.

Gizmo is a male black cat with a
bushy tail. He is all black with a
white patch on his tummy. He is a
much loved family cat. Please
contact us if you know of his
whereabouts.

And now how do I remember him? Holidays. A day trip to the
seaside. The smell of seaweed. The sand. Jess and I running along
the frilled lace-edge of the sea. No. No, there was no sand. I feel
hard shards through the soft rubber soles of my shoes. Rocks.
That was it. There were rocks, black, clutching. Skeins of shining
weed, their tiny bladders so tempting to little fingers. Squeeze
hard and . . . pop! The low growl of the ocean, rumbling through
your chest. I am jumping from rock to rock, leaping over pools
where soft translucent bodies hide from the light. I stop, balanced
on a perfect crag, and peer in. The water in this pool is still, clear.
Through my reflection I see a pale shell, buttery against the dark
rock. I dip the tips of my fingers into the water, lower my hand
towards the coil. What if the animal is still in it? What if it

moves? The water reaches my wrist, my forearm, my elbow. My hand stings with the cold. I hadn't realised the water was this deep, the shell looked only inches from the tips of my fingers before I plunged them into the pool. I bend closer, clutching hard at a cluster of razor-lipped barnacles at the edge. The water is almost up to my armpit when a thin scream almost causes me to lose my grip and tumble head first into the hollow. I look up quickly. My sister's head floats into view along the top of the rocks. She is giggling. I look back into the water. The shell has not moved. I hold my breath, as though preparing to dunk my head beneath the surface, plunge my arm in up to the shoulder, snatch the shell from its nook and dig it deep into my pocket, my skin numb. Then I stand and turn, leaping back towards the shocks of wiry grass and mats of starry clover which border the beach, as the wet shell soaks through my pocket and makes a dark patch on the side of my jeans.

When I get back to our food-littered rug Dad is nowhere to be seen and Jess is still smiling. She is prodding a pink crab which she has corralled between the cool bag and assorted Tupperware containers, plastic cups and bottles of drink. The animal is crouched, half sheltered under an empty crisp packet. Jess raps its shell with a plastic fork. It waves its antennae, but otherwise remains still. She pokes one of its legs, and the crab waves a delicately-serrated claw in her direction.

'Smells horrible around here.'

Jericho is sitting on the edge of the rug, watching Jess torment the crab.

'Don't know why she's so interested in that animal. It's hard. It's stinky. Not worth the effort.'

'She doesn't want to eat it,' I whisper. 'She's just playing with it.'

I turn to my sister.

'Jess, why don't you let the crab go? You could carry it in that tin, just throw it into one of the pools.'

'I'm keeping him as a pet. I'm calling him Tantrum.'

'You can't keep him, Dad will . . . Tantrum?'

'Yeah. Good name, isn't it? Tough. Like his shell.'

'OK. But Dad still won't let you keep him.'

She looks at me sideways and grins. Jericho rolls his eyes.

'I'm not going to tell him.'

'But . . .'

'I'll stick him in the empty sandwich box in my bag. Dad'll never know.'

'He'll know by the smell,' Jericho moans. He bares his teeth, shakes his head.

'Jess, you can't.'

'Why not?'

'Well, it needs to be in the sea.'

'It's not in the sea now and it looks OK.'

'I mean, it needs to be near the sea, so it can go back into the water whenever it wants.' Sudden inspiration. 'That's where it lives.'

Jess shrugs off my reasoning. I admit, it wasn't that persuasive. I'm too busy worrying about what Dad will say when he finds a live crab crawling around the car on the way home.

'Oh, leave her. Come and play.'

Jericho bounds off over the grassy dunes towards the black rocks edging out to sea. When I reach him he is crouching low over another rock pool, sniffing the water delicately, the tips of the long curls which frame his head touching the water's surface and floating there like golden weed. He puts out his pink tongue, touches it to the water and jumps back snorting and shaking, droplets of water flying from his mane. Unfortunately, the ledge of rock on which he stands is narrow and his back legs slip into another pool. Before I can reach forward to grab him, he is up to his neck in seawater, blowing and grunting and growling and thrashing and splashing while I squat there with tears of laughter stinging my eyes at the sight of him. He drags himself out of the pool, turns his rump towards me and shakes, making me as soaked as if I had fallen in with him. When he's finished he snorts hugely. I can't stop laughing.

'Don't know what's so bloody funny.'

I've managed to control myself at last, rub my nose and try to wring the water from my hair. He looks a mess and, worse, is beginning to smell like wet dog. A tug of fierce love pulls at my heart.

'Oh, Jericho. Don't ever leave me.'

He snorts again, begins licking his paw ferociously, as if trying to rasp the fur away.

'Why can't we go somewhere dry? It's boring here, nowhere to run around. It's all picking your way through this bloody sharp danger zone stuff.'

Rasp, rasp. Then he stops and looks at the rocks between his feet.

'And don't tell me to never leave you. It's up to you. You'll forget me one day and that'll be it.'

He looks towards the purple horizon where the sea meets the sky. I feel the remnants of my smile slide from my face into the shimmering pool below.

'Don't be silly. Of course I won't forget about you.'

For a few moments he doesn't move or speak.

'Yes you will. You'll forget about me.'

He turns to look at me, his golden eyes somehow dimmed.

'One day you'll wake up and there'll be something else. Something. Someone. One day it won't be me. You'll see.'

I have nothing to say to him.

'And when that day comes I won't be any more. I just won't be.'

My heart clenches. I feel he is speaking some truth, a truth I don't want to hear, so I brush it away with a forced giggle. Which sounds like a sob.

Jericho blinks at me and then shakes his head. A lopsided grin is thrown my way as he gets up and stretches each leg in turn.

'Come on. Let's find something horrible to distract Jess.'

He walks off, almost dainty, as he picks his way between the still pools of seawater, careful not to slip and fall again.

I'm not sure what he has just told me. I don't understand it. So I push it away and stand, balancing on the rocks for a moment before heading off after him, pulling at my trousers where they are wet and cold and clinging.

Rizzo has gone missing. She is
orange tabby-striped
and friendly.
Please please call if you know
anything.

I woke late this morning and drank three cups of strong coffee in quick succession. Trying to sit and read after that was impossible because of the caffeine in my blood, which has had me zizzing around the flat like an anxious bluebottle on speed. So I decided to put my unusual energy to use and began to clean the cooker. Only half the hob was sparkling when I ran out of steam and had to sit down again.

I phoned the police, more out of habit than out of a genuine desire to see progress. The answer was as I expected. *Ms Irving we will let you know as soon as we know anything.*

I rummaged half-heartedly through the fridge, finding nothing more appetising than half a jar of gherkins, an ancient bagel and an enormous bar of dark chocolate. So I had a gherkin sandwich. Followed by half the chocolate. Followed by mild nausea.

I phoned Shiulie, but she wasn't in so I left her a rambling message. Then I remembered it's Tuesday and she will be at work. Like all other normal people.

After a brief tussle with my unruly hair in an attempt to make myself presentable to the outside world (unsuccessful) I have given up on the idea of going out and am now slung across the arms of my favourite chair, one foot rising and falling in time with the lion's side on which it rests. My heel warms through his fur.

I try to remember what I ate for dinner last night, but my short-term memory seems to have deserted me. No scene comes to mind.

Jericho snorts in his sleep. My foot is thrown into the air with his sudden intake of breath, and my heel lands on his ribs rather more heavily than I'd hoped. I try to raise my foot, hold it high, tense my calf muscles against the certain mauling coming their way. My leg trembles with the effort, and I wonder why the muscles in my lower leg are named after young cows.

The lion snarls quietly, baring a scimitar-like incisor, but doesn't wake.

I relax my leg again, let its full weight rest on Jericho's hide. My mind wanders, and I'm sifting and shuffling the sand of my memories around in my mind trying to pull out recent recollections of my father. But all that remains when the fine sand and dust have disappeared through the mesh seems to be the nuggets of my youth. My mind feels as if there are tiny holes through which thoughts and memories disappear when I'm not paying attention. I will hoover a room, or butter my toast, or cut my fingernails and I will almost immediately feel the memory of it leaking slowly through the gaps. And what am I left with? Not much. The occasional twig. A length of twisted root. A couple of pebbles, round and hard and perfect as day. These are the pictures and sounds and smells from my childhood mostly. I can't remember what I'm meant to be doing at work. I can't remember when Mum last came round here. I can't remember the last words my father spoke to me. But I find, suddenly, that I don't really mind. The thought makes me raise my eyebrows in surprise and I stretch my arms up and over my head.

I look briefly for the remote control before the doorbell rings. Jericho starts and lifts his head, eyes still half-closed.

'What the bloody hell?'

I push my bare foot into his mane, dig deep with my toes, try to encourage his head to the floor. It's like trying to calm a grumpy boulder.

'Go back to sleep.'

He grumbles as his head sinks slowly towards the carpet, but I can't hear what he's saying. He rubs the side of his head against the floor, snorts once, twice into it and at last rests his head. I rub my toes against his head for a few seconds more, loving the heat, the rough of him.

The doorbell rings again, the echo down the hall lasting a few seconds longer this time. But I don't get up. I don't really want to see anyone. I'm quite happy here.

I let my head fall back against the chair and close my eyes. My breaths slow and are soon keeping rhythm with the lion's.

We sleep.

Missing from Cornwall Road. Small
black and white cat answering to
the name of Beauty. She never came
home on Tuesday. She was wearing
a pink and white collar with a metal
heart shaped tag which had Beauty
on one side and a telephone number
on the other which unfortunately is
no longer correct. We miss her so much
and should you have any
information please contact us.

The world is not as I thought it was.

I have been viewing it through a filter. It is like a kaleido-scope, splitting and fracturing what I see and hear and smell, what I experience, exploding outwards, colouring and re-colouring things, tinting and changing, morphing, stretching and squeezing everything around me. My memories fold in on themselves like origami; they are pretend paper creatures, lotus blossoms and swans, dragons' heads and grasshoppers, scorpions and parrots, delicate pieces of paper become something they are not, dolphins and gryphons, owls and giant squid, all sucked into the centre of something formless and dark like starlight into a black hole while I remain dazzled by the vortex around their edges.

*

The world is not as I thought it was.

Thought it was all hard edges, sharp corners, rank smells. Digs in ribs with iron-shod sticks. Cold hard floors and whip cracks and burning hair and empty bellies and loneliness. Pain. Broken teeth and broken claws. Cramped legs and stiff shoulders. Taste and smell and cold, cold feel of concrete and metal.

But it's changed. Its edges have softened. Melted. The metal and hardness are gone. Now it's full of the soft, warm creature smell of her, salty-sweet, dreamful. Full of her fingers that tug at my mane and the pit of my stomach. Full of her tiny heart which beats flutter-quick against me as we lie together. Full of food, fresh washing, of lavender. Full of the shine on her hair. Full of the shine in her eyes. Full of her.

If you see Birdy my chocolate cat please
please let me know. He is shy but sweet.
I miss him so much.

The air of the kitchen moves around me sluggishly, as if intoxicated by the smells it carries; onions frying in butter, ground cumin, fresh ginger, chillies, lemons. Steam curls from the pot of boiling rice and beads the tiles behind the cooker with tiny droplets of water. Jess stirs large pieces of garlic in the pan.

I am sitting at the kitchen table gazing out of the window at the row of rug-sized walled gardens below me.

'Peripheral vision really freaks the hell out of me.'

If Jess has been talking to me before now I've not heard a word of it, so this statement comes as a surprise. She must be talking to me, as I am the only other person in the room. Well, the only other human person. The lion sprawls in a far corner underneath a drooping ficus plant and on top of Jess's favourite soft toy. A snake. Which has a skin of plush green velvet and a felt forked tongue and shiny black eyes. I can only just see the tip of its tongue poking out from underneath Jericho's belly.

'You know what I mean?'

She turns to look at me, continues stirring the contents of the pan.

'Yeah. Well, no. Not really. Why does it freak you out?'

She tosses her head, pushes her fringe out of her eyes with the back of a greasy-fingered hand. Looks up at the ceiling, as if the answers she seeks have been lifted there by the rising steam.

'It's like, there's this whole other world just out of reach, which only exists when we're not looking at it straight on.'

She stares at me, expecting a reply. I stare back at her.

'When we look at it askance. Like this.'

She widens her eyes and turns from me as far as she can while looking at the chair next to me. Her green irises quiver at the edge of her eyes.

'I love that word. Askance. Sounds so old fashioned. *Askance*.'

She mouths the word a couple more times, then turns back to the cooker and picks up the wooden spoon again, frowning and groping for words to describe the otherworldliness of looks askance.

My sister finds strangeness in the most mundane places. In the crumbs at the back of the bread bin. In the drops of water clinging to the sides of the sink after the washing up has been done. In the creases and rumples of her pillow case, still warm after a dreamless night's sleep.

She spins suddenly to glare at the plant in the corner of the room.

My heart stammers in my chest.

'OK, like, if I look straight at that plant and Sidney the Snake underneath it, all I see is the plant and the snake. Yeah?'

Sidney. Jesus.

'Marn?'

She waits for me to process the information.

'OK, yes'

'Right, but then if I look a little to the left of the plant I can still see it, but it looks totally different. It looks like there's more there. *More than meets the eye.*'

She enjoys her pun, chuckling to herself as she lowers pieces of chicken into the pan, then shuffles them around in the browning butter. My stomach growls but I feel a cold breeze blow through me.

'What do you mean, "totally different"?'

I clench my teeth, then force my jaws to relax again.

'Well,' she says as she adjusts her position so she is looking at the wall to the left of the ficus, 'the plant looks huge, and it's sort of moving, and the snake looks huge too, like an enormous beast crouching there. Just crouching there and waiting.'

She stops. I press the heel of my hand to my forehead to try and contain the pressure which is building there.

'Waiting to pounce.'

Jericho snorts in his sleep, kicks a back leg. I'm reminded of sleeping dogs. The ones we are always warned should be left to lie. Jess squeezes her eyes closed and shakes her head.

'Then I look directly at the plant,' she looks back at the plant, 'and it's a normal plant again. Not a particularly healthy one, but then you're shit at looking after stuff. I'm surprised it's lasted this long.'

She sprinkles green leaves of coriander into her pot, stirs and wafts the fragrant steam towards her nose. The food burbles gently to itself. The vice clamped around my head eases off slightly.

'Anyway, it's weird. Things just appearing like that when we can only see them out of the corner of our eye.'

A splash of some dark, sticky liquid.

'It's rude; just materialising out of nothing. Could at least have some warning.'

Another waft, another delicate sniff.

'Like I said. Freaks the hell out of me.'

A pinch of coarse ground black pepper.

Jess laughs suddenly, drags her fingers through her hair.

'Or am I just imagining things? Being mad. Go on say it, I'm just being a mentalist, aren't I?'

She begins to laugh again, but the sound dies quickly, the smile fades from her lips as she looks at the potted plant and her squashed snake. She is still for a moment. Then she shrugs and picks up the two deep bowls she has filled with her aromatic concoction.

'There. Looks gorgeous, smells gorgeous, tastes bloody gorgeous. Eat in here or in front of the telly?'

I'm watching the lion snoring, his ribcage ballooning with each huge breath. The lowest leaves of the plant stir in the warm breeze of his snores. I feel Jess sigh pointedly at me. Her feet are not moving yet I still feel the psychic foot tapping.

'Marn. Where do you want to eat?'

I want to curl up beneath Jericho's elbow, nuzzle my face into his warm fur, let his breathing lull me into darkness.

'Sorry. I don't know. Don't mind.'

'Well, get a couple of trays and we'll eat on our laps. Attenborough's on in ten minutes. Something to do with polar bears.'

She sighs happily and I trail after her to the sofa with two plastic trays. We settle down. My sister picks up a dripping drumstick, tears most of the meat from it with one bite, growling theatrically to herself.

'I love polar bears. Vicious sweethearts.'

I look down at my food. The smell of it brings water into my mouth but for some reason I don't feel like eating.

'Mmm, smells great, give it to me if you don't want it.'

A golden muzzle nudges my hand.

'No, go and get something yourself.'

Jess turns to look at me, oil dripping down her fingers.

'What?'

Um.

'Nothing.'

Her gnawed drumstick hovers in front of her chin. She searches my face.

'You said something.'

Er.

'No. I didn't.'

She doesn't move. Jess can remain motionless for what seems like a feline amount of time. Just watching and waiting.

'Oh, look, I don't know. I might have. So what?'

I am gruff with her now, covering my back. Jess does not speak, just tightens her lips into a line.

'I might have done. Just mumbling to myself, nothing important. Just watch your . . . thing.'

I wave my fork in the direction of the flickering TV.

She considers me for a moment. Places the chicken bone back into her bowl and puts one finger after another in her mouth to suck off the grease. She looks at me while her thumb is in her mouth. I have the random thought that neither she nor I sucked our thumbs when we were small. I wonder why some children do that and others don't.

'Look, Marn. I'm kind of worried about you.'

She sniffs, taking her time, obviously trying to find words which aren't barbed.

'Talking to yourself. It's not . . . normal.'

The 'normal' is half-whispered, as if it's a shameful disease, and not at all something to which one should aspire.

I'm about to make some excuse to put her mind at ease, put her off the scent, but I've obviously taken too long.

'OK, don't tell me. You're "tired". Yes?'

I give her a fraction of a nod.

'Yeah, well, that's bollocks as we both know, but I can't force you to spill your guts.'

She pauses. Looks towards the kitchen, ponders.

'Actually, *technically*, I probably could. I'm stronger than you and a carving knife would do the job nicely . . .'

'Jess!'

She turns back to me and licks her knife. Grins.

'Alright, I won't. 'Cause I'm not that kind of a sister, am I?'

'What? The homicidal, butchering kind?'

She laughs and her eyes flick back to the screen where huge white paws are clawing their way out of a snow-dug den.

I offer a silent prayer of thanks for my sister's short attention span and concentrate on my food.

She asked me here. She did. *She* asked *me*. She asked me because she needs me, see? I can't say no to that, can I? Yes, so I did make a bit of a fuss when I got here, but only to get her attention. Just to make sure she took notice. Of me.

You know the thing about the circus? Some animals fit in to performing, some don't. That runt of a bastard Blossom. *Blossom.* Tells you all you need to know about it. He was a cat. Irene's cat. She kept him in her trailer. Never got his claws pulled. Never got put on a chain, never had a collar round his neck or got stuck with metal spikes. Never whipped. Never beaten. Just stroked and given cream. He loved to take the piss about that and all. Bastard. He'd preen himself just out of reach of our cages, talk to himself a bit too loudly. What a beautiful day it was, you should see those white white clouds and that blue blue sky and oh! those silly pigeons which made great sport, not to mention the mice which were perfect for sharpening one's reflexes. Bloody bastard. Sometimes Irene would feed him in our enclosure. He'd lick his cream slowly, look me straight in the eye. Once he brought in a mouse he'd caught. Dropped it in the corner, watched while it shook. Patted it with a paw to see it scamper, jumped on it, picked it up again. Shook it around a bit. Tossed it into the other corner, then jumped on it again. I tell you, it was a full ten minutes he played with it before snapping its neck with a quick bite. Then he prodded it, sniffed it, grinned at me. Turned tail and slunk out of the tent. Left the mouse dead in the sawdust. It lay there until we packed up and left. Bastard never ate a scrap of it. Waste. Evil, spiteful bastard, like I said. With a taste for torturing things.

Alright, I'll get back to the point.

I've got nothing to be ashamed of, you see. Staying around, watching over her. It's my *job*, isn't it? I could bugger off any time I fancied. Could get up, show her my arse, bugger right off. Not a backward glance. If I wanted to, of course. All that before, just a bit of a lark. A bit of a giggle, you know? Me making a fuss, pushing her over like that. After all, it's not like she has some kind of hold over me. I'm still here by my own choice. She's just a little bit of a thing, couldn't keep me here if I really wanted to leave. How could *she* make me stay? Bloody stupid idea.

So, no, I'm not ashamed of anything. Especially not of being chained to her side. Which I'm not.

Ashamed. Don't be so bloody ridiculous. Makes me laugh. Really does.

Clifton was last seen two weeks ago in
North Rd
He is a male white cat
Long fluffy tail
Sorely missed

On the journey home in the car I worried terribly about what Jericho had said to me, my hair still wet with seawater, Jess's eyes red from weeping over the return of Tantrum to the rock pool. I worried about me leaving him, finding something else to occupy my time. What else was there to interest me? Who else would I spend time with if not with him? But then again, what if he was right? What if I did find something, someone else? What if I walked away one day, forgot all about him? What if he left and never came back?

It wasn't possible. I knew I'd never, never stop needing him. And I couldn't think what else could ever be as important to me as he was. So I talked myself out of it. He'd been wrong before. I couldn't remember when, or what about, but we were always bickering and arguing so I reasoned that he must be wrong about a great many things all the time for us to argue. He would surely be wrong about this too.

Our days of that long summer carried on in the same way. Golden, hazy, hot. We would spend hours trailing through the meadows behind the house, having given Jess the slip and leaving her squalling and stomping in the back garden. We would chase each other through the woods, me hiding in low trees and pelting him with twigs and leaves when he got too close. Later I would pick bits out of his mane as we sat in the shade under the trees, while he licked and licked his splayed paws. Sometimes I would knot daisies into his hair and the tuft of his tail, severing the brave green stems from their roots with my thumbnail. I remember plaiting his mane.

'Oh, let me!'

His eyes glowed.

'Bugger off.'

'Please.'

'Plait your own hair.'

'Go on.'

'No!'

The magic word would do it.

'Oh, please.'

The magic word and strategically deployed fingers scratching in the region of his forehead. His eyes narrowed. It was working.

'Mmrmph.'

That was it.

'Yes, that means yes. OK, lie down and keep still.'

He lay on his side, compliant, quiet. A lamb. He shut his eyes and breathed deeply. His breath smelled familiar. It reminded me of slightly off milk when it goes sweet and fragrant and of the liver Mum insisted on cooking for me. The liver made me retch. I'd carve it into tiny pieces to hide under the tines of my fork. Even though mum noticed it appeared on my plate every week.

My fingers searched towards the roots of Jericho's mane, pulled clumps of hairs apart, separated locks, ordered and tamed them. Then I began to twist, slowly at first, then more quickly, as the greenfly danced around our heads.

As summer carried us along though it seemed as if I had more energy than he did, that we would be pelting through the fields and I would suddenly have to stop for him to catch up. Before he would have matched my pace or even outrun me with his long, loping strides. I would stop, hands on hips, and watch his heaving sides as he jogged towards me.

'Don't need to go so fast,' he would chide, as he caught up and collapsed at my feet. 'Always too fast. What you trying to catch?'

I would notice that he would not run around as much as he used to. He would stop mid-stride, as if startled by something, then step forward hesitantly, sit down. Nothing I could do could coax him back to whatever game we had been playing, so I would join him, stroke him, whisper special words into the furred cave of his ear. And his head would nod and his eyes would close and his breath would come noisily. After a while he would get up, turn without a word and walk slowly back home. I didn't think much of it then.

We would return home, clothes and fur burr-studded, my toasted arms and his moist nose pearled with pollen. One day Jericho told me stories of Africa with its exploding upside-down trees and hyenas whose jaws could bite through steel and stripe-flanked horses and the shimmer and flicker of the heat which made the swaying herds of wildebeest seem as though they floated feet above the savannah.

'Trees don't explode for no reason. They need to get bombed, or hit by lightning, or something.'

Jericho looked at me with hooded eyes.

'They do explode. So there.'

'But how?'

'That would be telling.'

This was unsatisfactory.

'What kind of tree? What's it called?'

I thought this would catch him out. I had forgotten he was as adept at fabrication as I was. Bone of my bone.

'It's called a Baobab. It explodes.'

'But how do you know about Africa? You've never even *been* there.'

The sleepy eyes widened.

'Been where?'

'Africa.'

'Have.'

This was confusing.

'But I thought you were born in the circus.'

He stretched a huge paw.

'Was.'

Most unsatisfactory.

'But . . .'

'Doesn't mean I don't know about Africa, though.'

I had no idea what he was talking about by now. He sighed.

'Anyway, 'm tired. Go away. Need sleep.'

I watched his tawny flank rise and fall and wondered why Jericho was so often tired these days. And summer drew to a close, gathering the swallows in its darkening skies. They called to each other, speaking of their plans for hotter shores where the great trees waved their roots at the sky and clouds of fat black flies patrolled the wide savannah.

*

Jericho was right.

The leaves were burnt-looking and dry, pooling around the bottoms of tree trunks, when I got up the morning of my first riding lesson. I was so excited I was unable to eat more than a mouthful of breakfast. Horses! Real horses!

I felt high up sitting on the spotty grey pony, so high, with my legs stretched by the animal's barrel chest and the warm smell of him and I loved it. We walked round a sawdust ring and turned and walked back round the other way while the instructor called to us to sit up, no, sit back, no not that far you'll fall off, heels down, *heels* down not toes, and slapped her tall black boots with her riding crop. When the lesson was over I slid off the pony's back and led it to the stables. The clicking of horse shoes on concrete and deep, snorting breaths. A boy stood in my pony's stall, bent-backed and swinging pitchforks of fresh straw around so that dust flew from the metal tines like smoke tendrils. He looked to be a couple of years older than me, maybe fourteen or fifteen. I watched silently from the entrance. When he was finished with the new bedding he leant the pitchfork against the wall outside and took the reins from my slippery grasp.

'Hi' he said.

I couldn't think of a response instantly and he led the pony into the straw-lined stall.

'Hi' I said to the grey's backside. I watched the top of the boy's dark head bob above the pony's back as he removed the saddle, teased the metal bit from between the pony's yellow teeth and hung up the bridle on a peg outside. He pushed his glasses further up his nose with the back of a grimy hand and took a thick brush out of a rubber pail.

'Do you want to help brush him down?'

I didn't reply but he must have seen from my expression that yes, please, I would love to help brush him down. He showed me how to use firm, circular strokes along the animal's flanks and underside, smaller, gentler ones on his legs where bone sat just below hide. I loved the way the pony shivered its skin at me if I brushed too gently and tickled his side.

'That's it', he said.

How to use the special soft brush on the pony's face, stroking the soft-as-velvet chin, caressing the tender skin around the eyes. How to comb the wire of the iron-grey tail and mane without pulling too hard.

'You're a natural. I think he likes you.'

I smiled up at him from underneath the wide belly and he smiled back. He rested one dirty-fingernailed hand on the pony's rump and watched me quietly. I liked that he didn't try to talk to me too much. I thought, this is where I would like to be forever, please, just here, with this steaming pony and the acrid smell of horse sweat and this boy with the smiling brown-green eyes. No boy had ever smiled at me like this before. I wondered what his name was but didn't ask. He told me anyway.

'I'm Jem. What's your name?'

I told him.

'Cool.'

I thought his name was cool too and wanted to ask what it was short for, but didn't.

When the pony had been groomed Jem put the brushes away.

'See you', he said, repositioning his glasses, and sauntered towards the tack barn with the saddle in the crook of his arm and bridle slung over his shoulder.

I came home in a haze of happiness smelling of horse and straw and was so exhausted by the time I climbed into bed that I was almost asleep before my head hit the pillow. My last thoughts were of a pair of smiling eyes and a pair of strong hands brushing a flank, down and round and down again.

My new love: part human, part horse.

It had been a long day. I hadn't thought about Jericho once.

And by the time I remembered him the next day it was too late. I didn't see him again.

Mimi my cream Chinchilla cat
is a real lady and
Wouldn't have gone off
on her own
She is quite nervous
around strangers
Light blue collar with tags
Please call if you have
seen her or
Know someone who has

'What are you up to?'

'Not *up* to anything. Patrolling.'

Patrolling. Keeping me in or keeping something else out, I wonder. He circles the hydrangea bush, pushing his head deep in amongst the twigs, rubbing his face against the branches and leaves. Then he turns, a couple of petals still clinging to his lashes, lifts his tail and sprays the leaves. Well, that would keep the cats off. If there were any, that is. I'd forgotten about the cats. Poor old Knuckles.

The phone has been insistent this morning. I've not answered it, though I have a suspicion it will be Leo calling, asking how I am, when do I think I'll be returning to work. He's been good to me. Too good. Signed off weeks of absence on full pay, it's now gone down to three-quarters of my salary. I don't need any more, though. Why would I need more? It's just me and Jericho here.

Jericho resumes his perambulation around the rapidly withering garden. I watch him for a while, pulling the long sleeves of my old dressing gown down over my hands to warm them and hugging myself. Lounging in a deckchair on a bright but chilly November morning somehow seems like a normal thing to do. Watching my friend – who also happens to be a talking lion – also seems to be a normal thing to do.

'We're alone,' he tells me.

I look around.

'I know.'

'Just telling you. Just reassuring you, that's all.'

I nod slowly.

'OK. Thanks.'

His pacing is beginning to annoy me.

'I consider myself reassured. Really. See?'

I present him with my open palms. He glances my way but continues shambling around the lawn.

'Jericho. Come here.'

He does one last turn around the potted lavender and lumbers towards me. I open my arms to the huge beast. Flesh of my flesh. He stands over me, lowers his face to mine. His whiskers tickle my nose and I sneeze. Which makes him stumble backwards and sit down too suddenly on his haunches. He sneezes too. We sit and stare at each other for a couple of seconds before dissolving into laughter. The laughter rolls up from deep in my belly, breaks from my lips and I feel almost as if I've never laughed before.

Then I let the laughter tire, stumble and fall away. I rub my nose with the back of a cold hand. I sigh and look away, over roofs antlered with aerials and chimneys.

'D'you remember?'

His voice is quiet. I look back at him.

'Do I remember what?'

He isn't looking at me, but at the bulbous thickened knuckles which raise the amber hairs at the end of his paws. The swellings look painful.

'Oh, things. Us. The stuff we used to get up to.'

His voice trails off. I don't know what he is talking about. I mean, I do. I remember many things of which he could be speaking. But I don't know what exactly he is talking about. The particulars. The colour and the smell and roll of the seasons, yes. The hard edges and skin prick of the moments within the hours of a specific day, no. My memory is lazy.

'When we were kids.'

'We've both been grown for longer than we were kids. What about what we've been doing *since* we were kids?'

Jericho has not spoken of his life, his existence, apart from me. I had assumed that wherever he has been, whatever he has been doing has been peaceful. That he resented being here with me. But that was then. For the last couple of weeks he seems to have grown used to it. To me. He is no longer angry, no longer tells me that I have done something terrible, that it's all my fault, that he needs to go. To leave me. Again.

He looks up at me from underneath white sprouting eyelashes. Licks his nose with his great pink tongue.

'But what about now? It feels right. You here. Me here. Us together. It feels good, Jericho.'

He shakes his mane as if plagued by insects, and sighs. Looks away over my shoulder. He says nothing.

'Doesn't it?'

He lays his chin on his paws.

'Yes, my love. Yes it does.'

His eyes close slowly. Then open only halfway to look at me.

'That's exactly the problem.'

> Poppet is a black and white
> female cat
> who is very pretty and friendly
> we need her back and are very
> worried
> Please call if you have any news.

Shiulie is silent for too long. There is nothing I can say to make it better. Nothing. And so I say

'Jesus.'

She sighs, bites her lower lip, hard.

'I know.'

Her hand flutters around her throat like a bird with a broken wing, finally alighting on a lock of hair which lies against her collarbone. She brushes it away over her shoulder.

'Jesus.'

I put my hand on her knee and leave it there because I don't know what else to do with it. Then when I think it's been there long enough I lift it away and fiddle with my bracelet, a chain holding a tiny golden swallow.

I cannot take this in.

Jesus.

Shiulie appeared at my flat five minutes ago, finger not lifting from the buzzer until I had opened up. I was tempted not to answer, envisaging a drunk, a salesman or worse; a Jehovah's Witness standing on my doorstep. That, and the fact that nine across had been frustrating me – *Five recommended per day*, five letters – and Jericho was being singularly unhelpful.

'Meats.'

I peered over to the shadowed corner in which Jericho sprawled like the fresh kill of a Ryder Haggard hero. My pen hovered in mid-air.

'What?'

He yawned hugely.

'I said "meats". Five letters. "Meats"'

He snorted, rubbed a paw over his nose.

'Simple, see?'

'Yes, I know you said "meats". What I'm asking is whether that's your suggested answer to the crossword clue, or are you just repeating your favourite word?'

He showed me one of his long incisors.

'Well, if you don't want my help you can bugger off.'

'Well, kitty, I might just do that.'

A low growl as he rolled over, nearly squashing my collection of small potted cacti which live next to the radiator.

'Don't. Call. Me. Kitty.'

I looked back at the page in front of me, searched out the clue and sucked on the end of the pen. There was a 'mrrmph', and another, quieter 'mrrmph' as he settled down and began to snore.

I was considering putting his suggestion on the page when the doorbell rang. Jericho growled quietly. I swore quietly. Neither of us moved. For a full thirty seconds the bell kept ringing. Jericho lifted his head from the carpet and turned blazing eyes on me.

'Will you stop that bloody noise.'

It wasn't a question.

'Certainly. And you can stop telling me to bugger off.'

I got up and headed downstairs. A slim, dark shadow through the glass pane in the front door. It must be Shiulie. I opened the door. It was Shiulie. And it was also not her.

'Dilanzdedilanzdedilanzded.'

'Shiulie?'

What's wrong with her face?

'Dilanzded!'

'Shiu, what's wrong? Christ, what's happened?'

She said nothing but pushed past me into the house, fled down the hallway and up the stairs two at a time as if all the beasts of hell were at her heels. Her hair was almost completely covering her face in long, tangled locks. She was usually so careful about her appearance. I ran upstairs.

'Dylan. It's Dylan.'

She couldn't look at me. Stared only at the white knuckles of her balled fists.

'What? What's Dylan? What's he done?'

A quiet voice from beneath the curtain of hair.

'He's done it.'

Done what? He could have been arrested in Central America. He could have been injured. He could have done anything.

'Dylan. He's dead.'

Anything except that.

Suddenly her words were rushing and jumbled and falling over each other in their frantic attempt to be the first to fill the shocked silence in my flat. White noise was all that filled my head until her words finally reached me. He said he would take it easy. He said he would stick with his dive partner. But he didn't. He said he would be fine. But he wasn't. He's not coming back.

Shiulie rushes on, voice half-drowned by her sobs, but something, some soft tendril has been demanding my attention, stroking the base of my mind. I shake my head, but it remains. Something won't let go. Something she said, a loose grouping of words almost lost in the breathless confusion of the rest. What was it?

And then the tendril clutches my neck. Squeezes.

'What do you mean he never came back?'

Shiulie is staring at the glass of wine clutched in her hand as if she has never seen such a thing before and is internally debating with herself what she should do with it. I must have opened the bottle, got two glasses, filled them. I remember nothing about it. She turns bloodshot eyes on me.

'They haven't found his body yet, Marn. They've not found him.'

She lowers her eyes again, hiding them behind wet lashes and strands of hair.

'They will, though. They'll find him.'

We are silent. I imagine the deep blue cold of the ocean; Dylan's body shifting gently in the current like a giant frond of live coral, until the searchers come to claim him, come to lift him gently to the surface and away from his underwater realm. My hand finds its way to Shiulie's lap again and twines its fingers in hers. We sit like this, hip-to-hip, in the darkening room.

Dilanzded, I thought. *Dilanzded*.

*

The screaming in her head. It shook me up, startled me like a whip crack to my bones. Unlike a whip crack it carried on and on and on. Drowned out all other noises. Had to shake my head, concentrate, to shut out the racket. Then I heard the high-pitched voice, tremble in the throat. I thought to myself, I thought something's gone bad here, something's gone very bad. Got up in time to see her half carrying that black-haired Shiulie into the room. She was in a bad way, that one. Mine was silent as a tiny scared animal. Worse, that is. Much worse to hold all that screaming inside your head. Dangerous. Though not as bad as the screaming that brought me here. That pain she knows well. She lets herself feel it, but doesn't let it show on her face, in her eyes. Yet. That other thing was something else. Too deep even for her to hear.

Poor scraps. Look at them; holding on to each other like they've been orphaned in a storm, rocking each other in the raft of their arms. She's a good one, that black-hair. Feel almost responsible for her too. Almost though, not quite. One's quite enough trouble for me. And with all this noise I can barely hear my own thoughts.

It's up to me. I'll think of a way to make it better.

Give me a moment.

LOST

Since 09/09

'MOUSE'

Persian cat.

Larger than normal.

Male (intact).

All grey.

Brown eyes.

Missing from Staffordshire Terrace.

Have you seen this cat?

£££ CASH REWARD.

We drive to Ruth's in silence. Expecting and dreading howls of grief, smashed plates, hair ripped out at the roots. We expect to find human noise shattering the air, so savour the quiet within the humming car. The quiet before the storm.

I concentrate on the small details to anchor me here, to stop me spinning up, up and out of the open sunroof. A finger smear on the inside of the passenger window, low, near the seal. Shiulie gripping the steering wheel. A dry leaf trapped underneath the wiper blade. She is biting her lower lip. A loose wire, blue, hanging underneath the glove box in front of my knees. A shining at the outer corner of her eye. A loose spring digging into my left thigh. The peeling corner of the MOT sticker on the windscreen.

She'd called me that morning. A clipped exchange.

'Marn. It's me.'

'Hi.'

'Do you want to come see Ruth with me today?'

'OK.'

'I'll pick you up at two.'

It was only after I'd placed the receiver back in its cradle that I had realised what I had just agreed to. A personal visit to the young, grieving widow. Such an old-fashioned word, 'widow'. Was it not only old, bent women who were widows? Did Ruth now have to wear thick black tights? A dark knee-length skirt? Was her hair suddenly surprised at finding itself silvered, curling from beneath a black scarf? Was her back bent, her face cragged, were her fingers gnarled and twisted like old roots? What would we find? What would we—

'I said we're here, Marnie. You asleep? Come on.'

She watches me wrestle with the seatbelt. My struggle pulls my strategically-placed scarf aside. For a moment Ruth is forgotten.

'Flaming Nora, what have you done to yourself?'

She is looking at the bare skin just below my throat.

'What's that on your chest? Those marks.'

This is not the time to be explaining. There is no good time to be explaining.

I reposition my scarf.

'Nothing.'

I'm covered again, and lucky that we have more important business. Shiulie sighs.

'Later,' she says ominously, and is gone from the car.

I clamber out into the flat sunshine which shouldn't be here. Ruth's house is still standing. It has not been swallowed up by the earth. It is still a pale duck-egg blue. One, two, three. I count the windows. Not one smashed. All still there. Nothing is different. Nothing has changed. Why not? Why is the paint not peeling, why is the chimney still standing and why—

'Marnie for bleeding Christ's sake come on.'

Shiulie calls me from the front door and I aim myself at her impatient frown. She rings the bell. Too loud. It will wake the ghosts. But it only shrieks so loudly because the door is ajar. And the door should not be ajar. The door should be shut, closed, bolted.

'Frig' says Shiulie, as she nudges the front door with her finger tips. It swings wide. The hallway is empty, sunlight filtering towards us from the open garden door at the far end.

'Frigging frig', she says.

She turns her brown eyes on me, then looks back into the house. We stand there, transfixed by the empty corridor, uncertain where to go next. Into the tunnel? Away? What does this signify, this door which should be closed to the world instead of inviting it all in? What should we do with a door which acts in this way, which does not behave, swinging freely, mischievous, teasing?

I feel an exhalation from the end of the hallway, a great sigh. Shiulie hesitates on the threshold, poised like a dancer on the balls of her feet, head cocked as if listening for signs of life. I grab her by the wrist.

'Come on.'

And I'm pulling her towards the light at the other end, our shoes clattering on the bare wooden floor, heading towards the sunshine.

We emerge into the sunlit garden, and stop. After all the noise in our heads there is quiet. Nothing ripped, nothing torn. No shreds and tatters blowing in the breeze. Nothing shattered and jagged on the ground, no windows smashed, no crockery broken.

Ruth sits in the middle of a neatly-trimmed lawn. We stare at her without speaking. She is looking at what she holds in her hands, concentrating on it. Gradually her focus shifts towards the presence of two people who have invaded her silence. She looks up at us, as we stand, frozen on the patio. She blinks. She smiles. We smile too, dutifully, back at her.

Shiulie takes a couple of steps onto the lawn but stops. She can't go any further without stepping on them. She tries not to look confused. She fails.

'What are you doing, Ruthie love?'

Ruth smiles, and looks back at her hands.

She is holding a T-shirt. It is orange, with bright 70s-style letters: *Strictly for My Ninjas*. It is large, too large to be hers, and I know I have seen it before. It is large, and it is empty. Ruth holds it in her hands and gazes at it as if she might find her man in there, somewhere, somehow. She turns it over, pulls open an armhole. Stares at it. Smoothes it closed again with the flat of her hand.

There are clothes spread out, covering most of the neatly cut lawn. Socks, trousers, shirts, T-shirts, jackets, boxer shorts, jumpers, hats. A large rosemary bush is now a tie rack, all the ties hanging in neat rows, stirring slightly in the breeze. All these clothes. All Dylan's. All empty. All laid out tidily, as if waiting for inspection.

Ruth looks back up at us, eyes wide, as if expecting bad news. She looks from me to Shiulie and back again. Her eyes plead.

'He's not here. Is he.'

It is not a question, although it feels as though there may be some small part of her which believes we might just say *Yes love*,

235

of course he's here. You just need to look hard enough, you'll find him, he's here somewhere.

My eyes blur and sting.

Shiulie steps over a pile of jeans and wraps Ruth in her arms. 'Oh God. Oh Ruth. Jesus God.'

I sit on the crazy paving and look at Ruth's face and listen to Shiulie sobbing into her shoulder. But Ruth's eyes are dry. She looks towards the house and at each window in turn with expectant eyes. Dylan's pale face does not appear behind any of the panes; his nose freckled from too much sun, his eyes shining and full of stories of faraway places. Ruth gives Shiulie a couple of comforting pats on the back and untangles herself from her friend's grasp. Walks over the clothes, trampling them into the grass. She rests a hand on my shoulder for a moment as she passes.

And as she disappears into the cool shadows of the house I hear her calling. I struggle up now, the blood rushing painfully back into my calves, tingling in my ankles, my toes. I need to go to her, to give her some small comfort, she is calling me, she needs me. But it is only when I have stepped from stone to wood that I hear it is not me she is calling. Nor is she crying out to Shiulie, who sits amongst the tumbled garments, her face in her hands. Ruth calls out, over and over, never raising her voice too loud, never shrill, never desperate. She calls gently to someone who could just be in the next room, just beyond the wall which divides them. She calls to her lost boy.

'Where are you?'

I struggle to draw breath past the lump in my aching throat.

'Where are you?' she calls in the empty house as she walks from room to echoing room.

'Where are you?'

No one answers.

Female cat one year old, white chest,
brown and black colouring – very
fluffy tail lost in KENTON area
DAISY ST – NO COLLAR

Nitrogen narcosis is the technical term. That is what will be written on the death certificate, what the other divers will whisper to each other, afraid of speaking too loud for fear of it happening to them. 'The Martini Effect': another phrase for the same potentially deadly phenomenon. A very different group of words, a very different effect. Sounds fun, even stylish, very James Bond.

I try to investigate, to make sense of this, to find some meaning in this crazy thing. I cannot believe that this has happened, that Dylan has lost himself somewhere in the inky blackness of the sea on the other side of the world because gases forced their way into his blood stream and built up to a level where he was, effectively, too pissed to make rational judgements. Something to do with depth and compressed air and something else, I forget. One Martini for every fifty feet. I hate Martinis. Alcohol so bitter it makes my tongue stick to the roof of my mouth, mixed with alcohol that tastes sweet without being sweet. Fragrant. Nasty. Not deadly, though.

I won't believe it. This sort of thing can't happen.

But apparently it can.

This narcosis, this deadly cocktail, seems like a pleasant enough way to end your days. I must believe this. I must believe that as he swam with his friend he began to feel light-headed. Tipsy, as my mother would say. Started making wild gestures, spinning round too quickly, breathing too fast, kicking downwards, forgetting about his depth gauge, ignoring the pressure around his eyeballs. Deeper, deeper. He didn't notice his friend's growing alarm, but waved him down too, to be with him, to discover the unplumbed depths, the unseen creatures. The real dark of the underwater realm. Deeper, now not just tipsy, but roaring drunk with the heavy black water, pushing down further, further, why was Jon not following? Jon, his dearest friend, why was he trying to pull him back? Not to worry he'd have such stories to share with him when he returned from the blackness, such stories of sea monsters, Kraken and giant squid – and wait – what was that squirming just out of reach in the blank depths – giant tentacles and eyes disappearing from him, quick, deeper, one last push to catch up with it, such stories he would have to tell Ruthie, his Ruth. Deeper, deeper, in one final blustering bet with the five oceans pushing down, becoming more euphoric the further away from the light he gets. Until, at a depth that his body can no longer take, he passes out, a beatific smile on his face, his regulator undulating in the deep current like the weeds which cradle him in their ghost-fingered grip.

I have to believe that this is how it was. I have to believe he died with joy in his heart, adventure on his lips. That at the end he knew he would bring back stories for his family of the wonders of the ocean, stories more precious than rare gems and shells lined with mother-of-pearl.

The last sign Jon saw of his friend as he disappeared into the gloom was the frantic shower of quicksilver bubbles spiralling Dylan's last breaths from far below, to burst against Jon's mask, his cheeks, tickle his forehead and scalp, teasing their way through his hair to leave him for the surface.

The rescue party went down as soon as Jon raised the alarm. After three days, when the search was finally called to an exhausted halt, Jon had to be dragged from the water and held on the dive boat to stop him jumping overboard to continue. He sat, pinned between two silent rescue divers, staring at his white, pruned feet, while the craft made its way back to land and the sun rose over the sea.

Dogs have two favourite words: *gosh* and *wow*. You don't need to hear them, you just need to look at their faces: 'Gosh, a leaf!', 'Wow, a wall!'. Idiots. Oh, I forgot blimey: 'Blimey, my tail!'. They get excited about everything. Cats, though. They're slippery, devious. Sneaks. Yes, technically, I'm a cat, but a good-sized one. Couldn't be sneaky if I wanted to. Too bloody big.

Anyway, this morning while I was waiting for her to get herself out of her bath, I was examining the tree in her garden (tall) and her shed (rotting). I heard 'Wow, blimey! Cats!'. Now this made me stop what I was doing. Cats? I thought. But they've all gone. They *should* all be gone. Just me left here. There shouldn't be any bloody cats still around, if you know what I mean.

That's when it came pelting through the bushes. Tiny dog thing. Sharp white face, short legs, teeth too big for its head. Shot out from between the plants, flew along the fence – 'Wow, wow, WOW!' – and caught sight of me. Tried to run backwards while it was still running forwards, tripped, somersaulted. Got up, stood staring at me. I stared back. It grinned. I didn't. It stopped grinning, hung its head, whined. That's when I grinned. That dog spun so quickly on its hind legs I thought it'd twist its head right off. Off it went, scrambling back the way it had come.

Like I said, idiots.

Today she's going to bury a dead person. She must've finished washing. I can smell flowers from the open window. Lavender. She smells of lavender. She says it helps her sleep. I've not seen much evidence. I watch her from the corner of the room, turning in her bed, throwing covers off. Tugging them back over her small body. Mumbling. She dreams when she does sleep. Kind of dreams that wake her up in the dark morning hours. Kind which don't let her back to sleep once she's woken. Kind which she tries to keep from me. But I see them. I see them wind themselves in her hair, hover over her bed. I see them. I see them all.

It's up to me to drive the bad dreams away. Up to me to see her safely through. But how? How, when I can hardly work myself out? I'd lick her like a cub. Nuzzle her until she purred, if I could. If she could. If she'd only tell me what to do.

Big old useless bloody lug, I am.

Here she is. Pulling the front door closed behind her, checking her bag, walking down the path, stopping to check her bag again. Turning back to the house, stopping at the door. Half pulling keys from the bag then shaking her head, banging the heel of her hand against her forehead. Wish she wouldn't do that. Always hurting herself in little ways. Walking back down the path, hesitating at the corner then finally walking away down the road. Her dress is dark, thick. Scent of lavender trails behind her.

She needs help. My help. Need to do something for her. Somehow. Stupid old bugger, though. What? Must be something. Must be. Wouldn't be here otherwise.

I'll follow her. See what she's up to. Make sure she doesn't get herself into any trouble. She needs me around, and I'll figure out what to do. We're a good team. Marnie and Jericho. A good team. I'd forgotten that.

Our Ginger Tabby Rupert has gone,
last seen on Blakeley Road, he is shy
because he was mistreated
by his previous owner.
He can't have gone far.

What a beautiful day.

That's the kind of thing he'd say now. He would be right. It is windless, frosted, the sunlight so sharp you could cut yourself on it. He would always look up – up and out – at the sky, at the clouds, at the rain, and call them beautiful, while the rest of us were looking at our feet, kicking at stones and grinding our heels into the dust.

And here we are now, looking at our feet which stand next to a deep hole in the ground. A hole which he will very soon inhabit.

Dylan's body was found two weeks after he went missing, the curious waves nudging him gently up the beach, over and over. I imagine a strolling tourist wondering at first at the man sleeping on his stomach at the edge of the water, head resting on one outflung arm.

The vicar's hands are red and look sore, as if he himself has toiled for hours alone to dig the grave. The prayer book he holds shakes ever so slightly as he reads. I'm sure he never knew Dylan, but somehow it helps to think that he might be upset too, just a little. His voice rises and falls in the unnatural sing-song lilt of experienced religious orators.

One man to speak words of comfort.

The balls of my feet are aching now, it feels as though we have been standing for hours. Shiulie sniffs against my shoulder. The freshly-dug earth is rich and clayey, smells of metal. I can almost understand the desire small children have to stuff it in their mouths.

Four men to lower the box.

The coffin is in the hole and the white satin lowering ropes dropped in, gently, almost apologetically, on top of it. They lie there, pristine.

I feel Jess at my other shoulder, her fingers grasping the fabric of my skirt, holding on. Just.

Now the words are finished. People begin to shift and move, slowly, so as not to jar the silent moments. They stoop, one-by-one, and straighten, swing their arms out over the grave and then leave. One-by-one they sow their earthy seed and retire.

I feel the thudding clods of earth land on the coffin lid as if they were landing on my own.

One-by-one they fall as mourners file past the open grave. I feel Shiulie stoop next to me. She rises again, crumbling the moist earth between her gloved fingers, then reaches out and lets it fall with wide open hands dusting each other, the wind catching pieces of soil and flinging them away over the grass. I follow her automatically, clenching the mud in my fist so hard it squeezes out between my fingers. I hold my spread palm over the hole but only a crumb of the earth falls. The rest sticks to my palm, the crevices between my fingers, as if delighted by the sudden light and freedom and afraid of returning to the dark, dank ground. I shake my hand, then wipe my palm against my side. There will be mud there for a long time I think. Jess drops a small paper fish, folded from a single piece of gold wrapping paper, into the hole. It glints from the pile of dark earth, until another handful of soil covers it.

I have tried not to look at Ruth too much, but I can't get the picture of her out of my mind. Standing still at the side of the grave, her face closed, betraying nothing. Dry-eyed and ashen-faced with the certainty of her loss.

I will think of the sea monsters – Dylan swimming there, chasing the eyes in the dark, ecstatic with the thrill of the chase – and the stories he will return with grasped in his dripping fists like a harvest of pearls. I will remember him like that.

My kitty Zak disappeared October 8.
He disappeared in Cloud St. He
likes to wander so could be
anywhere by now. He is male
domestic short hair. Zak is all white
with yellow/green eyes.

Something's digging into my lower back. Could be a book. Probably a book. Not sure if I really care right now. It's uncomfortable but I can't be bothered to move.

An hour or so ago we were sprawled over a couple of beanbags, Jess and I, tea lights ablaze around us, tumblers full of red wine. Circling the issues like a couple of cats stalking prey. Getting closer, closer as the levels in our glasses fell, rose again, fell.

'What are the cops saying?'

Cops. As if we're in an American sitcom. Jess was winding a brown lock of fringe around the middle of her index finger. Tighter, tighter. Her fingertip bulged purple a couple of centimetres away from her eyes. I didn't reply. I was hoping she would forget her question. She's been doing a lot of that lately.

'Marn. Have they called?'

'Who?'

Her eyebrows rose up her forehead.

'What do you mean "who"? The cops. The bloody police.'

She dragged out the vowel sounds. Po-leess.

'No. No, they haven't called.'

'Have you called them?'

I had to meet her gaze then, stop pulling at the thread unravelling from my jumper.

'No. I haven't called them.'

She unwound the hair from her strangled finger. Stared at me through narrowed eyes.

'Why?'

Her question so totally lacking in inflection it was as if she had given up expecting a convincing answer before she even asked. I let out a sigh.

'You seem to have forgotten him already. It's as if you've got better things to do. Why haven't you called them?'

'I just haven't. There's no point in hassling them constantly. They'll call if they have news. When they have news.'

She got up suddenly and walked over to my phone. Picked up the receiver, held it out to me.

'Phone them.'

'Jesus, Jess, it's almost midnight . . .'

'Phone them.'

'Jess, please . . .'

'Phone them.'

My voice swelled to fill the room. It surprised Jess. It surprised me.

'And what the fuck are they meant to do? What, Jess? Tell me. No really, do tell me, because you've obviously got all the good ideas here. Why don't you share them with me? There's no sign of a struggle, a fight, anything wrong at his flat. At all. Nothing. He's a grown man. What the hell are they supposed to do?'

Both standing, glowering at each other. How had we got here?

'He's just gone. There's nothing anyone can do. We'll just have to wait.'

Both shaking.

'There's nothing more they can do, Jess. Nothing *I* can do. Nothing.'

Silence. I taste those empty words. Drying my tongue like dust. She doesn't deserve this, any of this. Give her some hope. Give her something to cling to in this deluge, a piece of driftwood, a floating branch, anything.

'Jess.'

There is nothing to hold on to in her eyes. Mine falter and slip from her appalled face and I end up staring at a corner of peeling wallpaper. I really should paste that down again. Or repaint. Maybe just push a book shelf in front of it to hide the scar on the wall. Hide it away, pretend it's not there.

I pull myself back to my sister, trying to reassemble my thoughts before I speak. But the barbed words are stuck in my throat, and before I can think of a way to console her (there is no way, no way) she spins, snatches her jacket from the chair back and flings herself through the door.

She leaves behind her a space the size of a fist in my chest. Nothing will make this better. Jericho is nowhere to be found today and I find myself sitting by my overflowing bookshelves, the scattered piles of books leaning against the walls of my living room, searching frantically for my other companion. A soft toy monkey is swiped unceremoniously from piles of roughly stacked books, photo albums, old papers, magazines, never to be thrown away. You never know when you might need them. The disgruntled animal, one leg twisted underneath its body, gives me a final withering glance from under a crazily-striped brow, before being kicked under the chair to commune with the shadows.

'Yeah, same to you,' I mutter. I sneeze and wipe my nose across the back of my hand. My cheeks are burning. A precariously-leaning stack of ancient *National Geographic* magazines is felled by my elbow; unread yet ragged copies of *The SAS Survival Handbook*, *A Tale of Two Cities* and *French Provincial Cooking* are flung across the sofa, taking with them a half-eaten bar of chocolate and a bunch of dried red chillies. *Jonathan Livingston Seagull* and *Justine* meet the same fate. An old sandal emerges into the light from under a pile of leaflets for horse riding tours of distant Mexican canyons. Candles gutter on the carpet, the tiny flames which had surrounded Jess and me in a protective glow close to extinguished. At last my prey is routed from its lair underneath a stack of last weekend's newspapers. The large book is without a cover, yet the inside page still bears its title: *Roget's Thesaurus of English Words and Phrases*. Standing in the half-light I run a hand over the words, tracing the letters one-by-one. I sit legs crossed, and edge my back to the cool wall. Open the book, any page will do. Read:

435 Blueness: N. blueness, blue, cyan, azure; blue sky, blue sea; sapphire, aquamarine, turquoise, lapis lazuli; bluebell, cornflower, forget-me-not; gentian blue . . .

My lips move, weave the colours into a mantra, the cyans, azures calming my heart, each word a whisper of tranquillity. I begin to read out loud to the tumbled books, the dusty hangings, the empty chairs.

purple, blue and red; imperial purple; amethyst; lavender, violet,

heliotrope, heather, foxglove; plum, damson, aubergine; Tyrian
purple, gentian violet; amaranth, lilac, mauve; purpure

Rolling the words around my mouth, I bask in their phonetic sensuality, in my own meaningless eloquence. I let the colour swirl in front of my eyes until it has a life of its own.

. . . amaranth, lilac, mauve . . .

A glass marble silently rolls across the floor and comes to rest against my bare foot. A pair of yellow eyes gaze through the doorway at me on the floor, me reading, me, throned in chaos. Me weaving my kaleidoscopic spell. And the lion listens, chin propped on forepaws, legs curled under heavy body, eyes wide and glistening as skeins of colour blossom from my mouth like warm breath on a cold day. A low rhythmic rumble begins from the doorway.

My voice fades. I look up at my spellbound audience briefly, close my eyes and lean my head back against the wall, clasping the book to my chest. I can feel a wisp of hair rising and falling against my nose in time with my breathing.

Bluebell. Cornflower. Forget-me-not.

*

So she stops reading, falls asleep, right there on the floor against the wall. I go over, lie next to her. Try and give her what comfort I can. Which isn't any. Useless, I am. The dreams still find her, and I'm powerless to stop them.

Soon she jerks awake, sits staring at the window. Doesn't say anything. Just sits and stares. I close my eyes, can't bear to see her look so haunted, and get to thinking about how it might have been.

Apparently we like to hang around in groups. Females do most of the work; hunting, bringing up the babies and such. Males play around with the little'uns when they feel like it. When they don't they snarl, bat them away. The fellas get to show off, lie around, rut with the females. They get the best bits of every kill. The first parts, the still hot, quivering haunches of antelope or wildebeest. Sometimes even before the bugger's heart has stopped, before the tremors have died away. You can feel the pulse in your mouth as you tear at the neck. Thick salty-sweet blood running down the back of your throat. Gentle shock of bone crack in your mouth, marrow squeezing out between your teeth. Black clouds of flies you breathe in when your mouth is wide open, trying to cram as much meat and bone and hoof and hair in as possible. Occasional snarls at the bouncing vultures trying to grab scraps of the quickly cooling meal.

Then rolling over, licking your chin, red-stained, standing slowly, walking unsteadily, drunk with meat and blood, towards the nearest thorn-tree shade. Look at me. So fat. So beautiful. So beloved. Shake of the mane, a glimpse back at the half-eaten carcass almost invisible under a mound of lioness flesh. A row of panting cubs, whiskers bristling. Sitting and watching others eat and their bellies growling as loud as their feasting parents.

Course, I've never actually experienced any of this. I've watched over a shoulder. She loves the animal programmes on TV. Loves them, that Jess. As if we're any different. As if we're anything special.

Prides. That's what they call groups of lions. Prides. A pride of lions. Yes.

I'm not sleeping. Not even dozing. Just watching. Yes, I've got my eyes closed. Don't need eyes to watch. To watch over someone. Watching is best done with eyes closed. Puts others off guard. Especially humans. They think you're asleep, see?

Ears and nose. That's best for watching. Now this one here, she thinks I'm asleep, even though she knows me so well. Or thinks she does. Can smell her tiny, careful movements, careful not to wake me, disturb me.

But watching over her: it's not enough. Not nearly enough. Something's got to be done. And soon. See, her mind is blank sometimes. Like now. She's searching back, back, always back. When she goes far she finds what she's looking for. But when she looks over her shoulder, to what happened only a few days ago, it's like she's trying to see through a pile of damp straw. I can't help a snarl escaping from between my teeth. But it's OK. She thinks I'm just dreaming.

> JESSICA lost CAT
> JESSIE is black with a
> WHITE chin. She has a RED
> collar. If you find her PLEASE
> call me on . . .

A missing cat with my sister's name. Feels spooky, somehow. But a perfect ice-breaker after the raised voices and slammed doors of last night. I was expecting not to see her for a few days, for her to have sloped off to Roo's, or even back to Mum's, but her movements in the kitchen just after four this morning pulled me from my sleep. I am glad she's back. I am determined to make an effort with her. I may even try to say sorry.

'Looks like you've gone missing now,' I quip as my sister shuffles into the kitchen for breakfast. I turn to show her the latest poster and am about to follow up this comedic gem, but instead can only stop and stare. I realise my mouth must be hanging open. I shut it. My initial thought is that she has suddenly broken out in a virulent skin rash. This idea is quickly pushed aside, though I still can't quite grasp what I'm seeing. She sits down at the table, carefully pushes her fringe out of her eyes and drags the plate of toast towards her.

'Morning.'

I don't reply. Her hands look fine. I glance quickly at her bare ankles, which are also pale and unblemished. She butters her toast thickly, dribbles on some honey and crunches into it. Then she notices the lost cat notice on the table and smiles wryly as she reads the name.

'Oh right, geddit now. Funny. They just keep on coming, don't they?'

Her hair is brushed, tidy. She flaps her toast in front of her face and continues.

'Catnappers, must be. Is that a word, do you think? Catnappers. Catnapping. "Hello Ms Irving, and what do you do for a living?", "Oh, I'm a catnapper".'

She stops to consider this. I continue to gape, silently.

'Or maybe catnappers are people who chip bits off cats. You know, like flintknappers, they make stuff out of flint by knocking bits off it. Maybe catnappers make stuff out of cats.'

She stops.

'Talking crap, eh? I'm just a crapnapper.'

She meets my wide eyes and somehow manages to carry on eating through her grin.

The reason I am staring – gawping – at my sister is that her face is covered in large white spots, some slightly smeared, each about the size of a five pence coin. She looks like a diseased clown.

'Jess.'

'Mmm?'

'Are you OK?'

Why, why must I ask such stupid questions?

'I'm fine.'

And why, why must she lie to me?

'But . . . what's that on your face?'

She shrugs.

'Nothing.'

Of course.

'Jessie. Sweetheart. There's . . . white stuff on your face.'

'Mmm.'

'What is it?'

She sighs, fanning the cat poster in front of her face as if the heat of my words are suddenly stifling.

'Spots.'

'I can see they're spots. But.'

I'm not entirely sure what to ask. A 'why' would imply that she has done this to herself, deliberately defaced herself, something that points towards trouble. 'How' and 'When' are irrelevant. 'Who'? No. After a moment I go for the hard one.

'Jess. Why? Why did you . . . do the spots?

She stares at her toast.

'If you're planning on running away to join the circus don't you think you should practise putting on the make up?'

My feeble attempt at humour fails, as I knew it would. She just swallows the remains of her breakfast and wipes crumbs from her dressing-gowned lap onto the floor.

'Is this because of last night? You know, I feel bad, I'm really . . .'

'Wouldn't understand.'

She is probably right.

'Try me.'

Those eyes on me again, like pools among moon rocks. She looks as if she has tried to erase parts of her face. It must be grease paint. Jess turns back to her plate, pushes it around the table with the tip of one finger. Bites down, hard, on her lower lip.

'Jess.'

'I'm ugly.'

This I was not expecting. For once, I would like to be able to 'rise to the occasion', as they say, I would like, just once, to be able to say something helpful, meaningful, profound, on the spur of the moment when faced with the shocks, the horrors which seem to be coming thick and fast these days. Just once I want to cut to the quick and show that I can deal with whatever life throws at me. Just once.

'What?'

Evidently, this will not be that once.

'You heard me. I'm ugly. U. G. L. . . .'

'Jess, you're not! You're . . .'

'I am. I'm foul and disgusting. Can't you see it? I mean you wouldn't tell me, obviously, you're my sister. But you know I am. You see it.'

See what? What am I meant to be seeing? She tucks a lock of hair behind an ear, carefully, so as not to smear the marks on her cheek. They are thick, opaque. Where does one buy grease paint from?

'Every time I look in a mirror this face glares back at me. You haven't got any idea what it's like to look like this. You know I'm ugly, deep down. You know. You just wouldn't tell me. You haven't got the guts.'

'I don't . . . how can you think . . .'

'Everyone sees it. They stare, I know they're talking about how I look. So I decided on a strategy. Pretty simple, really. *Distraction*. That's the thing. Distract people from my face. From my hideousness.'

She looks at me as if she expects me to understand it all now. As if it's all been made clear. I don't reply. She takes a deep breath, as if preparing to explain something simple to a child.

'If I've got large white spots all over my face people will focus on those rather than on me. See? You did. It works. They won't see my repulsiveness.'

All this stated so calmly, as if she has been planning this for months and is now able to explain her actions with total confidence. She seems almost serene. Is this what those days of panic, locked in the bathroom have been about? The constant checking of hair, face in any reflective surface? The biting of the fingers, the pulling out of eyelashes? The broken glass of the bathroom mirror? Where did Jess go? Where did my sister go?

When Jess and I were a lot younger, me ten, her four maybe, we shared a craving for salt. Chocolate couldn't tempt us. Plates of biscuits would be left untouched. Slices of moist cake pushed around plates, squashed and hidden under spoons. Our unusual tastes were a problem at school friends' parties, where ice cream and jelly, smartie-covered chocolate logs and iced buns were a staple. Instead we would devour whole bowls of salty knotted pretzels in a single sitting, hide bundles of tiny sausages in paper napkins for nibbling on later. Our favourite salty snack was chicken stock cubes. We became cat burglars in our own home driven by our desire for the perfect gold-wrapped lumps. I would pilfer just one from the packet in the top cupboard in the kitchen, balancing precariously on a high stool for the treasure and then hurry away to bed, the savoury plunder in the depths of a dressing gown pocket. Once the lights were out and we were assured of privacy, my mother's goodnight kisses still cooling on our foreheads, we would join each other in bed, unwrap our treat, divide it solemnly in half and eat the sticky mess, licking our fingers and giggling. Tiny, bird-like bites; too much of it in your mouth at once would make your eyes water and your tongue stick to the roof of your mouth. We would huddle together with our booty, whispering, plotting. Together.

'Foul and repulsive, foul and repulsive. Foul. And. Repulsive.'
She is singing these words to herself quietly, over and over.

'Jess. Did something happen to you last night?'

She turns her green eyes on me. I have always envied those eyes.

'Nothing happened.'

And she smiles.

Suddenly my eyes are stinging and I feel my cheeks heat and colour. I can't cry in front of her, so I cover her hand briefly with mine, show her what I hope is a sweet and understanding smile and hurry out of the room. As I leave I hear her humming a simple tune, tea being poured from the pot.

I walk the streets for a while, slowing my breathing, trying not to think of her spotted and dotted. Defaced. I stare in the window of the second-hand book shop, wonder idly if I should go in and search for something my father wrote. I turn away from the idea, decide a layperson's psychology or self-help book would be more suitable, something to explain my sister. Instead I walk on and buy sausage rolls in the bakery next door. I forget Jess has become a vegetarian and will not eat them. I shall have to eat them myself. I buy a Sunday paper, fight with it, drop it all over the pavement outside the shop. I am out of money so I walk home, slowly. The living room is darkened by the heavy closed curtains, lit only by the flickering green light of the TV. Jess has fallen asleep on the sofa. Tiny cartoon ninja girls whizz around the screen behind her head. It is bonfire night on Wednesday and I wonder whether Jess will have replenished her spots for the big event. Maybe she will have changed her mind by then.

I retreat to the kitchen where Jericho snores by the window. I sit at the table with the newspaper on my lap as the light seeps from the room and watch him twitch in his sleep.

Have you seen Pie?
White with dark tabby ears and tail
and dark spot on her back. Seven years
old with a pink sparkly collar. She
has a couple of small bald patches
under her fur on her back.

Neither Shiulie nor I had wanted to go out to watch the fires and the explosions and the flame-lit processions through the old streets. We had talked earlier in the year of avoiding the dramatic pyrotechnics in the neighbouring town and hadn't joined the drunken revelry for over five years. Dylan had tried to persuade us to come with him, year after year: it was his favourite event. This time we would go without him. We would go for him, send him off in style. Ruth would not come.

We wrapped ourselves up in our thickest jackets and woolly hats. Shiulie filled a hip flask with whisky, filled our pockets with gloves and we set off. And swaddled in this way we find ourselves in a small town overtaken by pyromania and seemingly overrun by countless warring factions, all brandishing flaming brands. Dylan would have loved it.

There is so much smoke my eyes water and sting. Cerise blooms across the fogged night sky like a sudden bruise, seconds before the explosive boom reaches us.

'Ooh.'

Blurred green lines draw themselves across the redness and a white flash heralds an almighty crack sounding in the heavens.

'Ahh . . .'

My neck is beginning to ache as I bend backwards, trying to make out the shapes in the sky. A night sky which is clogged with mist so that only the shadows, the trailing ghosts of fireworks can be seen. The sharpness and focus of the bonfire nights I remember from the past seems dulled and blunted by the blanketing greyness, and even the sounds seems muffled and echoing. The only thing which has not had its keenness dulled is the familiar comforting smell of the dark explosive powder.

Ooh. Ahh. Those are the sparkling ones, my favourites, like showers of diamonds, or tiny stars falling from the sky.

'Whooooaaa . . .'

This is Shiulie. She is holding my hand, squeezing and crunching my finger bones together each time a new colour smudges itself across the sky. Our hands are still frozen, despite the many pairs of gloves. She is jumping up and down on the spot with cold. Or excitement. Or impatience. Or all three.

A loud crack sounds somewhere near my ankles, making me jump. Only one of the thousands of small bangers which will be let off tonight.

Another banger replies, this time further back into the crowd. Shiulie is now standing on tiptoe trying to see over the sea of heads. Then turns to me with an excited grin, the lights jumping and dancing in her eyes.

'Come on, move your arse. Let's find ourselves the best seat in the house.'

Surely the street residents have the best vantage point. I can't imagine she is going to hijack one of the houses along the bonfire societies' procession route. She squeezes my hand again then lets it drop, the better to employ both elbows in clearing a path for us through the heaving press of bodies. I plunge in after her, only momentarily hindered by someone standing on my left foot.

Ambulances and police linger at the outskirts in the shadows. Blazing tar barrels roll down the cobbled streets.

An elbow punches me in the side. Even through my padded jacket the sharp pain makes me gasp. I plunge on through the crowd with Shiulie, tripping over feet, standing on other feet, pushed and shoved by excited arms and hips and hands. Flames seem to be all around us, cans of beer held aloft to greet the burning effigies of men and women and demons.

Suddenly we are out of the crowd and on the edge of a park, heading up a steep incline, away from the revellers. I can now walk without dodging people and prams and dogs. This is unexpected.

'Shiu, where are we going? I thought we were looking for somewhere to watch from.'

She puffs on ahead.

'We are. But somewhere we don't have to get punched in the head to get a view. We'll have a view of the whole buggering arsed lot of them!'

We climb upwards, following a dirt track getting steeper and then sweeping round a corner so the view of the flames is completely obscured. Steeper still and I find my boots slip on the loose stones of the path. Shiulie's denim-clad backside strains ever upwards in front of me. A large rock skitters from underneath my sole, sending my face earthwards. My palms and my knees meet the jagged stones of the path and I yelp.

'You OK?' from above.

I'm about to answer but a growl echoes from behind me on the path.

'Go on, shift yourself. I'll push.'

Shiulie scrambles up the path and disappears around another bend. A firm pressure against my behind surprises me but pushes me forwards. I struggle upwards, helped along by the grunting support from below. Flashes light up the sky beyond the hill we are climbing, making a corona around its crest. I reach the top, palms sweating and throbbing, legs complaining, and I gasp.

I hadn't realised how high we'd come. The hill drops away suddenly beyond an iron railing to reveal the town below. Just ten feet away Shiulie has already climbed over and is sitting on the cliff edge dangling her legs. I sidle closer. Sit on the stringy grass and shuffle forwards on my bum until I'm close enough to the edge to hang my feet into the air. A hundred feet or so below lies the outline of the rough chalky path.

'Not bad, eh?'

Not bad at all. About twenty others cluster along the lip of the steep drop, some standing against the continuing rise of the hill, but most sitting on the railing's edge, huddled in sleeping bags, padded coats, many with hip flasks or steaming thermos flasks. There is talk, but it is quiet, whispered almost. Normally, a night-time town seen from above would be sketched by the rows of street lights. This one is drawn in rivers of living flame, each fed by smaller glowing tributaries. From our perch we see all the fiery processions, there must be fifteen, twenty of them, snaking through the crowded streets. And barely visible at the town's heart the bonfire. Surely thirty feet tall, a dark pyramid waiting for fire.

'He'd love this, wouldn't he?'

I nod. It is beautiful. It really is. It may just be the warmth of the whisky nosing its way through my body but suddenly I'm feeling almost OK. I'm feeling alright. Not ecstatic. Not over-joyed. But I'll settle for alright. It's such an alien feeling I grin widely, and a real smile stretches the muscles in my cheeks in all kinds of ways I had forgotten. I imagine my skin as a dried mud face pack, pulling at my cheeks as my face expands, then cracking and falling off bit by bit. It's suddenly incredibly funny, this skin-peeling, whisky-bodied moment and I yell with laughter. I laugh and laugh and laugh.

After a while I notice Shiulie staring at me, a smile on her face and firelight in her eyes. She swigs at the hip flask, never taking her eyes from mine. She wipes the back of hand across her lips and holds the silver bottle towards me.

'You, my dear, are a fucking nut job. In my professional opinion.'

And she leans towards me and butts me with her shoulder.

'Crazy!' she yells into my face.

We guffaw at each other. And others sitting over the precipice join in the laughter, because they have no choice, looking over their shoulders at us cackling above the flames and fires. And we laugh and laugh. And my skin falls away. And I laugh. And then tears are running down my face and then I don't know whether I'm laughing or crying any more but I carry on because I have no choice, it's all I can do.

A warm, heavy weight presses on my lap. I touch it with my hand. The fur is thick. I hold on to it as the laughter ebbs away and I wipe my eyes on the back of my jacket sleeve.

'She's right.'

I'm still hiccoughing the rest of my fading giggles down.

'What?'

Hot breath against the side of my neck.

'Nut job. What she called you. You are one.'

I turn to look into his eyes. Which glow brightly in the lights tonight.

'Yeah. You're probably right.'

I put an arm around his neck and rub the short fur behind his ear. He lowers his head so I can reach better, and rumbles at me quietly. We watch the flames below for a while in silence, the three of us, Shiulie and I passing the flask of whisky between us, Jericho sitting motionless at my other side. After a particularly long swig Shiulie holds the flask out in front of her over the drop.

'Here's to you, you silly bugger. I'll never know why you decided to call it a day in that bloody underwater realm of yours, why you thought it would be a good idea not to come back to your girls, but who can decipher the strange workings of the male mind. Certainly not me.'

She pauses as a volley of red stars explode over our heads.

'And you missed some fucking good whisky.'

She tips the flask and a thin trickle of liquid falls into the darkness, lit orange and red by the firelight below.

'You stupid bastard,' she says.

'Bastard,' I whisper.

More people are now reaching the top of the cliff, struggling up the same path we had taken, giggling and whispering and complaining and play-fighting. Shiulie has noticed a small group of friends toiling up the last of the slope. She waves the flask over her head.

'Oi! Dickheads!'

This gets not only theirs but everyone's attention. She heaves herself up using my shoulder and bounds over to the knot of steaming jackets and coats. I watch her envelop each of the people in her arms, slap them on the back and launch into jubilant exclamations. Her hands fly at her sides as she talks, sometimes coming to rest on a shoulder or arm but then swooping away again like airborne embers. The others laugh with her and I look at her and wonder at her easy charm, her lightness. She waves me over but I pretend not to see. I still feel OK.

My hand – the one which had been buried deep in the warmth of lion fur – is scratching at Jericho's head, but suddenly I feel the strength seep from me. My fingers drop slowly towards the cold ground as the body beneath moves away. He is still rumbling, but this time louder, more intensely. And something else is there. It could be menace.

'You're still as beautiful as you were then, you know.'

These are the words I hear from somewhere above my head. I twist round and look upwards but can't make out a face in the shadow which hovers over me. The voice though, I cannot mistake. Even though it is a year since I last heard it. Even though I had hoped never to hear it again. You're still as beautiful as you were then.

This is untrue. I do not think, nor have I ever thought of myself, as beautiful. I mean, look at what Roget has to say about the word:

> . . . dazzling, delicate, delightful, divine, elegant, enticing, excellent, exquisite, fair, fascinating, fine, foxy, good-looking, gorgeous, graceful, grand, handsome, ideal, lovely, magnificent, marvellous, nice, pleasing, pretty, pulchritudinous, radiant, ravishing . . .

Dazzling. Ravishing. Exquisite, for God's sake. No, not me. Not me at all.

I do recognise the voice. The voice is Will's, and Will *is* beautiful (fascinating fine foxy). Will is the beautiful man who was Shiulie's husband until he ended their marriage without warning a couple of weeks before their first wedding anniversary. Which was almost a year ago. Will is making me blush like a schoolgirl when I should be setting the dogs on him, laying the mantraps, charging the Tasers. It's just as well it's dark so he can't see my reddening cheeks.

I struggle to stand up without falling over. He steps back to give me room and I look to where Shiulie has been entertaining her friends. I can't see them. I pray that she won't return before I've had a chance to get rid of Will. Preferably over the edge of the cliff.

My eyes have grown accustomed to the dark after what feels like hours of staring at bright, orange lights and I struggle to make out Will's features through the squirming yellow images burned onto my retina. Suddenly his face is lit green by the fireworks which flash behind me. I look into his (delicate, delightful, divine) eyes to see whether he's having me on. But I don't know how to tell. Isn't he meant to be scratching some part of his face, tugging at an earlobe, if he's lying? Or is it that he should have his arms crossed in front of him? I can't remember, but he's not tugging or scratching or folding. Nor is he smirking, laughing or anything else which would obviously indicate a joke.

We stare at each other. Why can't I say anything?

'Will. There you are. It's so bloody hard to find anyone in this. Come on, we're supposed to be meeting Stiffy.'

A blonde girl with small eyes has taken Will's (handsome, ideal, lovely) arm, and is pulling him gently away. I have been unable to utter a word. I should be spraying him with vitriol for the broken heart of my friend, and for the sudden warmth which grips the back of my neck and spreads forwards to circle my throat. I should at the very least throw whisky in his face. I would love to see him in pain, physical pain. Not as good as seeing his broken body on the rocks at the bottom of a cliff, but a start, a definite start.

He wriggles away from her grasp but mumbles his assent.

'OK. I'll be there in a sec'.'

The girl wanders off. Will's gaze lingers on mine a moment longer.

'Good to see you again, Marnie. You're looking well.'

He swallows a gulp of his beer, then bites his lip. He leans closer.

'I'll give you a call some time. You're still at the same place, aren't you?'

I mutter something which he takes as a yes.

I feel his fingers brush the back of my chilled hand. They warm parts of me they shouldn't.

'Great. See you soon, yeah?'

I throw the whisky in his face, following it with the flask, then knee him in the groin and knee him in his face as he crumples to the chalky path. Apologise to the assembled revellers, what with this being a peaceful celebration and all, but rather than the frowns and police sirens I expect, I receive rapturous applause and clods of earth and large rocks thrown at my prone prey for good measure. I could still do it.

'Take care, gorgeous.'

He cocks his head to one side, narrows his eyes at me and smiles.

I never even said one word to him. I let him say what he liked, let his eyes take their time wandering over my puffa-jacketed body and I said not a damn word to him. The only thing I did manage to do was spill some whisky down the front of my jacket.

He turns to follow the blonde girl towards the highest point of the cliff edge and he is gone. I can still feel the ghost of his touch, and with Shiulie only moments away too.

'I could have done it for you. No trouble.'

I glance towards the level of my hips. Jericho is circling me like a starved beast.

'I'm getting pretty bored anyway. Bit of well-deserved disembowelment always livens things up, I find. What do you say?'

'Just leave him. Go and find something else to do.'

I'm trembling so hard I need to sit down. Then I catch sight of Shiulie. She stands with one hand on a hip and the other outlining balloons in the air with her hat, head thrown back and laughing. She hasn't seen him. I could take her home now, ensure that she is safe, safe from him, safe from harm. As far as I know she has not had any contact with Will for months. I need to make sure it stays that way. But how do I make sure he doesn't contact me? The thought of him turning up unannounced while Shiulie is with me is almost too much. I walk over to the group, stand at its outskirts uncertainly for a few long moments until Shiulie notices me and flings an arm around my shoulder.

'Kitten! We've run out of goddamn booze, and I need to get pissed as a catfish if I'm to survive tonight. Dylan would have expected nothing less.'

'Shiu . . .'

She notices the dark stains on my chest.

'Have you been drooling again? Come, let us find more alcohol.'

'Shiulie, haven't you had enough? I was hoping to head home soon.'

She wheels on me, looks at me as though I've lost my mind. Bursts out laughing.

'The fireworks haven't even started properly. Dylan would be horrified. More importantly, I'm not really pissed yet, and Dylan would be even more horrified at that. So don't start talking about wimping out.'

She settles her chin deeper into her scarf, sinking her mouth behind the fluffed wool. Her eyes crinkle up and I know she is smiling behind those crimson folds. Then her gaze shifts and lights on something beyond my face. Her eyes widen slowly as her eyebrows pull together. The scarf drops from her face to pool around her shoulders. Her mouth is open. I turn to see Will standing at the far end of the cliff with an arm draped around the waist of the blonde girl, who is smiling, playing with his hair. He runs a finger down the side of her neck. I watch Shiulie implode. A round man barges past her, making her stumble. One end of her red scarf drops from her shoulder and into the mud. She drops her gaze to her boots. She seems for a few moments to be talking to them, reprimanding them for getting so dirty, why didn't they keep to the cleaner grassy bank, she'll just have to go and clean them when she gets home now. She looks up again, turns her head and meets my eyes. She mouths something and pulls a lock of black hair into her mouth. Then walks towards me, past me, sets off on the dark path down the hill.

Lilou – dearly loved and missed
Tabby, grey, black and brown
markings
Long Haired
Female
Black collar with diamante studs.
Reward for ANY information.

'Bollocking *space*, for fuck's sake! He needed *space*. I mean, have we ever heard *that* one before? Whoreson wanker! *Space!*'

The word is spat into the low bushes next to the bench. She is shaking with rage and the tears aren't long in coming. But she doesn't sob. Just stands there looking up at the sky without blinking, eyes streaming, as if having a staring match with the stars.

We walked down the hill in silence. The low clouds had dissipated, revealing a deep inkiness pricked with tiny lights. She walked quickly and I followed, as flashes of colour lit up the sky behind us and delighted shrieks carried on the air. I said nothing. There was nothing to say. I followed her through the crowds, almost losing her a couple of times, to the first pub she came to.

She headed straight towards the bar, elbowing the crowds out of her way.

'It's her, Marn, isn't it? He was having a bloody affair. Wasn't he?'

'I don't know, Shiu, I really don't know . . .'

Her hands are shaking. I'm afraid she might crush her pint glass like a polystyrene cup.

'A year, Marnie. We weren't even married a year.'

Her hands clutch at her jeans. She turns huge eyes on me.

'What did I do wrong?'

This so desperate, so imploring, almost a whisper. So simple. Her whole marriage summed up in five words of her own assumed guilt. Tears roll down her cheeks, pool in the hollows of her collarbones, then spill down her chest to trace dark paths down the front of her shirt. But she doesn't blink. I am afraid to touch her, lest she collapse under even the gentlest of touches. I can't bear her trembling silence.

'Shiulie.'

My fingers close on her smooth brown wrist, gently, gently, she is a wild thing now. Let me help you. Tell me how.

My touch seems to break something in her. She closes her eyes slowly and takes a breath which shakes her whole frame. The tremor reaches my bones. What can I do?

Another wracking sigh.

'Space,' she whispers.

'Fuck,' she whispers.

'Drink,' she whispers.

*

This is why I didn't want to come back. Hearts torn. Minds ripped. Weeping. Pain. Didn't want any of that again. Had enough the first time round. Had enough with Marnie. Had enough with Marnie to last a long, long lifetime. She loved so hard, so much. Nearly broke me. The brown girl, though. Shiulie. Hair so black it's blue. No knowing which way she'll go now. No knowing what she could do. She might just sit down on the grass, hold herself together with her arms. Or she could find a knife and carve herself an unforgettable banquet out if him. No knowing. No knowing at all.

Not my thing though, is she? I mean, she's nice and all, good to my Marnie, but really not my thing. Can only have one thing at a time. Although. Look at my little bit. Look at her. She's breaking inside, I can hear the cracks. She's hurting. Not just from the other one's tears, but something else she doesn't want to admit to herself: that he hurt her too. Now that I *can* do something about. If she'd let me. If she'd ask me. So maybe I could do something for them both, something that would kill two birds with the one jagged stone, as it were. We'll see. I'll keep my eye on her a while longer, bide my time.

I'll think of something.

*

'A pox on him.'

My glass stops on its way to my mouth and I turn to look at Shiulie.

'And on his family. And on his shitty dog. And on her.'

Go on: rage at him. At the injustice of the world, at the inconstancy of lovers.

'Shiulie!' I say, hiccoughing loudly, and then bursting out laughing. I can't help myself. Especially after too many long swallows of whisky and jugs of warm brown ale.

'Well, what do you expect me to say? Bastarding bugger. Crapping tosser. A plague on every one of his houses. And his poxy buggery car.'

She stops. Sniffs loudly. Gulps the contents of her glass.

'Cocking car.'

Sniffs again and grows still. From the way her eyes have narrowed to mere slits I'd say she has just had an idea. From the way her nose has crinkled up I'd also say the idea has something to do with Will's car. Will's red Fiat Coupe which he loves more than life itself.

Shiulie turns her red eyes on me. Faint black lines of melted mascara meander down her cheeks. I lift my hand to rub them away but she shakes her head impatiently.

'He loves that bloody car more than life itself, wouldn't you say?'

'Well, yes, I could say that. Yes.'

It's a beast of a car with a throaty warble at rest and a roar to put the most ferocious jungle cat to shame when it's revved up. His baby, his dearest love. I'm not sure I want to know the shape and colour of this idea.

'I've an idea. You'll love it. If you love me, you'll love it.'

'I bet I won't.'

'I bet I bet I bet you will,' she half-sings. Her eyes are shining, her lips stretched taut over her perfect sharp little teeth. She jumps up and, without turning to see if I'm following, disappears into the crowd. I've not even had time to swallow the beer in my mouth.

'Oh, I already do,' says a rumbling voice from the region of my right hip. I feel a blast of warm air on my thigh through the fabric of my trousers. My fingers find his mane, twine themselves into it.

'Hmm?'

He tugs himself away from me.

'I *love* her idea, very bloody much. Come on girl, last one to the car park's a bloody buggery tosser.'

*

I saw it. I saw it in her head and I know what I have to do now. I know where to find it. Close. It's around here, somewhere close.

I'll track it down until I find it.

And when I've found it, I'll kill it.

I'll kill it dead.

ZOE a golden tabby female five years quite
small for her age last seen
Thursday night. Zoe spent most of
her time around the home so not like
her not to return. We
all miss her terribly especially her
son and our dog. please if you know
anything about her contact us.

'What the hell is that?'

Another bystander, a stranger made bold by the chaos in front
of us, whispers this in my ear. She is referring to the car. I know
her face will be drained of colour, like mine. I know her jaw will
be hanging slightly open, echoing my own.

The car was once red. It is Will's and it is lying on the pitted
tarmac like road kill. The tyres have been slashed and deflated,
all four of them. The skirts have been wrenched free of the main
body of the car and lie splayed like broken ribs. All the glass is
shattered. The driver's side door has been peeled open and one
of the wing mirrors dangles like a gouged eyeball. The roof is

deeply dented. It looks like a huge weight has dropped on it from a considerable height. Smaller dents and gouges run the length of the body of the battered machine. A dark and pungent liquid pools underneath and spills, slowly, towards the group of people who have gathered to stare.

'What the hell is that smell?'

The car was once red, but now it is mostly brown. Smeared with—

'Shit. It's covered in crap. It's like someone's run a herd of bulls through here. What the fuck?'

The car's bonnet and roof are indeed covered in crap. She gives a low whistle.

'Bloody hell. Someone was *really* pissed off.'

I wonder how Shiulie would react, seeing this. The last time I saw her she was headed back up the cliff path, walking fast, shoulders hunched up beneath her ears. I haven't gone after her, not yet. I'll leave her in peace, hunt her down later. She needs some time to rage on her own.

A tap on my shoulder. I turn. It's the blonde girl with small eyes whose arms were wreathed around Will's waist earlier. Her face is blanched, the cords of her neck standing out above the tiny sequins stitched into the neckline of her sky blue jumper.

'Hi. I'm Jen. Sorry, but I saw you talking to Will earlier, and I thought you might have seen him. Do you know where he is? He's going to be gutted when he sees this.'

It is not long until he is found. Sometimes, it seems, searching and finding are so simple, so easily accomplished.

There is no scream, no shout for help from the small thicket behind the temporary car park. It's more that a sudden hush blankets us, a silence descends over the gathered people. We head towards the noiseless trees, where a small knot of people have congregated, most standing, a couple crouching. Jen the blonde stands looking down at something at the foot of the tree. Arriving at the hushed group I am somehow not surprised. Not shocked.

He's sitting rod-straight, back leaning against the trunk of a tree. His jacket is gone. That bark is rough, must be uncomfortable. His hair is short, perfect. His eyes are blue. Perfect. I've thought about those eyes a few times, rather too long, rather too hard. Inappropriately. This was when he was Shiulie's, so I could never tell her that sometimes, just sometimes, his eyes on me would make my heart rise to my throat. Just sometimes.

His hands lie relaxed in his lap, his legs stretched out in front of him on the grass. His eyes fixed on something far, far away.

A crouched man talks slowly and loudly at him, shakes his shoulders, first gently, then more roughly. Will doesn't seem to hear him. He doesn't seem to hear anything. He just gazes through us all, through the damp air towards the horizon.

My stomach is heaving suddenly and I need to turn away but can't wrench my eyes from Will's slack face. I've seen faces like this before. Empty, staring faces troubled my dreams, invading my sleep from the hospital where Dad was taken. I need to find Shiulie and get her home. Then I need to find Jericho.

'Bitsy' – White Chinchilla Persian
Missing – Devon View – four years old,
long-haired, male.
Silver collar.
Reward.

I pace my living room in the late morning sunshine, water dripping down my cheeks from hair not properly dried. I shake, though I am warm. I shake because I didn't find Shiulie last night and I didn't take her home. I shake because I should have looked for her earlier. I shouldn't have let her out of my sight in the first place.

It was a group of young boys standing under the cliff, surreptitiously smoking cigarette stubs under their hoods, who noticed bits of chalk and flint and root falling from the edge above, not me. It was they who ran to the St John's Ambulance to tell them they thought they could see something hanging over a ledge, halfway down the cliff face, it looked like a shoe, or a foot. It was them, not me. It was this gang of boys who led the way, pointing and shouting 'There, look, they're up there!' Not me.

I must stop losing people. They seem to come back broken, ruined. If they come back at all, that is.

Somehow Shiulie fell. She fell from the edge of the cliff, ending up on a ledge many feet below. The ledge saved her life. Only just, and in a way I couldn't have. Jess has listened to my garbled story of last night, shocked gasps spilling from her, eyes wide, head shaking from side to side.

'She'll be OK though, won't she? I mean, she's fallen down that bloody cliff, but they found her in time and she'll live, right?'

This said in a rush from behind her hands.

'Yes. She'll be alright. I don't know.'

'Will she go blind?'

'Jess, I don't know. I hope not.'

I can't stop shaking. Jess sighs and runs her fingers through her hair.

'I'll go see her. I'll take her some of that biltong they've just got in from the shop on the corner. The spicy stuff, she'll love it.'

'I don't think she'll be chewing biltong for a while yet.'

Jess purses her lips.

'Poor thing.'

Poor thing. I lost her and when I found her she was broken.

'She's had her operation?'

'Yes. Her mum said she'd be awake this afternoon, to come by then.'

Jess chews on a fingernail.

'Bloody hell though. I guess that Will won't be breaking any more hearts in a hurry.'

'Jess!'

'What? It's true. He can spend his time being dressed, and washed, and watching daytime TV, and the nurses will pinch his pretty bum and feed him with a plastic spoon. He'll love it. If he knows what's happening, that is. He was bad news. Everyone's best off without him.'

I should stop pacing around my living room and sit down but the implications of yesterday's events are looping and skydiving around the inside of my head.

'Including you.'

She says this softly, as if I'm not really meant to hear it. I stop at the window, turn towards her.

'Including me what?'

She smiles crookedly, wags a nail-bitten finger in my direction. She's painted what remains of her fingernails blood red in the hope that this will discourage her constant gnawing. From the red flecks on her teeth I can see that it's not made much difference. At least the spots have not appeared today. This gives me a slight feeling of relief, but you can't get complacent. You can never be sure what might happen next. I pull my dressing gown cord tighter, run my fingers through my wet hair and shoot a glare at her. This does not stop her.

'Don't pout at me like that, you know exactly what I'm talking about. Didn't take a genius to see. You had a crush on Will. Don't deny it.'

No.

'I will deny it. I absolutely will. I didn't have a crush on that bastard. Where the hell do you get these ideas from? Look, I'm going to visit her in hospital in a while, let me concentrate on that.'

I turn towards the window again. I do this partly to hide the flush which has suddenly crept up my throat, pounced on my cheeks, my ears. And partly I just want to remember his face. I hear Jess humming softly under her breath, shuffling through the pile of magazines on the floor.

She is right, of course. She is always right. I don't know why I bother to try and hide these things from her as she seems to know me better than I know myself. But this time Jess has only just scratched the surface. My mind wanders from my impending hospital visit.

I'm remembering one evening two or three years ago. Shiulie and Will were newly engaged. My friend spent her days sparkling with happiness, and I sparkled too, reflecting her light, her heat. But something of my own kind of shimmer must have caught Will's magpie eye.

Shiulie was visiting her grandparents in Delhi, had left me with kisses and promises of exotic and fragrant gifts. One afternoon Will invited me for a drink in the local pub. To talk about wedding preparations, flowers, honeymoon destinations. He said he wanted my advice as I'd known his betrothed since we were both children. I met him among the clouds of hanging smoke, him still ruddy-cheeked from the frosted winter air, me girlish and blushing under his laughing eyes. Eyes so blue they seemed pried from the azure haunches of a glacier. We bought each other drinks, I smoked the cigarettes he rolled for me, dipping his tongue towards the papers to seal the orange strands within, not allowing me to take them from him but insisting instead on placing the finished cigarettes between my lips himself. I didn't feel guilty. There was nothing to feel guilty about. I held my head low as he lit each one so he wouldn't see me trembling.

He talked about Shiulie's beauty, her adventurous spirit. Of how he had found the best girl in the world, would have the best wife and, eventually, the best children. I found myself, after a while, only half listening to him. I pretended instead that this fine man was my own. That he was talking about me, Marnie, his beautiful, brave girl. So I didn't really notice that he was leaning closer, closer. That his hand sometimes rested on my shoulder or my knee for just a little longer than was necessary. That I felt his warm breath on my cheek a little too often.

No. That's not true. I did notice. I did notice, and I did like it. My skin sang under his light touches, as I tried not to imagine Shiulie surrounded by wedding gifts, bolts of sequinned silk and Indian sweets made from yellow marzipan, ground pistachios, creamy coconut.

We talked, Will and I, until the lights went out and we were ushered homeward by the landlord, ash bucket dangled threateningly in front of our faces as we hurried to climb into our jackets. Will said he would see me home, that there may be all sorts of monsters lurking about at this time of night, all manner of teeth and claws in the dark, and young girls couldn't be too careful. Young girls. We laughed about that, laughed great clouds of steam and, arm in arm, we walked slowly back to my door. He pulled his collar up around his ears and thanked me for listening, for my superlative wedding advice. I thanked him for the cigarettes and alcohol. And then he left, singing under his breath. I watched him walk away under the lamp light, then turned and went inside.

'No you didn't.'

The blue and white ceramic cat I've been turning over and over in my hands, a gift from my mother's holiday to Portugal last year, falls from my fingers and shatters on the floor. I spin round, crunching shards of pottery beneath my slippered heel, almost falling over my own feet.

'I may not have been there, but I can see it in you, see it written there clear as daylight. He didn't leave at all. Well, not until the next morning anyway. And you call your sister delusional.'

Jericho is lying on the floor by Jess's feet. She has been turning the pages of a magazine, unaware that a warm tawny hide rests only centimetres from her bare, fidgeting toes. I only just manage to stop myself from shouting out at him as he lifts a paw to wash behind one enormous ear. Jess's hand, halfway through flicking over another page, has stopped at the apex of its movement, hovering over her lap as she slowly raises her eyes to mine. Lowers them to where the rubble of coloured cat lies about my feet. Then, with a wrinkling of brow and widening of eyes, she returns her gaze to the glossy pages on her lap. Gives a low whistle through her teeth as I gather the broken pieces together. I'm still staring at the lion, though, and not looking where I place my knees. A sharp sliver slices easily through towelling, through my skin. The pain draws a hiss from me and brings Jericho struggling to his feet. He lumbers towards me, tries to steady my leg with his paw and lick my knee with his huge tongue.

'I'm OK, it's fine, just leave me the hell alone will you?'

I am not really aware that I have said this out loud until Jess gets up silently, drops her magazine on the sofa and stomps out of the room. I try and follow her but a slab of lion bars my way, trying to still me, to clean my bleeding leg. His tongue rasps over my knee as I struggle feebly to get past him and pull Jess back.

'Whatever you bloody well want,' she calls from the hallway. I hear a last word which sounds like 'biltong' flung at me before the front door slams shut.

I nearly call out to her, but don't. I stand there amid the ruins of one of my least favourite ornaments, with an old lion tending my wound as gently as if I were a newborn cub. My hands clench in mane fur as strong as wire and twist and twist. The tears don't come. But sometimes I wish they would.

The cat is in the bin, my sister has been gone for an hour and my knee throbs under the sticking plaster. The lion reclines on the sofa, a hind leg overflowing onto the rug, looking at his front paws. I lie on my back on the floor and stare at the ceiling. The room is awash with purple shadows.

We are silent. I am afraid.

What did you do to him?

I hoist myself to my elbows and look between my raised knees towards the sofa, where my old friend sits, sphinx-like, and contemplates his twisted knuckles, his breaths rippling the hairs on his feet like wind through corn.

What did we do to him?

Gemma and I used to compete when we got bored in maths. As the teacher drew arcane symbols on the blackboard, cryptic signs of dark magic which we would never understand, we would pass tiny folded notes to each other describing the various ways in which our imaginary friends would best the other.

> *Smiff would jump on Jericho's neck and STRANGERLATE him to death with all his long mane fur . . . !*

> *Well Jericho would squish Smiff under his ENORMUS feet before he could get on his back anyway.*

> *But Smiff would run away quickly before Jericho caught him and make a spell that FREEZES JERICHO stiff for ever!!!!!!!*

> *Jericho would bite Smiff's head OFF before he could even say the first word of the spell.*

> *And Smiff would jump into Jericho's mouth when he roared and pull all his TEETH out so he couldn't bite!*

> *Yeah but Jericho would SWALLOW SMIFF HOLE, and he'd be trapped in his tummy FOR EVER!!!*

> *Well Smiff would jump up and down in Jericho's tummy so he felt sick and then he would SICK HIM UP all over the CARPET!! AND he would run away really quickly and jump into a tree*

because lions can't CLIMB TREES and he would throw pine combs down on his HEAD until he fell over!

And we would giggle into our sleeves and drum our heels against the chair legs and not once did we get caught.

What would Jericho do to Smiff now, I find myself wondering. Hold his tiny body down and pull his head off slowly? Arrange his viscera in amusing patterns on the floor? Terrify him into catatonia? What happened? He looks like a badly-upholstered old armchair. He would never really hurt someone. He couldn't.

My mind fills with the image of the beaten car, those haunted eyes.

He couldn't.

But where are the cats? And where is Will? What night-time jungle does he find himself stranded in? What echoing shrieks haunt those dripping trees? What fiery-tailed birds hang upside down from those moss-laden boughs and scream into his sweating face? What soft fingers reach from the shadows to twine in his hair until he pulls away and runs, not looking back, crashing through dangling creepers, over low tripping undergrowth, past oozing leaves the size of umbrellas, running, running, but knowing something gains on him gradually, and it will not tire, it will not stop, ever, while his legs feel as though they move through tar, through quicksand, through fire, through fire, and he will fall in the end, he knows he will fall, and in a rush of dank fur and claws it will be upon him and tearing through his clothes, his flesh, and the last he will see are those eyes, those eyes burning into him. Those golden, glowing eyes.

Jericho feels my gaze on him, returns the look briefly, snorts, then closes his eyes. He seems suddenly crumpled and pathetic, a tired battle-worn old tomcat trying to get comfortable on doll's house furniture. A sigh judders his rangy frame. Dear old puss.

But I can still smell the dark rotting things in the dead leaves under my feet. A cold shiver runs through me.

I get up quickly, scoop up my jacket from where I've dropped it on the floor.

'I'm going out. Don't follow me.'

He lifts his head as if it weighs more than his neck will comfortably carry.

'Where you going?'

I don't meet his eyes. Keys, where are they? Shoes. Quick quick. Shoes on. Come on, he's getting to his feet.

I find my keys on the arm of the sofa and, clutching them hard in my fist so the jagged points dig into my palm, I run out of the flat, banging the door behind me and dropping down the stairs two at a time. Tumble into the front door, wrench it open so the cold air slaps me in the face. A brisk jog down the road.

I am moving faster than I need to. Do I think about those great jaws, those powerful rolling shoulders? The stalker in the jungle? I could smell the decay, the air too thick to breathe, the heavy sweetness of burst, rotting fruit somewhere below me as I lay there and watched him doze on my sofa. I felt the slash of thorns, felt the warm drip of water on my face, heard the burrowing of fat grubs into cool flesh as he lolled there. How?

I don't want to join Will in his endless nightmare so force myself to breathe, to walk slowly. I laugh. Lions don't live in the jungle anyway. But my laugh is thin, insubstantial, disappears as soon as it leaves my lips. 'Lions don't live in the jungle', I say out loud to myself. Two teenagers pass me and snigger to each other, rolling their eyes theatrically and waggling their heads from side to side. Look at the crazy lady. She's nuts.

When I was a child I would indulge myself in revenge fantasies. I would play events over and over in my mind, scenes in which I was wronged, a victim, and twist what I knew to be the facts until I came out victorious. I changed the endings of what had happened, again and again, substituting my own humiliations and hurt with what I felt were justified reprisals. It would make me feel differently about myself, rewriting my own endings, making them happy ones. It made me feel alright, for a little while at least. But when you're grown up you need to be careful. When you're grown up you can think of much, much worse things, much more terrible retributions. We should keep these to ourselves, bury them deep, deep inside where no one, not even ourselves, can get at them.

But what happens when you let them out? When you let your daydreams of pain and mayhem loose?

> Please help! 'Mickey' can't find his
> way home! Missing from Griffiths
> Park since mid-October – light grey cat
> w/ white and dark markings on his
> face, belly and tail, green eyes.

Not her eye, I'm thinking. Please, not her eye.

The ward is light and shiny and full of voices. The glossy floor is like an ice rink. I am kindly requested to clean my hands with cold gel every few feet by large signs which cover walls, doors and even the floor. By the time I reach Shiulie's room antiseptic hand wash is all I can smell.

The door is open. I have heard from her mother about her injuries, but this hasn't prepared me for the battered, bandaged form lying in the bed. I tiptoe in and glance at Shiulie's mother, who stands over her on the other side. Her eyes skitter across Shiulie's face, taking in again and again the cuts and grazes which map out a few brief moments of violence. She bends and brushes a stray hair from Shiulie's forehead, rests the palm of her hand against her cheek then turns and disappears from the room, with just a tiny nod in my direction. She shuts the door behind her so quietly I do not hear it.

I stand by the bed and take in the wreckage of her face. A thick wad of cotton wool covers her right eye, held in place by a bandage which has been wound around and around her head. Her nose is covered with a padded, taped beak. Her jaw is swollen and red, a tangle of scrapes and cuts cover both cheeks and her chin. Her visible eye is closed, oddly perfect and unscathed, dark lashes lying quiet on her damaged cheek like a cat sleeping in the rubble of a war-torn house.

What has happened to you?

Shiulie's mum has told me she may not wake while I am here. The drugs make her sleep a lot, she told me as she rubbed her hands against each other, over and over. The drugs meld the real world with her dreams, she said. The dreams bleed into her waking moments so it is good she sleeps. She needs to sleep.

I drag a plastic chair over and sit by Shiulie's bed in the half-shadows. I sit with my hands clasped in my lap, my knees together, my feet flat on the floor to anchor me to something solid, something stable.

I lean close to her ear and try to say her name out loud, despite the pleas of her mother not to try and wake her, but it comes out as a strangled sob. Shiulie sighs in her sleep and turns her head away from me, but her eyes remain closed. I am glad for her continued sleep, and wonder what my sounds will be translated into in her dreams. Then I notice her hair. Most of the back of her head has been shaved, and another piece of thick wadded cotton lies taped to the naked patch. I know that under this dressing lie thick, black stitches which pull at the bruised skin, holding it together. I know also that under the dark tracks of thread there is a crack in her skull, a tiny one, but one which spiders out across the pale, veined bone. And I know that she also has a broken arm, a broken collarbone, a shattered kneecap, a broken nose, extensive bruising, cuts, scratches and scrapes, some of them deep. And something badly wrong with one eye.

She stirs again under the sheets and the stiff blue blanket.

'Shiulie?'

A noisy breath forced from her nose, a small moan, and her eyes flicker open. They remain unfocused until I take her fingers in my hand and repeat her name. She turns her head and looks at me.

'Ha,' she says.

'Ha,' I say.

I stroke her fingers with my thumb, careful not to disturb the needle taped to the back of her hand. I follow the snake of the plastic tube which winds its way up to the dangling bag which drips its liquid into her, slowly.

'How are you doing, clumsy?'

She smiles. A small, tentative smile.

'Not bad. My depth perception isn't what it used to be though,' she says, vaguely gesturing at her patched eye.

Her voice sounds muffled, as if she is talking through a mouthful of rice, and her words come slowly. She forms each deliberately, careful not to let sounds get swallowed or dropped. She speaks in much the same way when she has had too much to drink.

'Shiver me timbers, me hearty.'

She chuckles, then frowns.

'I'm having weird dreams, Marnie.'

She squeezes her eyes shut and opens them again, stretching them wide.

'What kind of dreams?'

Her eyes close again but she continues to speak.

'One had a huge bonfire. We were all throwing books on to it, you were there too and you were laughing, and I tried to stop burning all the books but couldn't. Then there's one where I'm pushed off a cliff by some sort of large animal with enormous teeth. Then in another I was on a boat trying to hide from something. And there were flying fish.'

The corners of her mouth crinkle in a smile.

'Silly,' she whispers.

She stops talking. Her eyes remain closed. If I'm squeezing her hand too tight she doesn't complain, but I notice my fingers trembling. I make an effort to relax them, one by one. I stay like that, holding her hand for a while. She may have fallen back into her dream-tumbled sleep, but I need to ask her something.

I need her to tell me her dream.

'Shiu.'

'Mhmm?'

'That dream, the one about the animal on the cliff.'

She opens her eyes and stares at the motionless ceiling fan.

'Big animal it was.'

I need her to tell me what happens in the dream.

'What happens?'

She sighs and shifts slightly. Fixes me with her good eye.

'You alright Marnie?'

I want to beg her.

'I'm fine, don't worry about me. Just wondering about your dreams.'

She sighs again, smiles another slow smile and closes her eye again. I give her fingers a squeeze. She is quiet for a moment and I'm about to whisper her name to check whether she's fallen asleep, but then she begins to talk. Her eyelid flickers as she watches her memories unfold against the dark.

'There's not much to it really.'

She stops. Then,

'I'm standing near the edge of the cliff. I'm drunk, and don't care if I fall. The thought goes through my mind that I do want to fall and break my neck. That would show him.'

I shake my head.

'So I'm standing there, watching the flames moving about below. I turn around and see someone moving in the shadows. They're in some sort of costume, and I think that they must have escaped from one of the processions in town. I call out to them, but they don't respond.'

Shiulie shifts and licks her lips.

'Can I have some water?'

I pull the small wheeled table towards me, half fill a plastic cup with the tepid water and hold it to her mouth. She takes a few small sips.

'Thanks.'

Again a pause so long she might have fallen asleep.

'What happens then?'

'I shout that they can fuck off then, wave my flask around, generally behave like an arse. And I go back to watching the fires and finishing my whisky. And then they rush me.'

She stops, eyes open again, scanning the wall at the far end of the room.

'What do you mean they rush you?'

'It's a weird costume. But then I see it's *not* a costume. It's an animal, a bloody great lion of all things. But I'm not scared because it's not looking at me, it's not looking *for* me, it's looking past me at something else. Someone else. And then it rushes past me, too close, because I get shoved and I'm falling and falling and there doesn't seem to be any end to it. The sky's all lit up with colours. Then the falling turns into floating and all I can think is that I dropped my bloody flask and the booze will all get wasted and it should be *me* getting wasted and now I'll have to go back down to town and buy more whisky.'

Her voice gets quieter and quieter until she stops. She tests her scabbed and swollen lower lip with the tip of her tongue. She looks over at me. I am trying to control the muscles in my face.

'That's all. A big old smelly lion out hunting, on bonfire night. And me floating around in the sky.'

She bursts out laughing and, just as suddenly, stops herself.

'Morphine will do that to you every time.'

I have dropped her bunched fingers onto the sheet and stare at them lying there, still, like a litter of newborn mice. The only thing I want to do now is crawl under the bed and bang my head against its metal leg until I pass out.

'They don't know whether my eye will heal. Did you know that? I may be blind in one eye for good.'

There is nothing I can say to that.

What has he done to you?

'I'm going to go to sleep now, I can't keep my eyes open any more. Thanks for coming to see me.'

She lets out a long sigh. Her fingers twitch and are still. She sleeps.

I have heard it whispered by her mother that if Shiulie's head had not hit the large rock on the ledge below the big drop, she would have carried on downwards, and probably been killed. Her fractured skull, while almost killing her, also saved her life.

What has he done to you Shiulie?

What have we done to you?

I lower my head towards the bed, kiss each of Shiulie's finger-tips, one by one, and let my cheek rest gently against her warm hand.

I'm sorry, I whisper. I won't let you get hurt again. We don't need anyone else after all, do we? No one else.

We'll be alright.

Been lying here under the window stretching my old legs since early morning. On my own. Draught creeping up and down my shoulders, like it doesn't have anything better to do. Been staring at the inside of my eyelids once I got bored staring at the walls and the floor and the sofa and the bloody potted plant. Don't feel like getting up and about. Just fancy a good lounge. It'd be nice to have a little company to lounge with, though.

Wish she'd clean this place sometimes. Been trying to count the objects underneath the sofa, but when I lay my head on the carpet the dust makes me sneeze. And the number of notebooks she's got lying around? I'll have to talk to her about that. About time she started using them properly.

She left without eating breakfast. Looked my way from under all that hair, threw me the crumb of a smile and left. I'd wondered whether she was growing tired of me. But she smiled. Just a little, but it was still a smile. So everything must be OK. I was a little worried. But she's OK. We're OK.

She doesn't want to be followed, I can smell it on her. She's in one of those moods. A brown and purple state of mind. I mean, it's only natural after what she's been through. The death.

That bloody fella. Have to say I'm pretty pleased with myself though. I did right by her. Proved myself. After all, I never killed him. Restraint, that's what it is. I'm able to pull back, to keep a lid on the old temper. Subtle, that's what I can be. I was worried about her reaction at first. She refused to speak to me for a whole day, didn't even look my way. As if she was surprised. As if she hadn't wanted it. As if she was afraid. Of *me*. Imagine!

As if she had nothing to do with it.

But she did. She knows deep down she did and wanted it too. I could feel it in her, deep down there, her heart and her guts were crying out for it. If no one else was going to do anything about it then I had to.

Course it's really the other one she's upset about. I understand, and I'm sorry about what happened to her. Didn't mean that to happen. But she's alright, she'll be fine. It wasn't really my fault. She shouldn't have been standing in my way. She'll be OK. Marnie'll come round.

Something gets to me, though. Just a bit. Seems I can't feel her thoughts, her mind, as clearly as I was able to. Before. Like she might have closed herself a bit. Turned in on herself. Just a bit, mind. But then I think to myself, oh you soft, slow, clawless old bugger, of course she hasn't. She couldn't. She wouldn't.

She hasn't thanked me yet. She hasn't even talked to me about it yet, but she will. She'll open that door, stand there for a while, look sheepish. Then she'll smile and run over to me and throw herself on my neck and hold me and tell me no one, no one, has ever made her feel so safe, so safe. She'll beg me never to leave. And she'll tell me she's not been talking because she's been trying to figure out the way to ask me to stay forever, and we'll have a laugh about it, and I'll cuff her around the head, gently like, and she'll scratch my ears and I'll rumble at her to show her I'm happy.

She'll beg me. She'll beg me to stay. And I'll say yes. Yes, my love, my cub, my life my flesh my heart, of course I'll stay. I'll stay always. Without you I'm nothing.

That will be that. There it'll be.

She'll be back soon. You'll see.

Bourneville – rescued as feral kitten
Would like to know he is OK. Black
male, 'fluffy', about 2 yrs old, long
hair. Last seen November 5th when
moved house, but he had other
ideas!

The calloused concrete bench, knuckled with ancient pebbles, presses my flesh. I imagine the tiny stones embedded in the old cement patterning the underside of my thighs, tattooing them with roughness. The leaves of the beeches jostle each other to dance with the breeze high in the treetops, but the air around me is still and heavy with the smells of damp earth, rotting leaves, frying meat.

Do you ever get the feeling that all the time you thought you were progressing, moving forward, making some headway, you were actually walking in a loop? Like the students in that film, lost in the woods for hours. They thought they were going in the right direction, that they would soon be safe, but as the sun set they came upon the same fallen tree they'd been at hours before. All that effort, sweat and tears for nothing. That same tree which, with its prone, broken form, spoke of the futility of trying, of impending madness and possible death. There was crying and trembling and screaming.

I thought I had lost the one I needed. Then I thought I had found something to fill the empty space; a warm, furred shoulder to lean my head on, purr me to sleep, to put the wrongs to right. But I think I've been doing the same thing as those kids in the film, only without the screaming. And the only thing I've come round to again is myself. There is no one else. There need be no one else.

I was obviously wrong about what I needed.

See? Nothing much changes.

The smell of grease from Woodie's Café coats the back of my throat. It's mid-morning; I've still not eaten but I'm not hungry. Not even the smell of bacon or the hissing sound of frying can tempt me today. Jericho would have moaned at me about not eating this morning if I hadn't slipped out quickly.

It would be the easiest thing in the world for him to find me, to track me down using his nose. He wouldn't even have to use his nose, he has found me here before. I'm sitting here beyond the terraced rows; at the edge of hilly parkland known romantic- ally but inaccurately as 'Bluebell Park'. I've never, not once, seen a bluebell on it. Cow parsley yes. Grass, yes. As many daisies as you can eat. But never any bluebells. They wouldn't last a minute, even if they did dare show their shy, drooping faces. Aggressive dogs, teenagers with enormous feet and muddy footballs, a whole world of trampled cigarette butts, half-crumpled beer cans and broken bottles rule here. Bluebells would be bullied by the resi- dent nettles, the knife-sharp thistles, the deceptively tender-looking dandelions.

I curl my fingers under the bench, put my weight firmly on the balls of my hands. The pebbles and sharp stones hurt my skin. The bones complain of the bruising, but I press harder. Isn't he meant to come when I'm hurting, in need? Aren't I a damsel in distress? The blood has stopped reaching my fingers. I lift my fingers from the cold bench and rub them as they tingle back to life.

Where are you, you old bastard?

A blackbird lands near my feet. It bobs around among the weeds, cocking its head at the sky, at the ground, at me. *What's going on here then?* Its deep black glows, blue-sheened, in the sudden sunshine and I notice that one of its wing feathers is pure white.

I cock my own head at the bird, smile at it. What, indeed, is going on here? I lean forward slightly and the bird bobs its beak, once, twice, then bounces away to listen for worms in the naked dirt. I let go a sigh which seems to come from the very depths of my heart. I smile.

I'll go home now and he'll say he understands and he'll grin his sabre-toothed grin and butt the side of my leg with his head and tell me to take care and eat something once in a while for God's sake and then he will turn and go. And I will be alone. As I need to be.

I'm losing my memory. Things are slipping from my mind. That's impossible of course. If you're made of memory, of ebb and flow of experience, how can your memory fail? How can I lose something of which I'm made?

So I'm not sure exactly why I feel this way. Like I'm being scraped too thin over the surface of something. Like my fur is thinning, eyes growing dim. Feels like I'm looking at things through thick glass. A bit more greased and blurry every time I wake. There's a weakness in my limbs. It's not always there, but I know it's waiting for me.

I'm sleeping more than usual. Can't seem to feel bothered about that though. Strange. And I'm spending more time on my own. She's spending more time on her own.

When I close my eyes it takes longer to see her face. To imagine the smell of the nape of her neck. Hear the hesitation in her voice. Takes me a while longer, a bit more effort, to summon these things. And when I do, it takes more concentration to fix them there, keep them close. She wavers in my mind. Just the other day I couldn't remember the colour of her eyes. No word of a lie. Whereas before, all I had to do was think of her, my little bit, my little fish, and in the dark, against the inside of my eyelids,

I could pick out the individual strands in those irises, the exact shape and depth of the darkness in pupils, name a hundred different shades reflected in her eyes, count her eyelashes, trace the red veins against the white. Now I can't even remember their colour. I think they're hazel. Maybe nut brown. But I can't be sure. Not any more.

Thing that worries me most is her closed mind. Can't sense her a lot of the time. She walks away and I feel the warmth of her leaving me. Leaving. My mind gets cold and slow and closed. And the air around me grows dark. And I'm alone.

I know she'll return though, we'll be together. What was it she said to me yesterday? How long did it take before her breathing slowed in the night and she slept? What were the dreams that folded around her, the ones that made her whimper and turn?

My memory, it seems to be going.

Missing from Jamaica Road,
A cat called Mr Knuckles.
Male, with short, ginger hair.
Orange eyes.
Scar behind right ear.
Please call Marnie with any
information.

Back at Dad's house I let myself in. I have rung the doorbell, once, but this time there is no kneeling at the front door peering through the letterbox. I walk into a silence which embraces me completely. In his study I sink into his hard leather chair, run my fingers along the grooved wood of the desk. My fingertips come away greyed with dust.

Faces cluster and peer out at me from the picture frames on the wall. I lean forward and scan the photographs again. A black and white holiday snap of my youthful mother holding me, a bawling, chub-faced baby. A faded studio portrait of an elderly couple, hands touching lightly. A small photo of my father standing in a doorway in a cream mackintosh and brown trilby, laughing at the camera. His hair is greying, his jowls puffed, but his eyes gleam.

And now I'm trying to think of him as Jessica does. I'm trying to find that spark of desperation which haunts her eyes. She has shocked me, shaken me with the colour and shape of her distress. But what shocks me more is that I find I no longer share her pain.

It is gone.

There is something of the past about him now, about my memories of him. As if he is no longer part of this world, and never really was. He is to me now almost a myth, a legend. A dark tale penned by the Brothers Grimm, or a surreal Russian folk tale about sleeping princesses and birds made of fire and Baba Yaga with her house that stands on chicken legs. A folk story to frighten the children, make them behave, eat their greens, go to sleep. He has faded and become transparent in my mind, as insubstantial as I once thought I was.

I realise now that he was never here, never really with us. Even when he was singing to us or cooking or giving us his strange lectures he was never really here. He was always missing. This physical loss is no different.

My sister worries at her memories like a dog with a bone that has long since been sucked of its juicy marrow, has long since given up its taste. I will succumb to this new and unexpected peace, will drift down underneath the warm blanket of things, allow myself to be lulled by the quiet, this new calm in our lives. Jess still paces, paces, like a caged beast, needing back the fingers of pain which accompany his presence, asking the night sky *Why is it so quiet? Where has the pain gone?*

I look out through the window. The plants droop over the path and a squirrel is flinging itself from tree to tree at the bottom of the garden.

You're not coming back, are you? That's OK. We'll be alright.

A slant of warm sunlight touches my cheek. I smile.

Go well, old man. Go well, Dad.

Where's the light gone? Can't be night-time yet. Sure it can't be dark. Why can't I see anything? It doesn't worry me so much. But, you see, I can't smell anything either. That's the real concern. Can't smell carpet, onions, even myself.

Can't smell her.

Maybe it's just I'm so tired. All the time. Just need a little sleep. It'll all be OK in the morning. The light through my eyelids'll wake me and I'll open my eyes and see her humped underneath her covers. There'll be snoring and the warm fug of morning bedroom and I'll stretch my stiff muscles and yawn and she'll stir and the covers'll move and she'll open an eye and peek at me and she'll smile and we'll be full of each other again and she'll say good morning my dear lion my dear Jericho and Mum'll call from downstairs come for your breakfast and Mum'll pick her up and cuddle her in her arms and I'll run out into the garden into the sunshine and we'll play in the sandpit with her toys and throw the ball and cover each other in sand and Mum'll stand at the kitchen window and watch us and smile and there is so much we will do so much and the long hot days of summer are only just beginning and we'll

FOUND – Large Black and White
cat.
Distinctive black smudge coming
from left nostril.
6–8 yrs (?) Short haired.
Timid.
Is he YOURS?

I'm awake. The dark is just beginning to pull itself apart and I
should still be asleep. The indigo light sneaking through the slats
of the blind tells me the sky is cloudless and moonlight-filled.
My heart is thumping but I don't know what woke me. Familiar
outlines of wardrobe, bookshelves are where they should be. A
tentative nausea creeps around my stomach as I lie on my back
and try to still my heart. This used to happen before he came.
I've not woken in the night for weeks now. I am used to sleeping
dreamlessly through the night, waking in the morning light, feeling
rested, awake. I close my eyes and revert back to my old habits,
breathing deeply, clenching and then unclenching my muscles in
turn. Toes. Calves. Knees. Thighs. There. My eyes are wide open

again. That's the noise again. There it is. I sit up too quickly, making the blood drain from my head. The room spins. A low yowl. Is he back? But it's not a thrumming rumble, or the deep rolling gurgle which used to shake my bed as he sang me to sleep.

He wouldn't make that noise. He wouldn't be able to make that noise.

There is something outside my window. Below my window. Something in the garden is calling for me. Something in the garden is waiting for me.

I pull my legs from the warmth of my bed. The room is freezing and I step through a cloud of my own breath to the window. Raise the blind. The moonlight sketches the tiny gardens below in black and white and grey, the sleeping backs of houses, the hunched shoulders of shrubs, the low wall at the end of the row of gardens. Which is somehow taller tonight. As though packages of differing heights are stacked all along its length. As my eyes accustom themselves to the darkness I am unable to stop the low noise escaping from my throat into the night. It is an animal noise, to answer that which called me to my window. That which calls to me now from the wall below.

Ranged along the low wall are cats. Dozens of them, surely forty, fifty. Sitting. Just sitting. Dream beasts with moon-filled eyes. Looking up at me. So still for a moment I think they are statues.

But no. Ears twitch. Heads shake and are dipped gracefully towards paws for washing. Muzzles gape in tooth-studded yawns, ribbons of hot breath curling into the night. Mirrored eyes wink on off on off through the darkness, scores of tiny torches signalling in Morse code, announcing the return of the neighbourhood's entire feline population. We have come home we have come home we have come home home home.

My scalp prickles with heat though the room is chilly, and I lean my forehead against the cold glass. A whimpering noise now, but this time from inside the room. Somewhere in my mind I think the sounds may be coming from me. But I can't be sure.

A list of names, images streams through my mind, the tattered scraps of photocopied faces, light eyes, dark eyes, notched ears, broken tails, striped fur, white fur, black fur, patched coats, the young, the old, the pampered, the rejected, Sandy, Mr Bojangles, Bitsy, Knuckles, Harry, Sausage, Scaramouche, Mickey, Mazzy, Pie, Balou, Tibbs, Bingo, Lilou, Jess.

They are back. They have come home. All of them.

They've come home.

And he has gone.

A nd again I am here, somehow I am here again, lying on my back, tough grass probing my shoulder blades through cotton. The clouds are like sheep, following each other blindly across the high, flat slate of the sky's early morning. Like sheep. Those blank eyes, those sawing jaws. That unseeing panic. I can feel the wires of the pylon, thick as my thighs, vibrating through my chest.

Again I try to keep my eyes open as long as I can, try to delay the eyelid blink which will shut out the view for the merest fraction of a second. My eye muscles twitch. Water gathers at the corners then spills and wanders slowly along my cheek bone to fall in soft cold drops in my ears. Like words.

I remember a distant day when a flock of sheep scattered in fear and wheeled around a field like a fleet of sailboats racing on the sea.

I remember a handful of thick hot fur, anchoring me, keeping me from spiralling apart.

I remember a low voice in the night. Telling stories to frighten me.

Bluebell. Cornflower. Forget-me-not.

And I look up into the blueness and it becomes white and I

fall into it and the thrum of electricity raises the hairs on my arms as I pass between the wires and my breath scatters the clouds and I fly apart a thousand shards piercing the sky and falling out and out and always I will remember.

I will.

I t's funny you should mention that sweetie, because I have a little story for you. I saw something wonderful once. I may be old and sagging and lumpy like the stuffing in this chair but I remember it like it was yesterday. Here, let me hold him for a little while. He's lovely, isn't he? What's his name? Fang? Sounds ferocious! What sort of dog is he? Ah, he's a wolf. He's lovely and soft, like a proper old-fashioned cuddly toy. Does he howl when it's full moon?

Let's see. I would have been a little younger than you are now. It was a couple of days after my sixth birthday. My parents had given me a tricycle for my present. I loved it. It was pink, with tassels on the handlebars, and I had a special Barbie cycle helmet in case I fell off and Daddy had tried to wrap it with shiny paper so I couldn't tell what it was. One Saturday morning Mummy took me out for a ride along the path. It was cold and I pedalled hard, trying to keep in front of Mummy, but she made sure she held tight onto the bike, and I couldn't go as fast as I wanted to.

We were going past the row of houses down the road when I saw an amazing thing. I couldn't really believe my own eyes, so I slowed down. And what do you think I saw? There was a lady. And she was on her hands and knees on her front path. And this lady had long brown hair which fell to the ground and I could only just see her big eyes peeping out from behind all that hair. She looked scared. And surprised. But mostly scared. And just you try and guess why. I bet you can't. Alright, alright, I'll tell you, don't set Fang on me! In front of the lady on the pathway was a great big old *lion*, just lying there staring right back at her. What do you think of that?

Well, I just had to stop and see what was going on. The lady stayed there on the path, and so did the lion. It was talking to her, but I was too far away and couldn't hear what he was saying. I knew it was a he, because he had a big floppy mane. That poor lady looked so shocked! Anyway, after a few moments she noticed me. She looked up and smiled at me. Except it wasn't really a smile. It was too faraway, as if she was really looking at something or someone else, not me. But I smiled back at her. I didn't want her to be frightened. I wanted to tell her not to be afraid, I could see he wasn't going to hurt her even though he was so big and so gruff.

Anyway Mummy got tired of waiting by my side – she couldn't see the lion you see, Mummies often can't – and she pulled on my handlebars, pulled me away. And off we went. I looked back as my feet went round on the pedals. The lady was still there, on her hands and knees, still staring at the lion, and he was still staring back.

I never told Mummy about the lady and the lion. She would have just told me to stop telling fibs. That there weren't any lions where we lived, they were all in the zoo, or in the circus. But I know what I saw. She was there, and so was he. But I never saw either of them again, even though I sometimes went cycling past the house. I'd purposely go that way, to see if I could catch another glimpse of them. Of the scared lady and her friend, the lion.

I wonder what became of them.

Anyway, that was a very long time ago. I know, it is a good story, I'm glad you liked it. Yes, of course you can tell your friends if you like.

Here you go, have Fang back. You take good care of him, and make sure you don't lose him.

You never know when you might need his help.

Acknowledgements

Special thanks to Sue Armstrong and everyone at Conville & Walsh, and Tom Avery and the good folks at Jonathan Cape.

To Valerio Vidali, thank you for bringing to vivid, beautiful life your dream of Alberto and mine of Jericho. To Alec Grant, without whom I never would have had the courage to begin this book, my deep and sincere thanks and affection.

My never-ending gratitude to Ellah Allfrey, without whose belief, persistence and encouragement my odd little book would never have been found.

Fierce hugs to my friends and fellow writists Al Brookes, Carol Bullock, Suzanne Donovan, Sarah Harvey, Russell McAlpine, Neela Masani, Dave Nwokedi, Adam Pirani and Umi Sinha, whose humour, motivation, boundless creativity and tough love kept me going.

And for Andrew, for putting up with me with such grace, patience and humour, my thanks and love. Also he really wrote the book. OK, not really.